TEMPERED JOY

Pamela S. Thibodeaux

"They that sow in tears will reap in joy." ~ Psalms 126:5

TEMPERED JOY
Book Four of the Tempered Series
By: Pamela S. Thibodeaux
Copyright © 2006

Publisher/Distributor:
Temperance Publishing; an imprint of
Pamela S Thibodeaux Enterprises, LLC
PO Box 324
Iowa, LA 70647

ISBN#: 978-0-9896728-5-6

Cover Design: Delia Latham (Delia Designs)

Previous Publications:
Oct. 2006;
ComStar Media, LLC.
Salem, Oregon, U.S.A.
ISBN: 1-933866-03-9

All rights have reverted to Author

Praise for Pamela S. Thibodeaux

"Thibodeaux leads the reader through from the first page to the last without once relinquishing control. She hooks them, holds them, and keeps them enthralled until the last line." ~ Review of **The Visionary** by Delia Latham, author of the "Solomon's Gate" series

"In His Sight caught my attention from the beginning and it made me wonder if I had given all to God as he gave all to me. Thank you, Pamela, for a story that I would readily recommend to anyone who needs that extra encouragement!" ~ Reviewed by Wendy for Happily Ever After Reviews

"Winter Madness is a wonderful romance and an excellent example of spiritual growth." ~ Reviewed by Dee Daily for The Romance Studio

"A Hero for Jessica is a good, sweet read charged with attraction but an emphasis on true love. I recommend it to women of all ages." ~ Reviewed by Violet for LASR

"Cathy's Angel is a short tale that is entertaining as well as inspiring. Well done!" ~ Reviewed by Marlene for Fallen Angel Reviews

"Pamela S. Thibodeaux's motto is "Inspirational with an Edge!" Her short story **Choices** lives up to those words and is well worth reading." ~ Reviewed by Gail for Night Owl Romance

"The Inheritance was my first Thibodeaux work; however, it will not be my last! Her approach to writing about everyday life, while struggling to maintain strict Christian standards and values, is a glimpse into reality which we all must face from time to time." ~ Reviewed by Brenda Talley for The Romance Studio

*"If you have ever considered Christian fiction bland, then check out the **Tempered Series**. It will be well worth your time."* ~ Amanda Killgore for Huntress Reviews

*"**Lori's Redemption** is fast paced, lots of action, gripping storyline ... I loved it. It's gone straight back into my TBR pile."* ~ Clare Revell author of "Monday's Child" series

"Through Pamela's blessed ability to find God everywhere, even in secular song lyrics, she has written devotions guaranteed to touch the heart and remind the reader of our True Love, the Rose of Sharon." ~ Endorsement for **Love is a Rose** by Linda Yezak, Author, Editor Triple Edge Critique Service

Dedication and Acknowledgements

Psalm 34 says, *"I will bless the Lord at all times; His praise shall ever be in my mouth."*

Jesus said, *"It is finished."*

As I come to the end of this series, I come with thanksgiving, I enter His courts with praise and I bless the name of the Lord most high.

It is my prayer that you–the readers–are pleased with the fruit of my labor and that God–my Father and the Father of our Lord Jesus Christ –is glorified in the efforts.

To my mom, Patricia LaLanne Sonnier, it is my hope that I'm half the mother to my children, grandchildren and great-grandchildren that you are to yours.

Also dedicated to my sons: T. J. (James III) and Bubba (Terry Jr.); may you always walk uprightly before the Lord so that He will bless the work of your hands and give you the desires of your heart.

And last but certainly not least, to my darling grandson, Sean Davyn Gabrielsen; may the joys in your life far outweigh the sorrows.

Chapter One

Alexis Jayne Morgan, better known as Lexie, frowned over at Ace Harris while her foster-father Scott Hensley, marveled on and on about Ace's accomplishments. Ace had competed in rodeos since before his freshman year, and won in every event from roping to bull riding. Now, as a junior, he held more titles than any other boy his age. Lexie grunted in a very unladylike manner. "A true cowboy."

"Lexie." Scott's voice held warning.

She ignored his tone and turned to him, eyes wide. "Well everyone knows, rodeo cowboys have rocks for brains and a death wish for a soul," she remarked, her tone a tad too innocent.

"Enough, Lex," Scott insisted.

"It's okay, Scott," Ace interrupted. "It's obvious she doesn't know what she's talking about." All afternoon he'd listened with his father while Scott talked of the return of their most recent foster child. He'd spoken fondly of the girl who had been in and out of their home for the past two years. *'She's bright and intelligent, smart as a whip. And, sadly, wise beyond her years.'*

Now all Ace could think was how moody she was. Within the span of an hour she'd gone from shy to happy to grouchy. Her opinion of rodeo cowboys grated on his nerves worse than the sound of a gate that needed oiling and challenged the very core of his identity. He met sarcasm with arrogance. "I'll have you know, *Miss Ma'am*, I've won enough money in prizes and scholarships to pay my entire college education. And all the while I've maintained a four-point-o average."

"Well, what do you know, a cowboy with a brain." She pushed her plate away and turned an imploring gaze on her foster-mother. "May I be excused?" A twinge of guilt twisted her heart when Katrina nodded.

A frown tugged at her mouth. The day had been a terrible one for her foster-mother. Despite Trina's best efforts, the boys Robert and Richard, ages four and seven, argued and whined and downright rebelled over the clothes she bought, and now here she was antagonizing Trina's guests. Lexie rose from her chair and paused to give Trina a hug and whisper and apology in her ear.

Trina turned to Craig after Lexie left the room. "I have no idea what has gotten into her. Lexie is never like this."

Craig chuckled. "It's okay. She's probably just feeling left out or outnumbered."

Ace snorted. "TFF." He referred to his favorite phrase: Typical Friggin' Female.

"Ace," his father warned in a tone similar to the one Scott had used with Lexie.

"Well, its true. Women!" He rolled his eyes. "God, generous as He is, had wonderful, loving intentions when He created them. But somewhere along the line something went wrong. They've turned into moody, unpredictable creatures."

"And it's all man's fault." Katrina defended herself, her foster-daughter and her species with flashing eyes and a challenging smile.

Ace grinned and rose from his seat. "Present company excluded of course," he retracted with a gallant bow and lifted Trina's hand to his mouth.

"Hey boy, are you flirting with my girl?"

Ace's grin spread to encompass Scott's barb. "Don't have to. She's loved me since the day we met. Huh, Trina?" he taunted with an impish smile.

His gray eyes shone like sunlight dancing off of sheet metal. Trina's heart melted. "Go on, Ace Harris." She shooed him. "Get out of here, with your devil-may-care grin and cocky attitude."

Ace chuckled and kissed her cheek then glanced at his father. "You coming with me or riding with them?" he asked then held his hand in a gesture of supplication for his father to toss him the truck keys.

Craig hesitated only a moment before he threw the keys to his son. He had no qualms about Ace going to the arena early since it was his habit to spend some quiet time with his horse, and in prayer, before a rodeo. "See you later. Be careful, Ace."

Ace grinned. "That's my name," he assured, as he headed for the door, "Careful Ace Harris."

Scott shook his head. "He's as bad as you were at that age. I bet Tamera has her hands full with the two of you. How is she anyway?"

Craig tossed his head with a laugh. Having his only son compared to him was the ultimate compliment. Or insult. Depending on who uttered the comment and the tone they used.

"Tamera's fine. She flew to Mississippi to close the sale of her house. We don't go there much anymore so she decided to sell it. Besides, she can't stand to watch her baby ride bulls," he remarked explaining the rare instance that his wife wasn't with them. "She goes to every rodeo and buries her head in her lap until it's over. She's always so proud, and relieved, but she can't stand to watch," he admitted with a chuckle.

* * * * *

Lexie watched Ace leave from her bedroom window. Embarrassment at her behavior washed over her in angry waves. She had absolutely no idea why Ace Harris affected her so except she couldn't stand arrogance and *that* he had in abundance. Still, his family and Scott went way back. More family than she was at the moment, although she loved Scott, Trina and the boys as the family she never had. She was thirteen the first time they met.

She had come home from a friend's house to find her father passed out. Unable to rouse him, she called 9-1-1. The ambulance took him to the hospital where Scott worked in

3

the emergency room. That incident marked her father's first bout with a near overdose of alcohol. He'd been warned then to stop drinking, that his liver suffered and would continue to deteriorate if he didn't. He hadn't listened.

Scott and Trina took her home with them that night and she had been in and out of their home for over two years since. Lexie hoped if her father didn't live she would be able to stay, at least until she finished school and turned eighteen. She leaned her forehead against the windowpane and absorbed the warmth from the setting sun, then closed her eyes, and took a deep breath. The scent of beeswax and lemon filled her nostrils. She smiled to herself and let the love she felt for her foster-family fill her heart and mind. She knew what she had to do. She rubbed the glass to rid the window of the oil from her forehead and tried to pray.

"Father in Heaven, help me," she muttered, though in all seriousness she doubted God heard, or cared, despite her years of religious upbringing.

She went downstairs, swallowed the lump of nerves in her throat and apologized. "I'm sorry, Scott," she said, and then turned to Craig. "My apologies to you also, Mr. Harris, and to your son."

Craig chuckled. His eyes danced with mirth. "It's okay Sweetheart. Every now and then Ace needs to take a tumble off the pedestal his mother put him on the day he was born."

"Craig," Scott warned. "How on earth can we teach the child manners if you so blatantly disregard her rudeness?"

"You're right," Craig agreed, then winked at Lexie, and continued. "I'll accept your apology on behalf of myself and my son. We'll keep it our little secret, though. Don't need him thinking he's won any more points, he's arrogant enough."

Her lightning-quick smile took his breath away and Craig couldn't blame Scott for being enamored with her, especially after hearing of the life she'd led.

Lexie turned back to Scott. "Can, *may*, I go to the hospital tonight?" She could tell by his quick frown Scott wanted her with them tonight and she anticipated his argument. "He's my father Scott, as long as he's still alive, I need to be there."

Scott sighed. She was right. A brilliant, self-made man described Lexie's father to a T. A computer genius, a modern-day gypsy who traveled with his company to set up businesses, train employees, and make a fortune. As with most human beings though, he had vulnerability, a downfall. Steven Morgan's downfall was alcohol and Lexie. Oh, he loved his daughter beyond reason, was often over indulgent with her. The one thing he couldn't handle was the responsibility of parenting. He never made time, the quality time she needed to feel loved and secure. He provided for her well enough, sometimes too well. She was spoiled and selfish and often undisciplined.

Scott watched her while she waited for him to give permission to spend the night at the hospital. Those expressive eyes were clouded with emotion. "Okay Lexie, we'll drop you off on our way to the rodeo. And," he added at her relieved expression, "We'll pick you up afterward. You don't need to spend another night there."

In an elaborate gesture, Lexie rolled her eyes but bit back her arguments. She understood Scott only wanted to protect her from the reality that her father may not wake up from this coma. She kissed his cheek. "Thank you."

He caught her hand when she turned away. "It'll cost you though."

She turned back, laughed at the glint of humor in his eyes. "What?"

He shrugged. "Oh, I don't know. What do you think Craig? We'll have to leave early and go out of our way to drop her off, and then pick her up."

Craig chuckled. He remembered the same game he'd played with his daughter years ago, and felt a tug at his heart. Though she'd given him two beautiful granddaughters, he still missed his little girl. "At the very least, a hug, and a kiss, oh, and, definitely a smile." He gave her one of his own. "That should just about cover it."

"Think you can handle all that, Lex?" Scott teased.

She tossed her head with a snort. "That's an awful lot for just a few minutes out of your evening," she drawled in her rich, south Louisiana accent.

He grinned. "Your dialect is charming."

"That so boy-O?" she queried in an intriguing combination of Cajun heritage and Irish ancestry which was more evident in her flaming auburn hair and green eyes than her forced accent.

Scott chuckled. "You've listened to too many wannabe Irishmen in your drama class," he drawled and pulled her on his lap.

Despite years of living in Louisiana, he still sounded like a Texan. Lexie giggled. "At least I don't talk like this," she taunted. Her nasally attempt at a Texas drawl made them laugh.

"Oh no, that does it." Scott tossed her onto the floor and followed to attack her with a barrage of fingers, tickling until she shrieked with laughter and begged for him to stop. He pulled her against his chest and accepted the hug and the kiss before he let her go. He rose to his feet then helped Lexie to hers.

Lexie smiled at him then at Craig. "Guess I'll go help Miss Kitty with the dishes."

Craig arched his brow in a curious gesture. "Miss Kitty?"

Scott laughed. "She heard me call Trina "kitten" one day. It's been Miss Kitty ever since. Sure you don't want to go to the rodeo, Lex?"

"Oh, please," she begged. "Spare me from any more cowboys."

Scott laughed. "There are cowgirls too."

She turned, grinned. "Do they compete against the boys?"

"No. The girls compete in a class of their own."

"She snorted. "Proves chauvinism still exists. I'll pass, thank you."

* * * * *

Ace won "All-Around Cowboy" for the third year in a row and considered the rodeo a smashing success. Another clash between him and Lexie occurred after they got home.

Scott's oldest son Richard, who had a bad case of hero-worship toward Ace, rode home with he and Craig. Lexie and Robert rode with Scott and Trina. Ace grinned at Scott with a teasing wink. A look Lexie missed. Then he turned to Richard.

"Race you to bed, Ritchie," he offered, as they walked through the door and toward the stairs.

Richard, who hated to be called Ritchie by anyone *except* Ace, frowned. Though he feigned irritation, the ritual occurred every time the two met.

"Don't call me Ritchie," he insisted. "My name is Richard, or Rick."

Ace bit back a grin. "Ricky, Ritchie, what's the difference?"

Lexie got in on the tail end of the conversation and flew to Richard's defense. Before anyone could stop her she was between them, shoving at Ace. "Don't pick on him you big bully. Pick on somebody your own size."

Ace hissed in frustration. "I wasn't picking on him you little idiot. It's an old joke, one that's been around longer than you've known him," he bit out, and then regretted the words the minute they left his mouth, especially when tears filled her eyes.

Lexie blinked, fought tears with fury, and pushed him away. "Maybe so, but I love him more than you can imagine and I'm telling you to leave him alone!"

Ace grabbed her by the arms while Richard called for his father.

Craig and Scott hurried in just in time to see the two square off and glare at each other, both faces taut with fury. Green eyes and gray clashed and each waited for the other to back down. A gentle hand on his arm stopped Scott from rushing in to rescue Lexie from Ace's fury. Fury evident by the throbbing muscle in his jaw. *Ace had to learn to handle his temper.*

"Ace."

Subtle warning edged his father's voice and forced Ace to swallow the bitter bile of anger in his throat. He choked it down, but it left a sour taste in his mouth. With a snort, he shoved her away. He turned on his heel and stomped out of the room.

Lexie was left to explain, which she did in very eloquent terms, leaving no doubt as to her fury, and embarrassment. The next morning when they prepared to head home, though Lexie was nowhere in sight, Ace apologized to Scott. "I'm sorry, Scott, if I've been out of line."

Scott accepted the apology with a chuckle, and grabbed Ace in something between a bear hug and headlock.

"It's okay Ace. I know you well enough to understand. Lex can be trying sometimes, but she's going through a lot," he remarked, defending the girl he already thought of as a daughter. Deep down he wanted to adopt her. He and Trina had talked often but hadn't discussed adoption with Lexie yet. It was too soon. So much still hung in the balance.

The Harrises said their goodbyes and headed home to Bandera, Texas. Ace rode high going into his senior year. About midway through, his whole world crashed.

Chapter Two

Ace clapped his hands together and blew on his fingertips for warmth. "One more time," he implored his father. "One more time, then we'll call it quits."

Craig nodded. "Okay Ace. That old bull is getting tired, so is this one."

Ace grinned. "Old my foot, you love it and you know it. Makes you think of your younger days."

Craig grunted. "My younger days were not spent chasing bulls."

Ace laughed. "No? Chasing what then?"

"Never you mind," his father replied with a grin while the ranch hands penned the bull in the chute.

Ace was gearing up for the last rodeo of the year before his final shot at the National High-School Championships. He'd been on top since before his freshman year and determined to stay there. When other boys practiced on mechanical bulls, he used real ones, because nothing compared to the feel of fifteen hundred pounds of muscle and madness beneath him. One could never predict what the bull was going to do. All he could do was prepare for the worst and hang on for all his worth.

Eight seconds was all he needed and eight seconds was his goal. Eight seconds that seemed like an eternity. He picked the biggest and meanest bulls on the ranch. When he stayed on, he picked another one, until he, the bulls, or his father gave out. Then he got up the next morning to repeat the process. High school, then college championships, and after that, the pros. He still hadn't convinced his mother that he could do it, that he wanted it. Just for a while. He loved her and understood her fears, and often used his whole being to tease her out of them. But professional bull riding was his dream. He knew it would have to be a short dream. His life was ranching. As heir to the Rockin' H, he understood what was expected of him. He understood the importance of it, and appreciated it. But this was something he wanted to do just for himself.

As a child he'd been the butt of many "shrimp" jokes. Born premature he'd always been smaller than other boys his age. Petted and coddled by his mother and older sister, and overprotected at every turn by his whole family, had not made matters any easier.

Time had given him height. Years of weight training and bull riding added breadth, width, and strength to his lean frame, and gave him a sense of self-respect and equality with his peers. He didn't think of it as egotism or pride, he loved the sport. He loved the animals. In his opinion bulls were one of God's most noble creatures and he enjoyed conquering something so majestic even if only for eight seconds.

His gray eyes missed little when it came to life. Despite the shock of blond hair that got lighter as he got older and his complexion darkened by sun and wind, he was the image of his father. Though not quite as tall, he held his own when pared up against men and boys his age and older.

Craig sent up a silent prayer when his son prepared to mount the angry, agitated, bull again. They'd been at it for days. He understood his son's need for acceptance, for identity outside of being Adam Craig Harris the Fourth. But, for the life of him, he couldn't understand why Ace chose bull riding to get it. "I'm going to go in and check on Mama, Ace. Wrap this up and come in. It's cold and getting colder by the minute."

Ace nodded in response to his father's words while he climbed the chute and then settled himself onto the bull. Taking a few minutes to concentrate only on the animal beneath him, he said a short, silent, prayer then signaled for them to open the gate.

The bull reacted as expected. He lunged from the chute and twisted and turned in an attempt to toss the unwanted and unwelcome rider.

Arm arched high, spurs egging his mount Ace rode for all he was worth. The ride was over in less than eight seconds. He ground his teeth in frustration then raced up the side of the corral when the bull tried to pin him to it. He turned the angry animal away with a boot between the eyes, careful not to sink a spur into its flesh, and frowned when the ranch foreman showed him his time. Two seconds short. He heaved a sigh and thanked the ranch hands for their help then headed toward the house. Tomorrow, he thought, there's always tomorrow.

Tomorrow didn't come.

Ace felt the coldness like a slap in the face when he walked into a too quiet house. His voice echoed off the walls when he called for his parents. His heart sank into his stomach when all he heard in reply were deep sobs from the den. He raced in and beheld a sight too painful, too horrible to describe.

His father knelt on the floor by the couch where his mother lay since that morning. It didn't take a genius to know she was no longer among the living. The whole room reeked of death. Dark. Dank. Its icy fingers clawed at Ace's heart and scraped his soul until his breath hitched in and out in an attempt to get oxygen through his body.

"Daddy?" He whispered but the word echoed in the room like a blast of gunshot.

Craig looked up. The sound of his son's voice penetrated the emotions in his soul. "Ace." He stood to block his son's view. "Call 9-1-1, Ace."

Ace took a step, one agonizing step, nearer. "Mama?" His voice quivered.

"Ace." Craig put his hands on his son's shoulders to stop him. "I can't wake her up, Ace." He spoke softly, gently. "Call 9-1-1."

Ace jerked from his father's grasp. "No!" Pushing him out of the way he knelt beside his mother's still, cold, form. "Mama! Wake up! It's me, Ace!"

He shook her none too gently. "Wake up, Mama!" Pulling her in his arms, he clung to her lifeless form while sobs ripped through him.

Craig stumbled blindly to the phone on the desk and called the emergency number. With all of his strength, he prayed for the ability to make the next call, thankful when his son-in-law answered the phone.

* * * * *

Stanley Morrison stared blankly at the phone in his hand unable to comprehend what he'd just been told; unaware his wife had walked into the room. Her voice pulled him out of the shocked trance.

"Who called?"

He turned, his face a mask of shock and disbelief. Tears filled his eyes. His hand trembled and he fumbled to hang up the phone. The emotions clouding her husband's eyes sent a shiver of fear down Amber's spine. She took a step back. "Stanley?"

"Amber," he whispered and reached for her. His mind searched for the right words, words to make the telling easier. There were none.

"That was your father," he said, his voice rough with unshed tears, raw with emotion. "Sweetheart, your mom, he can't wake her up. She's, oh, God, Amber, she's dead."

Amber stared up at him, her eyes wide, uncomprehending, while his words echoed through the room. A frown creased her brow. She shook her head.

"Dead, how; how can that be?"

Stan pulled her in his arms. "I don't know, My Sweet."

She pushed him away. "No. She can't be dead. There's got to be a mistake." Fear snuck in, stealing her breath. She pressed a trembling hand to her mouth to stop the scream that welled in her throat from escaping and shook her head again. The shock and grief in his gaze tore at her soul. "No, Stan, please. Tell me it's not true. It can't be true."

She began to sob. "Stanley, please," she pleaded, begging him to tell her something, anything, anything but the truth.

Stanley pulled her against his chest until the worst of the shock was spent. Hugging her to him, he suggested they bundle up the twins and head over to her parents' house. The ranch was a jumbled mass of confusion and hysteria when they arrived. Emergency technicians had tried in vein to revive Tamera while police took statements from Craig and his son. Shoving shock and grief into some deep corner of her heart, Amber made coffee and answered questions about her mother's medical history. When everyone finally left, taking Tamera with them, she sat in shocked silence with her father and brother while he made phone calls. Words rang in their ears and echoed in the house–pneumonia, pleurisy, congestive heart failure; words as foreign to them as autopsy. But that's what it would take for them to know the truth.

The next few days were as dark and dreary as the cold February weather. Scott and Katrina came from Louisiana to share the grief and provide much needed and appreciated support to their friends of a lifetime. Stanley reluctantly agreed to sing at his mother-in-law's funeral. He remembered her shining sapphire eyes when she used to tease him about that very thing. "Promise me, Stanley, you'll sing at my funeral."

Uncomfortable with the thought of losing her at all, much less soon, he would always laugh and kiss her cheek. "By that time I'll be too old to do a good job. My voice will crack and croak." He'd then give her a demonstration until everyone rolled with laughter.

Yet here he sat, a guitar in his hands, singing words of grief and pain, of hope and grace and the promise of eternal life. His wife, father and brother-in-law, stood behind him trying to hush the frightened cries of his two-year-old twin daughters.

Stanley finished the last song he could manage to sing, bent his head and choked on a sob. From the moment he got Craig's call, he tried to be strong for his wife. But now, this moment, strength deserted him. His shoulders shook and deep, heaving, sobs racked his frame. He felt a hand on his shoulder and looked up into the tearful gaze of Scott Hensley as he, too, struggled with grief in order to be strong.

Stan stood in line with the rest of the family and accepted condolences from everyone while friends and acquaintances shared their sorrow. One by one they filed past until only the family remained. He watched Craig rest his hand on the cold, mahogany coffin before falling to his knees. Sobs racked his huge frame.

Amber rushed to her father's side. "Daddy, don't. Come on, Daddy," her voice trembled with emotion.

"Oh, God! I can't Amber. I can't leave her. Not here. Not like this! God, *why*?"

Stanley watched Ace attempt to pull himself out of the gray haze of grief when his sister began to plead with their father who refused to leave his wife's side. He walked over and took Craig's arm.

"Come on, Daddy. Let's go."

A collective sigh of relief could be heard when Craig allowed his children to help him up. They clung together and cried. Arms entwined, they held on to each other and walked away. Stanley nodded in answer to the unspoken question in his wife's eyes. Yes, he would stay until she was safely lowered into the earth. Scott too, agreed to stay. Katrina took the twins and escorted the rest of the family home.

Without hesitation, Scott put an arm around Stanley's shoulder and accompanied him to the gravesite. They watched the coffin be placed securely in the ground and covered. Wreathes upon wreathes of flowers positioned upon the upturned earth showed how well-loved and respected Tamera Collins Harris had been.

When he and Scott walked back toward the truck, Stanley reached for the guitar which lay forgotten across the chair where he'd sat. His hand trembled; he hesitated and then, on a surge of grief and anger, smashed it, doubting he'd ever want to sing again.

Scott knew there were no words to ease the grief the younger man felt so he remained silent. Overwhelmed with grief himself, he put his arms around Stanley and held him until their sobs subsided.

"Thanks, Scott," Stan whispered. "I, oh, man, I don't know how we'll get through this. I've tried to be strong, you know?"

Scott nodded and forced the lump of tears down his throat. "I know, Stanley. But you don't have to be strong all the time. All of you will get by a whole lot better if you share your grief. Are you ready to head back?"

Stan shook his head and swallowed another sob. "No. Wish I never had to go back. That place is never going to be the same," he muttered. He rubbed a sleeve across his eyes, heaved a sigh and nodded. "Yeah, I guess we'd better head back. Amber's going to need all the help she can get."

Scott's heavy sigh spoke volumes. "You're probably right. Just remember, we're only a phone call away, anytime, day or night, as often as necessary. I can be here in a few hours if any of you need me to."

Stanley nodded his thanks and let Scott drive him back to the Rockin' H ranch.

Chapter Three

Craig eyed his son with a mixture of pain and fury. In the past two-and-a-half years, he watched in helpless frustration while their relationship deteriorated from one of mutual love and respect to mere shreds of the former, more often leaning toward hopelessness.

It wasn't unusual for fathers and sons to have a difference of opinion. That was a natural part of a boy becoming a man. But Craig knew he and Ace suffered from more than a difference of opinion. They suffered from prolonged, unresolved grief.

"Good Lord, Daddy, it's only a rodeo! One day, one night away," Ace insisted. "Besides, I'm nineteen, almost twenty, you can't boss me around anymore," he snarled, stubbornly defying his father's request not to ride this time, this particular bull. Hoping against hope Craig would accompany him and lend the support he so desperately needed.

In a time when father and son should have been drawing closer, grief tore them apart. Tamera was dead. Life wasn't the same and hadn't been since the afternoon Craig found her curled up on the couch where he'd left her that morning. Only that afternoon she wasn't breathing. Her heart had merely stopped, unable to take the strain of laboring to provide enough blood and oxygen to her overloaded lungs. God, in His mercy, saw to it she didn't suffer. She simply went to sleep and never woke up. Her death was quick, painless.

And it was cruel.

Neither father nor son had gotten over nor completely dealt with the shock. Amber, with two children, a husband and a career had no choice but to go on living. Ace and Craig merely went through the motions. Craig continued to run his ranch. Ace continued to rodeo. Neither really lived.

Ace rode more and more, competed in tougher ranks, rode bigger, meaner bulls and fought his demons the only way he knew how, with force. This time Craig feared, really feared for his son's safety. He shook his head with a sigh. "Please, Ace. Just this once, use the head God gave you. This bull is a killer."

"Then come with me." Ace insisted. "Be there for me." His father rarely accompanied him anymore. His father hardly left the ranch anymore. In a rare moment of understanding and need, he took a step closer.

"I miss her too, Daddy, but you can't stay stuck here like this. It's not healthy. It's not natural. Life goes on."

Craig frowned, muttered a curse. "You can't tell me how to grieve Ace. I don't need you hounding me too. Your sister does that enough. Besides, she's due to deliver that baby soon. I'm not sure I should leave her."

Ace snarled. "She's not due for months yet and she has a husband to look after her."

Craig sighed again. "You're right," he admitted, and raked a weary hand over his face. "Okay Ace, I'll go with you. But do me a favor, will you? Take the summer off. No school. No rodeos."

"To stay on top I've got to stay in competition."

"You've been on top since before high school. Give it a rest. Give someone else a chance. I'm worried, Ace. Your riding has been more and more reckless. And you look tired."

"You never worried before," Ace declared.

Craig shook his head, swallowed hard. He hadn't had to worry before. A tiny, strained smile tugged at his lips. "Your mother worried enough for the both of us. She's not here to do it anymore, so I have to."

He took the next step, one move closer to his son. "Please," he urged, his voice soft, broken. "I miss my son. We need this time together."

It was Ace's turn to sigh. He was tired. But, staying too tired to think was the only way he knew to fight the grief eating at his heart and mind. Maybe, just maybe, the time had come to stop fighting, to deal with it, and to heal.

Ecclesiastes 3 floated through his mind in bits and pieces...*There is a time for every purpose under heaven; a time to be born and a time to die...a time to weep...a time to mourn...a time to heal.*

One look at his father convinced him the time had come for both of them.

"Okay Daddy," he agreed. "Okay. I'll take the summer off. College will wait. Rodeo will too." He turned on his heel and headed out the door.

"Where are you going?" Craig asked, regretting he hadn't reached out and hugged his son.

"Bed down the bulls," Ace remarked, which meant he needed, or wanted, a few minutes alone.

"Don't forget we're having supper at Amber's."

Ace grinned, really grinned. Another rarity. "Thank God," he remarked. Neither he nor his father had ever really gotten around to learning how to cook. Oh, they tried, but it was always so much easier to go out or re-heat something Amber brought or sent over. So much more palatable.

* * * * *

Amber Harris Morrison finished her bath and put on fresh clothes. She pulled the butterfly clip out of her hair and shook it loose so that it cascaded around her like a cloud of black silk. She ran a brush through the long locks and watched them fall into place in her new style, long layers which framed her face and a wisp of bang that made her look eighteen instead of almost twenty-eight, and drove Stanley wild.

Which was why she was in her present condition.

She picked up the dirty clothes and used the towel to wipe the tub, sink and cabinet top on her way out of the bathroom. She stopped in the doorway of their room and checked on the girls who were down for their afternoon nap.

At four, the twins Kaitlyn and Ashlyn still slept together despite the two beds in the room. Identical except for the color of their hair, they were miniatures of their mother and grandmother, inheriting the porcelain-like features and brilliant sapphire eyes. Because of her dark hair, Kaitlyn looked more like Amber. Ashlyn, on the other hand, had thick, silky, blond hair, making her the image of her grandmother and though he tried hard not to show it, her grandfather's favorite.

A tender smile curved Amber's lips and she bent to press a kiss to each silky head. "Oh Mama," her heart whispered, "if only you could see them now." She sighed when the baby in her womb stirred. "If only you were here."

She bit back the emotions swelling in her throat and eyes, and remembered the days when she and her mother would sit for hours and just watch the girls in whatever they were doing, sleeping or playing. She remembered sharing with her their first smile, giggle, tooth, steps. And their first word: Da Da. Her mother had told her that meant the next baby would be a boy. She hoped so.

Pulling the door almost closed, Amber went into the kitchen. She couldn't afford the luxury of watching them this afternoon. She had too much to do. Her father and brother were coming for supper. She put a roast in the oven and a Christian music c.d. in the stereo then set up the ironing board. She hoped to catch up on a few things before Stanley got home.

Despite the sadness of missing her mother, her heart filled with thanksgiving and praise for all of God's blessings. *Heavenly Father, thank You. Be with my father and brother in their time of grief. Please God, help them heal.* Tears pricked her eyes. She blinked them back with determination.

You know I've tried everything I can think of, but I just don't know how to help them. Peace filled her soul as she communed with the Lord in the silence of her heart.

With the intensity only a woman has, she prayed, ironed, watched the roast, and listened for the arrival of her husband or family. All the while she kept one ear tuned to the slightest sound from the girls' room and one eye on the back door. Her smile welcomed him when her father knocked softly and opened the door.

"Hi, Daddy." She stopped, walked, waddled actually, around the ironing board and greeted him with a smile, hug and a kiss. Her heart clutched at the sadness that lurked deep in his eyes. But a closer look revealed a light of something else there—hope an easing of grief, or merely acceptance? Whatever, it pleased her to see it. *Thank You, God.*

Craig hung his hat on the rack by the door and returned her greeting with one of his own. "Should you be doing that?" he queried, and eyed the ironing board and dresses which hung nearby.

Amber rolled her eyes. "I'm pregnant, Daddy. Not an invalid."

"Does Stanley know you're ironing?" Craig asked, and grinned at her unladylike snort.

"Is he here?" she challenged.

He chuckled. "Where are the girls?"

"Sleeping and I'll thank you not to wake them. They've played hard all morning. They need this nap. *I* need them to have this nap," she admitted with a smile.

Craig eased into a chair and accepted a cup of coffee with a sigh. "Yes, Ma'am."

After she checked on the roast, Amber returned to her ironing board and eyed her father. "You look good today. Where's Ace?"

"Bedding down the bulls. Probably going to lift some weights too before he heads this way."

Amber smiled at the thought of her baby brother. At nearly twenty, he sported the same height and width of her husband, both men just shy of her father's six-foot frame.

"You mean work up an appetite?" she queried, her tone a mite too sweet. Craig chuckled again. Music to her ears.

"Probably so. He wants me to go to San Angelo with him this weekend."

"You should," she urged.

He held up a hand to ward off the familiar arguments. "I said I would. Are you sure you're going to be all right?"

"Daddy," she chided her voice tender. "Stanley will be here. Of course I'll be all right." They talked, voices subdued until, one after the other, the girls appeared in the doorway.

Flushed and tousled, Kaitlyn spotted her grandfather first. "Hey, PaPaw," she drawled and held up her arms.

"Hey, Sweetheart," Craig replied and lifted her onto his lap. He held out a hand and urged Ashlyn up too. "How are my girls this afternoon?" he queried and kissed each on the cheek.

Their attention was drawn to the door when Stanley stepped up onto the porch, whistling. Giggling, they curled deeper into his chest while Craig urged them in the familiar joke: "Hide. Hide. He's going to make you get down."

He picked up the newspaper and shielded them from their father's view. "Hello, Stanley," he remarked when Stan walked through the door.

Stan acknowledged Craig with a nod then his eyes honed in on and narrowed at Amber. "What are you doing?"

Amber heaved a sigh of exasperation. "I'm sitting with my feet propped up, embroidering."

Her voice, laced with sweet sarcasm underscored the challenge in her flashing eyes.

With studied calmness Stanley reached over and unplugged the iron. He arched a brow at his father-in-law when she hissed at him. "You know the promise I made you a long time ago about not beating her?" He continued at Craig's grin. "What'll it take to make you forget it?"

Craig shook his head. "I warned you."

Stanley shook his head. "Right." He turned back to his wife, walked over and took the half-ironed dress off the board and tossed it onto the un-ironed pile. He noticed the finished ones and ground his teeth. "Can't leave you alone for a minute can I, Amber Nichole?"

She slapped her hands on her hips and snarled. "Well, if someone wouldn't buy all these frilly, cotton dresses, I wouldn't have to iron them."

"Bag them up and I'll take them to the cleaners tomorrow."

She growled and rolled her eyes. "Oh, please. There's no need to take them to the cleaners when I'm perfectly capable of ironing them myself."

"Right, and after this baby is born you can iron all you want. But until then..."

"What? Are you going to dress *him* in frilly, cotton dresses too?" she interrupted.

He grinned. "No. But I'll make sure he has plenty of jeans and cowboy shirts for you to tend to." He took her by the hand, led her to a chair, and kicked a stool under her feet. "There, My Sweet, how about a glass of milk or juice?" he offered and chuckled at her feisty reply. Pouring himself a cup of coffee, he sat down.

"Where are my girls?" he queried as though he couldn't see them piled up on their grandfather's lap or hear their giggles and, despite their best efforts, notice them unhidden by the newspaper.

Amber cleared her throat and bit back a smile. "They were taking a nap."

He eyed Craig, a pointed lift to his brow, his eyes glittering.

"I've been meaning to talk to you. You know, when their feet touch the floor they'll be too big to sit on your lap." He grinned when the girls giggled and pulled their knees up to make sure their feet were nowhere near the floor.

Craig chuckled and bit back a groan when the two pair of heels dug into his thighs. "No way, they'll never be too big to sit on PaPaw's lap. They may have to take turns but..."

"Me, first!" Kaitlyn insisted, and snuggled into his chest.

Ashlyn, shyer than her twin, simply looked up at him with huge, pleading, eyes and a trembling lip. With a soft groan, Craig pulled her closer. "We'll worry about that when the time comes," he promised, and hugged her to his heart. "Until then you both can sit here anytime you want."

Stan and Amber shared a smile. Forgiven, he leaned over, his lips covering hers in a tender caress and whispered his love.

Ace arrived and Kaitlyn rushed from her perch on Craig's lap to throw herself into his arms. "Uncle Ace! Uncle Ace!"

Ace laughed and grabbed her up, tossing her into the air. "Hi ya, Squirt!"

"I not a Squirt!"

"Yes you are. You're a squirt and your sister's a peep squeak." He replied and attacked her with tickle monsters until she shrieked for him to stop.

Taking advantage of being the only one on his lap, Ashlyn snuggled deeper into Craig's chest. "I not a peep squeak. Huh, PaPaw?"

Craig smiled. "You certainly aren't, Sweetheart," he replied, wishing with all his heart Tamera was there. Ashlyn reminded him so much of her grandmother, it hurt. So much that all he wanted to do was take her home with him and never let her out of his sight. Irrational thoughts he knew, but the way he felt. If only he hadn't left Tamera. If only he had insisted she go to a doctor. If only. . . He choked back the tears and cuddled his granddaughter, stroking the silky blond hair off her face.

Her father's face was ravaged with pain, his eyes dark with it, his voice thick with it. Fighting tears of her own, Amber got up to check on the roast under the watchful eye of her husband.

After dinner was served and the dishes done, they retired to the living room. Stanley picked up his guitar and strummed the strings in a gentle caress. Amber's heart swelled as he tuned it. There was a time after her mother's death, when there wasn't much music in the house. The absence of music was Stanley's way of grieving, not to mention the fact he'd smashed his guitar to shreds in a fit of grief and anguish. At the request of the family, he sang at her funeral, his voice thick with emotion, tears streaming down his cheeks for the mother-in-law who had meant so much to him. But, as it usually does, time, faith, and living eased the grief and now music was as much a part of their lives as it had always been.

The influx of new country artists, male and female broadened his scope of music. There were songs for any occasion, to laugh, to cry. Stanley made it a point to never sing songs that made them cry. The best were those reflecting his favorite hobbies: seduce your wife or tease your daughters. Anticipating both he smiled. "Any requests?"

The girls jumped up and down. "Barney! Barney!"

He frowned. "Barney? That's baby songs," he teased, and stroked the strings in that same tender way. In a soft voice, he sang....

"I love you, you love me, and we're a happy family. With a great big hug..." he trailed off when they threw their arms around his neck. "And a kiss from me to you...," They pressed their tiny lips to his cheeks, kissing every hair-roughened inch, and then ran around the room hugging and kissing everyone. Raising sweet, excited voices, slightly off key, they finished the chorus with him.

"Won't you say you love me too?" Flinging themselves in their father's arms they thanked him with more hugs and kisses. Somehow Stanley managed to catch both without dropping the guitar.

Amber watched the display with tears in her eyes. She leaned over and put her head on Craig's shoulder. "Remember when I was that age?"

His smile was tremulous, his eyes haunted. "Oh, yes." He chortled, and kissed her forehead. "Your mother accused me of spoiling you beyond repair."

Amber knelt at his feet, her eyes searched his. "I miss my daddy," she said softly. "I need you back."

His eyes narrowed into slits of steel. "What do you want me to do Amber, run out and find another wife?"

Her face paled, she gasped, and tears filled her eyes. She flung away from him, ran into the bedroom and sank down onto her bed, fighting the sobs that shook her.

Craig regretted his harsh words immediately and rose to follow his daughter. Pulling her into his arms, he apologized. "I'm sorry, Sweetheart. I'm trying Amber. I really am. It's just so hard." His voice broke. "I loved her so much. And I miss her. It should have been me. If only it had been me, then she could be here for you."

"Don't say that!" she insisted. "I loved Mama but I would never wish it were you! Never! We need you, Daddy. Ace and I both need you. We need your strength, your wisdom and guidance. We need you, not this shell of a man you've become."

"But I can't teach Ace everything he needs to know. I can't teach him the things a mother could, like how to be tender."

Amber cupped her father's face in her hands. "Oh, Daddy, next to Stanley, you're the most tenderhearted man I know," she assured him. "Ace can, and has, learned enough tenderness from Mama and from you to make his own way. He'll grow up to be as much of a man as you are. He already is. Right now we just want and need our father back."

Back in the living room, Ace turned to Stanley, his eyes fierce, voice raw.

"She needs to leave him alone in his grief."

Stan agreed. "I know. But she worries as only a woman–a pregnant woman–can. She's worried about you too." Ace shrugged and tried to be nonchalant. But his eyes were haunted.

"I'm fine."

"Are you, Ace? Are you really?"

"I will be as soon as I get my father back. It's like he died that day too."

Stanley nodded in understanding. "That's what Amber says too. But remember, Ace, I'm here. If ever you need me, I'll always be here, for you as much as for Amber and your father."

Craig came back into the living room. An apology shone in the haunted eyes, hovered on his lips. Stan waved it away with a shrug, put down his guitar and went to his wife. He pulled her in his arms and stroked the length of silky black hair off her face.

She sniffled and buried her face in his chest. "If you dare play a sad song I'll break that guitar over your head," she threatened in a shaky voice. "No matter what they ask to hear."

He chuckled, pressed his lips to her forehead. "Yes, Ma'am."

As soon as everyone settled down Stan picked up the guitar again, strummed to the tune of every one's favorite songs but made sure they were all lively ones.

Chapter Four

Amber put away the dishes and started supper with a light heart. In the weeks since Ace's last rodeo she had seen a big change in her father and brother. They were healing at last. There were still moments, days even, when she would catch a shadow or glimmer of pain, deep in the identical gray eyes, but more often of late, they shone with laughter and joy.

Though healing had begun, neither showed an interest in learning to cook nor in hiring a maid to do it for them. They were coming for supper again tonight. Amber vowed, under the fretful gaze of her husband, to keep them fed as long as she was able.

Which wouldn't be much longer, she thought and rubbed her well-rounded abdomen.

As her pregnancy advanced into the last trimester, she was, and would continue to be, getting around less and less. Especially if Stanley had any say in the matter. He worried about her constantly as the due date for the baby got nearer, insisting she rest more and do less. He pampered her beyond reason, came in early and took more and more responsibility over the care of the twins.

Amber knew the Bible said for wives to be submissive to their husbands, and that it was out of love and concern for her and their unborn child he was so domineering. Therefore, she usually indulged him by giving in to his badgering. Usually.

Stanley opened the back door and got a whiff of the aromas which flowed from the kitchen. He frowned at his wife, his eyes narrow slits of shimmering blue. "What are you doing?" he asked when she pulled a ham out of the oven to baste it.

"I'm hungry for ham," she remarked all innocence.

"Right," he growled then took it from her and put it back in the oven. He shoved the door shut with a shake of his head. "Then you can send leftovers home with your father and Ace."

Amber blinked back tears at his frustrated tone of voice. "Something wrong with making sure my father and brother eat decently once in a while?"

"Your father needs to hire a maid to clean and cook for them. And you shouldn't do so much."

"I guess he can't stand the thought of some stranger in Mama's kitchen," she hissed, her eyes icy shards of sapphire.

Justly chastised, Stanley bit back his retort. He missed her too. Tamera's death had left a huge hole in their lives. Regretting his harsh words, he wrapped his arms around his wife. "I'm sorry, My Sweet, you know I just don't want you to overdo it."

Whether she admitted it or not this pregnancy wasn't as easy on Amber as her first one. She'd been sick a lot early on and had threatened miscarriage once. Despite that, she insisted she was fine, and did her best to fill the role of wife and mother as well as nurturing daughter and sister.

"I know, Stan," she admitted. "I'm fine. I rested for a while when I put the girls down for their nap," she soothed in an attempt to appease him.

"Good." He nodded his approval. "You should rest more. Stay off your feet. And I don't mean by sitting at your desk for hours at a stretch."

Though she hadn't sold anything lately, and though her time to work was limited, Amber still loved to write. Though her royalties were by no means enough to make them rich, she managed to write enough to keep herself happy, the public interested, and the publisher asking for more.

She rolled her eyes. "You're beginning to sound more like a father than a husband."

Stanley grinned, determined not to be intimidated by her tone. "What time are our guests expected?"

"Not for a while."

"Are the girls asleep?" he queried, his voice husky.

A loving, teasing light lit his eyes. Amber felt her cheeks grow warm. More so from the heat in his gaze in lieu of the warmth from the oven. "Yes."

Stanley took her in his arms and captured her lips in a thorough kiss. His hands ran over her in a teasing caress while his lips traveled over her cheeks to her ear then down her throat. Her soft sigh of pleasure raced through him. He chuckled and swung her up in his arms. He turned, caught a glimpse of Ashlyn in the doorway, and groaned.

Amber giggled.

Chiding her with a firm look, he put her down, pressed his lips to hers in a kiss of promise then went to kneel beside his daughter.

"Hi, Sweetheart, have a good nap?"

She shook her head, rubbed her eyes and held her arms toward him. Stanley picked her up and kissed her soft cheek. He sat, pressed her head to his chest in a hug, and brushed the silky strands of blond hair off her face as the last dregs of sleep evaporated from her eyes. Within moments, she chattered away, giving him a full report of their escapades of the day. He listened in earnest and gave her his undivided attention until Kaitlyn joined them. Somehow, he managed to give each equal attention and still keep a conscientious eye toward his wife.

Amber smiled and ran her fingers through his gold-tipped chestnut hair. She poured him a glass of tea and prepared the girls each a glass of milk then drew a plate of still-warm cookies out of the window. Placing them each two on a napkin, she served their daughters a snack then set the plate in front of her husband. Dinner would be a while yet.

As soon as they finished their snack, as well as the cookies Stanley snatched for them, they wriggled free from his grasp, anxious to go play while there was still plenty of time, but stood like dutiful little girls while their hair got brushed and braided to keep the tangles out. Then they were off, the door banging in their wake.

Stanley picked up the dishes and set them in the sink. He pulled his wife in his arms. "Now, where were we?" he queried in a soft, husky voice.

Although their lovemaking was postponed until that night, Amber indulged him with a few kisses and caresses. And, like a good little wife, she sat while he checked on supper.

Craig and Ace arrived promptly at five, their appearance announced by the delighted squeals of the twins when they were swung up into the air by a set of strong arms. Greeting them with hugs and kisses the two men swapped girls so each could be amply greeted by the other. They hung their hats on the rack by the door then Craig bent to place a kiss on his daughter's cheek. Ace did the same and kissed Amber's other cheek.

"Umm, smells good," Craig remarked, inhaling deeply the aromas filling the room. "You're turning into a mighty good cook, Stanley," he teased his son-in-law.

Stanley shrugged. "Not too hard. Be happy to give lessons," he hinted with a bold grin.

Craig laughed. "It'll be up to Ace to take them. I'm a disaster in the kitchen. Huh, Son?"

Ace answered with a snort and a roll of his eyes. "Talk about, can't even boil water. But I've learned how to make tea and toast. And eggs," he bragged, his voice tinged with laughter.

"Ugh!" Amber wrinkled her nose. "Tea, with eggs?" Ace laughed into her teasing sapphire eyes, his sparkled with mischief.

"We'd have milk if Daddy would learn how to milk the cow. Or drive to the grocery store."

Craig grunted. "I'm a rancher not a dairy farmer."

"Yeah," his son taunted. "A degree in agriculture plus a hundred years experience in no way enables you to make a list, drive to the store and pick up groceries in town. He can remember the horse feed but not the milk," he complained, with a wink at his sister who joined in the teasing and chided her father.

"All right you two, show some respect here. I am still your father."

"That's about all you're good for," Ace remarked.

"I'm still well able to take you to task young man and don't forget it," his father insisted.

Ace gasped in mock horror. "Heaven forbid."

The banter was interrupted by a shriek from outside when the twins ran up on the porch screaming. "A snake, a snake!"

The men scrambled for the door all at once. Somehow, they managed to squeeze through without breaking the frame, relieved to find only a worm. A huge night crawler had found its way into the sand box. Craig stomped around in the sand to make sure there were no more while Ace teased the fear right out of the girls. Stanley shook with laughter at the four of them and soothed his concerned wife. They returned to the kitchen and the girls rushed in to clean up before supper was served.

Afterward, Craig sighed and rubbed his stomach. "Man that was good. I'm stuffed. How about you, Ace?"

"Not me. I'm ready for desert."

Stanley took the plate of cookies out of the window and set it on the table. "Here, bottomless pit. Pig out."

Ace grinned and raced to finish his cookie before the twins finished theirs. Laughing and teasing, he taunted them until their lips were smeared with chocolate from trying to eat and laugh at the same time.

Amber chuckled and rubbed her stomach where the baby stretched and pushed against his boundaries. "Enough, Ace," she admonished. "You're spoiling them. Too many cookies before bed is not good for them, makes them crazy."

"That's okay," he remarked with a wink at the girls. "They'll go to bed like two little angels. Huh, girls?"

"No," Kaitlyn answered and eyed her uncle.

He arched an eyebrow at her, his expression firm. "What did you say?"

She smiled, not the least bit wary of him. "No. We don't want to go to bed like two little angels. We want to play," she insisted.

"Oh yeah, play what?"

"Hide and seek! Hide and seek!" they squealed in unison.

Ace grinned. "Well you'd better hide. And be quick about it. One, two, three," he counted aloud while they rushed from the table to hide.

Amber rolled her eyes. "Here we go. They'll be up for hours now."

Stan agreed. "Yeah, and he can stay here and tend to them too. We'll go home with you," he informed his father-in-law.

Craig chuckled. "Suits me."

"Oh, no, you're not sticking me with those two little heathens," Ace declared, forgetting just moments ago they were angels. He ignored the giggles which were a dead giveaway and made a show of looking for them.

At her husband's insistence, Amber rested while he loaded the dishwasher and served coffee. The three adults enjoyed intimate conversation while the three children played in the rest of the house.

As the evening wore on and the twins wore out, Amber sat with the girls while they took a bath. She helped them to dry off and dress and then ushered them into the living room to say goodnight to their uncle and grandfather.

Stanley carried them to their room and took his turn reading them a story while Amber visited with her father and brother.

"Oh, by the way, I talked with Scott today, "Craig informed his daughter. "They plan to come up for the summer. Trina's offered to help you with the baby and Lexie will help with the twins."

Ace snorted. "He waits until I've promised no rodeos and no school to invite her here."

"I can't wait to meet her," Amber remarked. Being so much alike, her father and brother agreed on nearly everything, and managed mutually satisfying compromises on the things they didn't, except this one subject: Scott's adopted daughter. It seemed the little lady had left both men with very different, very conflicting opinions.

Though they met her nearly three years ago, Amber had yet to meet Lexie. Her father had pulled out of his coma once again and Lexie went to live with him. The reprieve lasted only a couple of months before he had a relapse and died. After, she'd been placed with Scott and Trina who adopted her right away. For her last year of high school she attended an honor academy in north Louisiana. Upon graduation, she spent a year abroad, a trip made possible by the inheritance left by her father.

"Meet who?" Stanley asked when he came in from the girls' room on the tail end of the conversation. His question brought a smile to one man's lips and a snarl to the others. He grinned when Amber told him the news, anxious also to meet the little girl who had left such lasting impressions on Craig and Ace.

After his in-law's left, carrying huge bowls of leftovers with them as well as the rest of the cookies, Stanley urged his wife into a hot bath while he checked on the horses and the girls before closing up the house. He arrived in their bedroom to find her already snoozing.

"She sleeps," he whispered with a suppressed groan. Careful not to disturb her, he crawled into the bed beside her. She opened her eyes with a smile and reached for him. He pulled her into his arms and uttered her name on a breathless whisper of need. His lips covered hers in a tender, hungry caress.

* * * * *

Meanwhile, on the outskirts of Lafayette, Louisiana, Scott gave Lexie another run down on his friends whom she'd heard all about before, but, with the exception of Craig and Ace, had yet to meet.

"You'll love Stanley," he promised his voice thick with pride and admiration for the boy he'd grown to love and accept as part of the family.

"He's the most unpretentious man you'll ever meet. He's talented in more ways than one but doesn't have a smug or conceited bone in his body. His Thoroughbreds go to the Triple Crown races, his Quarter horses go to National championships in both rodeo and shows, his Arabians are known all over the world and his Walkers participate and win in the finest Equestrian competitions. He loves Amber beyond reason and simply dotes on those girls."

"Probably good he's not conceited or pretentious," Lexie remarked, her voice a mite too sweet. "His brother-in-law holds the market on that."

Scott laughed. "Be nice Lex. You haven't seen Ace in over two years. He's grown up a lot since then. So have you. Or so I thought," he teased.

She snorted. "Tell me about Amber," she urged, loving the way his eyes danced when he thought about his best friend's daughter.

"Amber is beautiful, in every way. She's got her father's height and long, black hair, and her mother's disposition. She's sweet and friendly, and never meets a stranger or someone beneath her respect. She's a beautiful woman and mother. She's shouldered a lot since Tamera's death but, so far, seems to be the one to keep the family going."

"And she's also a writer."

Scott nodded. A note of paternal pride laced his voice, "Yep, she doesn't compete in the same circles as the big names you've heard, but her writing is well above the rest."

"And you're opinion is in no way biased," she teased.

He chuckled. "Not me."

Lexie laughed. "I can't wait to meet her. I've read her books. They're interesting, unusual. They have more...I don't know, something the others don't."

"More soul," Scott interjected. "She writes from a spiritual stand point, mixing love, life and romance with faith in God. It's a new and interesting kind of writing. The day will come when it'll be in big demand. Mark my words."

Lexie propped her chin on her hand and regarded him with dancing eyes. "Tell me more. I don't remember much about Mr. Harris. Except that he adored his wife and children. Or Ace. Except that he's a chauvinistic jerk cowboy."

Scott rolled his eyes at her teasing. "Oh boy, Lexie, it's going to be a long summer if you go there with that attitude."

She grinned. "So change my mind," she challenged.

Three weeks later they sat on Craig's porch waiting and wondering where Ace was. So far everything Scott told her about Amber and Stanley, Lexie agreed with. They were beautiful people, sweet, kind, funny and hopelessly in love. Their feelings showed every time they looked at each other. From the first moment on, she felt like she'd known them all of her life, like she was a part of the family. The twins were absolutely adorable and she couldn't wait to spend more time with them.

"I wonder where in the world that son of mine is," Craig muttered and consulted his watch for the tenth time in just as many minutes. "He said he'd be here." What he didn't admit was the resistance Ace showed when he'd been requested to come in early.

"There he is! There he is!" The twins announced, bouncing with excitement while pointing to a horse wandering toward the house.

Ace stopped his horse beside the porch and dismounted. "Sorry I'm late," he shook Scott's hand and kissed Trina's cheek.

"Alexis," he greeted with a cool nod in her direction, and then turned back to his horse. "As you can see I got side tracked," he explained to his father while he untied a calf from the back of his saddle.

"What'cha got there Ace?" Craig asked.

Ace grinned, a cocky, arrogant, heart-stopping grin. A teasing light danced in his eyes.

"It's an orphaned calf otherwise known as a maverick," he answered.

Craig slapped his forehead with his palm. "Would you listen to that? The boy's a genius! Not even twenty and look how much he knows. Got a wise mouth too," he muttered under his breath, when the others burst out laughing.

"What happened?" Craig wanted to know.

"What's in the saddle bag?" Lexie whispered to Amber.

Amber frowned. "What?"

Lexie nodded her eyes wide. "The saddlebag moved."

Amber leaned forward to get a better look. Sure enough, the saddlebag moved again. "What's in the bag, Ace?"

Ace placed the calf on the ground, opened the saddlebag and lifted out a squirming pup. He carried it to the porch and held it out for them to see. "Seems a cow and coyote got into a fight, neither won. The cow bled to death. The coyote crawled off and died too."

"Ace, you can't keep a coyote pup. It'll never be tame enough to be around the children," his father chided.

"What did you expect me to do? Leave him out there to starve to death?" he demanded, eyes flashing.

"It'd been more humane if you'd shot him and put him out of his misery," Craig insisted, to the anguished cries of the women and children.

Ace shoved the pup in his hands. "You do it then," he insisted and turned on his heel.

Craig frowned. "That's real good, Son. Leave the responsibility to me."

Ace tossed a grin over his shoulder. Charming, boyish, lethal. Lexie stared in fascination at both he and the coyote pup.

"That's what father's are for," Ace taunted, "To clean up behind you when you fail at your responsibility." He picked up the calf and headed toward the barn. "C'mon Ritchie, you can help," he teased.

Ignoring the barb, Richard followed in his footsteps.

Lexie watched the exchange between Ace and his father with interest and noted the tender light in his eyes when he called Richard 'Ritchie.' He had certainly changed a lot since the last time she saw him. He'd been good looking then, in a rugged sort of way and despite his arrogance but now....

A flush warmed her cheeks when she realized how incredibly sexy Ace had become.

Chapter Five

Craig eyed the squirming ball of fur in his hands and cringed at the thought of killing it.

"You're not really going to shoot it are you?" Lexie cried.

His gaze cut from her anguished eyes to the soulful expression of the pup, which whimpered. He frowned. "Do I have a choice in the matter?"

His eyes begged Scott for help, but Craig could tell by Scott's grin there was no way was he stepping into that one!

"Please don't," Lexie pleaded, lifting wide, imploring eyes to his. "I'll take care of it."

Craig relented with a groan. "Okay, but only until its old enough to take to the zoo or turn loose."

Lexie petted and cooed and cuddled the pup as if it were a baby.

"What are you going to do with him now?" Scott asked her.

She smiled into his merry brown eyes and shrugged. "I don't know."

He chuckled. "You can look forward to getting up every few hours to feed him, Lex. Just like a baby."

"I don't mind," she crooned and rubbed her cheeks against the silky fur.

He laughed again. "Maybe Ace will fix you up with a box and some bedding, and a bottle."

"A bottle?" She asked and looked to Craig for confirmation.

Craig nodded. "Yeah, he's too young to be eating. C'mon Lex, let's see what we can find."

"I think there's an old bottle around here somewhere," Amber cut in. She rose from the swing and went in to look. She found a small baby bottle and brought it to her father.

Taking Lexie by the hand, Craig led her to the barn where Ace was busy feeding the calf. "How's he doing?" he asked his son.

Ace shrugged. "Took to the bottle right off. I guess if you're hungry enough, anything will work."

"I just hope this pup does as well," Craig remarked and turned back to Lexie. "Don't be surprised, or disappointed if he doesn't make it, Sweetheart. Remember, he's a wild animal. Most wild animals don't do well in captivity."

Lexie frowned, her eyes full of fear. "I won't," she promised in a soft voice. But her lip trembled.

Ace watched the exchange in silence. She still seemed a bit uppity, but the years had made a difference in Alexis Jayne Morgan Hensley. She'd grown up, he noted. His eyes swept over her in appreciation. In all the right places. Ace turned back to the calf and put a lid on his wayward thoughts. She was Scott's daughter.

Lexie listened attentively when Craig explained how to mix the milk for the pup. She cradled it in her arms, sat cross-legged in the hay and coaxed him to nurse. After a few spurts and sputters he seemed to get the hang of it.

Craig watched in silence remembering another woman, just as gentle, who had held a filly in her arms, cuddling and cooing while it nursed a bottle. His heart whispered her name: *Tamera.* A sense of peace filled his soul while he watched the young girl play mama to an orphaned coyote pup while his son did the same with the calf. They were a lot alike, these two young people. More than they suspected. More than they cared to admit. He'd seen the way Ace's eyes had swept over Lexie. This would be an interesting summer.

After the babies were fed, Ace bedded down the calf while Craig fixed a box for the pup. He would sleep in the room with Lexie for now.

Lexie carried the box and the pup back to the porch. Her eyes glowed. Her cheeks were flushed with excitement.

"I did it," she told Scott and Trina. "I got him to nurse."

"Remember," Craig cautioned. "Don't get too attached."

But it was too late. She was hooked, and determined to do everything in her power to keep the pup alive.

They watched the children gather around to pet him. Interest waning quickly, they opted for a game of hide and seek. Even Richard couldn't refuse the game, especially when asked so sweetly by the twins.

Kaitlyn, who'd been warned more than once to use the steps, glanced fearlessly over her shoulder at her father. Her eyes sparkled with mischief, her chin lifted in defiance. She ignored his warning yet again, jumped off the porch and ran to hide.

Stanley's eyes narrowed. "Looks like it's time for a demonstration in effective parenting," he remarked and followed in his daughter's wake. "Kaitlyn, come here!" he commanded, pointing to the ground in front of his feet.

Everyone watched her stop, turn, her expression woeful, and walk slowly toward him. Stanley squatted down and looked her straight in the eye. "Haven't you been told repeatedly to use the steps and not to jump off the porch?"

"What's repeatly?"

She had a habit of trying to side track him with questions. Stan knew this and bit back a smile, determined to remain firm. "Don't try it, Kaitlyn," he warned. "Repeatedly means more than once. Haven't you been told more than once to use the steps?"

"Yes, Sir," she admitted. Her lip trembled and tears rushed to her eyes.

"Don't cry," he warned. "You have no reason to cry yet, do you?"

She nodded and rubbed her little eyes. "You're mad at me," she whined.

Stanley ground his teeth, fought the urge to take her in his arms, and made another stab at disciplining his daughter. "Do you know why I'm upset with you?"

"Cause I jumped off the porch."

"Right, and what do you think I should do about it?"

She hesitated as though giving the question a great deal of consideration. Suddenly she brightened. "I think you should forgive me and give me a hug," she answered, knowing that's how he solved it when she and her sister fought.

Stanley heard the snickers from the porch and ducked his head to hide a grin. He coughed to cover a chuckle. He shook his head and rubbed his face. Raising his eyes heavenward he could almost see the face of God smiling at the innocent antics of the child. God, help me, he thought, wondering how on earth he was supposed to reconcile such sweet innocence with so much mischievousness.

Those whom He loves, He chastises.

The Scripture floated through his mind and Stanley knew without a doubt, left undisciplined, those sweet yet mischievous antics would become more daring and more dangerous.

"So, you think I should just forgive you and give you a hug?" He asked his daughter.

She nodded.

"How do I know you're sorry for disobeying me?"

"I sorry, Daddy," she apologized, her voice solemn, expression serious.

"Well..." Stan thought a minute. "I'm not the only one you should apologize to. Everyone on that porch," he pointed to them, "saw you disobey me. Do you want them to think you're a bad little girl who doesn't listen to her daddy?"

"No, Sir." She shook her head, her lip trembling again.

"Start apologizing then," he commanded. He watched her walk up on the porch. Beginning with Craig she apologized.

"I sorry, PaPaw."

Craig smiled down and stroked her dark head. "Thank you, Sweetheart."

"I sorry, Uncle Ace."

He winked. "No problem, Squirt."

"I not a squirt," she challenged.

"Kaitlyn." Her father's firm voice stopped her from engaging in the familiar banter with her uncle. Dutifully, she removed the smile from her face.

Ace glared at Stanley as, one by one, Kaitlyn moved on to Scott and Trina then Lexie. By the time she got to Amber, her cheeks were red, her lip trembled and tears clung to her thick, black lashes.

"I sorry, Mama," she mumbled in a heartbreaking whisper.

Amber hugged her daughter to her breast. "Thank you, Sweetheart. I'm proud of you for apologizing to everyone. Now, go finish your talk with Daddy," she said her tone gentle but firm.

With measured, careful steps Kaitlyn descended the porch via the steps and walked toward her father. She stood before him; hands folded in front of her, chin lifted high, blinking back tears, and waited.

Stanley's heart burst with pride at the little beauty which stood so proudly in front of him. He opened his arms to her, his smile tender. "I forgive you, Kaitlyn," he whispered, when she flung herself in them, her smile brilliant.

"Thank you, Daddy."

"I love you, Sweetheart. Do you know why I don't want you jumping off the porch?"

She nodded. "Cause I might hurt myself."

"That's right. Then I'd have to spank you for hurting my little girl," he teased, thrilled at her giggle. "Now," he put her down. "Run along and play with the other kids. And Kaitlyn..." His voice sharpened and garnered her attention once more. She raised glittering eyes to his. "If I even hear you jumped off the porch again, I'm going to spank you. Do you understand?"

"Yes, Sir."

"Okay." He patted her on the behind. "Go on now. Consider it a lesson learned."

With a fleeting smile over her shoulder, she ran off to play.

"That child's gonna be the death of me yet," he remarked with a shake of his head, followed by a chuckle. He walked up onto the porch and turned to Ace who was still glaring at him. "Don't you even start in on me," he warned.

"You're a mean old goat," Ace insisted. "Hateful, humiliating that baby like that."

Stan sighed. "You'd call me something else if I let her jump and she hurt herself. Wait till you have a child of your own. Then you'll understand."

Ace snorted.

"Did you let Amber jump off the porch when she was that age?" Stanley demanded of his father-in-law.

Craig grinned and winked at his daughter. "I told her not to. But she did it anyway."

"You see!" Stan insisted. "If you wouldn't have raised such a hard-headed child, I wouldn't have two of them trying their level best to take after their mother."

"I knew you'd find a way to blame me," Craig grunted, when everyone around him laughed.

Stanley continued to glare at his father-in-law. "Then on top of that, you cursed me the day they were born."

"Cursed you, how?" Craig asked, seriously puzzled.

"I hope they both have those sassy sapphire eyes and drive you to the brink of insanity," Stan mimicked, reminding Craig of his words the day the twins were born. "Well they have and are," Stanley concluded. "I sure hope my son has brown eyes," he lamented.

"That's highly unlikely," Scott informed him with a laugh.

"Thank you, Dr. Hensley," Stan remarked with exaggerated sarcasm.

Lexie giggled. "I like the way he says 'my son' as though he's doing it all by himself."

"Shut up Alexis," Stan insisted, with a grin into her sparkling eyes and tugged lightly on her flaming auburn hair. "Who asked you anyway?"

She laughed. "When's the baby due?" she asked Amber.

Amber sighed and rubbed her belly. "Anytime now."

"You have names picked out?"

She nodded with a smile. "Tamera Joy if it's a girl," she admitted and saw her father's eyes soften.

"I like that," he said, his voice thick with emotion.

Everyone murmured in agreement.

"We haven't decided completely on a boy's name," Amber admitted then glared at her husband. "I want to name him after Stanley, but he doesn't like his name."

"That's right. I will not have my son being called Art the Fart. I bloodied many a nose before the teachers got wise and just called me Stanley. I like Stanley Harris Morrison."

"And what will we call him?" Amber demanded. "Harry? I don't think so. Then we'll have to worry about him being called 'Harry the Fairy'."

Stan grinned. "We'll just call him Bubba."

"Not in this lifetime mister," Amber insisted. "No child of mine will ever be called Bubba. I know, why don't we call him William?" she suggested, wide-eyed. "William Stanley Morrison. Then we can call him Bill or Billy. Or BS." She leaned forward her eyes narrow slits of sapphire. "Cause he'll probably be as full of it as his father," she huffed.

Stanley grinned. "William Stanley Morrison. I like that, but not BS."

Amber frowned. "He'll probably be stuck with something like 'Billy Bob'."

Stanley raised her hand to his lips and smiled into her blistering blue gaze. "I promise to never call him Billy Bob."

"It's settled then?" Scott wanted to know. "Tamera Joy if it's a girl and William Stanley if it's a boy?"

They nodded.

"Look at that sunset Lex," he urged, and turned to his daughter, his voice thick with pride, as though he'd requested it especially for her.

Lexie watched the sky turn several brilliant shades of orange, peach and pink. Hints of yellow and blue stubbornly clung to the light. She could almost hear the sky sigh as the flaming orb slid below the western horizon. She turned toward the east and gasped with delight to note the moon already in its rise, full and glowing. The area around it brightened as colors bled from the sky and melded into darkness. A billion stars lit up the night. She sighed, the beauty overwhelming.

"I've seen some beautiful places in the last year," she remarked. "Especially Ireland, with its rolling green hills and remarkably blue sky. But life must have been wonderful growing up here." She looked to Amber for conformation. "With these wide-open spaces, big blue skies and all this raw beauty." Her voice lowered, eyes twinkled. "Masculine and otherwise," she teased.

Amber laughed. "You've heard the expression 'heaven on earth'?"

Stanley's chuckle cut off Lexie's reply. "That's right. That's why the first two letters of my name are the abbreviation of saint."

That brought another round of laughter. Amber sighed. "C'mon St. Stanley, round up your little angels and lets go home."

A sharp whistle brought the twins running. Amber rolled her eyes. "He calls them like he calls his horses."

He grinned. "Works doesn't it?"

She had to agree it did.

"Y'all don't have to rush off," Craig insisted. "Why don't you stay a while? Amber can rest and then we'll go out for supper."

Amber shook her head with a smile, kissed her father's cheek, and declined. "I want my own bed tonight. The girls rest better in theirs. Besides, we have a full day planned tomorrow with the barbeque and all. We'll see you bright and early," she promised.

"How bright and early depends on how late she sleeps," Stan admitted, and slipped his arm around her waist.

Amber glared at him. "And if you have your way that'll be till noon."

He chuckled but refrained from comment.

They said good night amongst hugs and kisses, and then went home.

Around midnight, Ace came in from checking on his calf. The soft sound of weeping drew him to the den. His heart thudded in his chest when he remembered the one horrifying time he heard weeping from that room, and the many times since. Times when he'd find his father in there, a drink in his hand, tears on his cheeks, a haunted look in his eyes, weeping and mourning for his mother. With soft, slow steps he approached the door, pushed it open and looked inside. His heart clenched at what he saw.

Lexie sat on the floor and cuddled the coyote pup which was dead, her face buried in his fur, sobbing her heart out.

Ace felt the icy reserve he'd built around his heart and his opinion of her begin to melt. "Don't cry, Lex," he whispered, and stepped over to her and pried the pup from her grasp. "We warned you he probably wouldn't make it."

"But he seemed to be doing okay," she sobbed.

"You don't know that for sure. Maybe he hadn't eaten in a while. Maybe he was sick anyway. Maybe the milk didn't give him enough nourishment. There could be a million reasons why he died."

"I don't understand why everything I love dies," she wailed. "My father, my best friend, and now this!"

Heart in his throat, Ace swallowed hard. He understood all too well how she felt. "I know, Lex. Sometimes it seems that way, especially when your dreams die with them."

She looked at him, her eyes devastated.

"I was so sorry to hear about your mom, Ace. I wanted to come. I should have. But I just couldn't bear it at the time with my father and all." His smile was tender, eyes haunted.

"Thank you," he whispered his voice hoarse with unshed tears. "I'll go bury the pup now," he offered. "Want to come?"

She shook her head no, curled up on the couch in a ball of misery, and wept.

Ace laid the pup back in the box, carried it outside and, with a heavy heart, buried it beside the barn. Going back into the house, he went back into the den to check on Lexie. Unable to bear her continued sobs, he pulled her in his arms, rocking, soothing, until the soft sobs subsided and she fell asleep.

He brushed the thick mane of auburn hair off her face and watched her sleep, overwhelmed with feelings he'd never experienced, never expected to feel. He tucked the covers around her and then went up to his room. Sleep, when it came, wasn't restful. Green eyes full of anguish haunted his dreams. He awoke the next morning feeling and looking haggard.

* * * * *

Craig walked into the kitchen surprised to find his son up and still in the house. "What's wrong, Ace?" The boy looked like he'd wrestled with the devil half the night.

"The coyote pup died last night."

"Aw, no, how's Lexie?"

"Devastated. She cried."

Craig smiled. "That's what women do when they're upset," he reminded.

Ace shook his head. "Not like that. It wasn't those few, forced tears that are meant to bend a man's will. She had her face buried in his fur and she was crying, really crying. Just...it was..." he shook his head and raked his fingers through his hair. She had shaken him to the core.

Craig bit back a grin. Ace had never been upset over a woman. He'd learned early that wealth and recognition meant too much to too many of them. A hard lesson for a young man that had jaded him. "I hate to hear that."

"You think Stanley's up?"

Craig glanced out the window and nodded. "If the sun's up, Stanley's up."

Ace nodded. "I think I'll run over and see if Sheba has an extra puppy."

"You might ask Scott first. What if Lexie goes off to college or something? Who's going to take care of the puppy then?"

Ace shrugged. "If Scott doesn't want it for the boys, I'll give it back to Stanley."

Craig nodded. "Okay."

Ace found Stanley outside as he hoped. "Hey, Stan, got any pups left?"

"Morning Ace," Stanley greeted. "Want a cup of coffee or something?"

Ace shook his head. "No. Do you?"

"Just one, a female I planned to keep for breeding."

Ace reached in his pocket. "How much, Stanley? I'll buy her.

Stan frowned. "What's the matter, Ace? You don't even like Rat Terriers, said they're useless," he remarked, and walked toward the barn.

"Lexie's pup died last night."

"Oh."

Stan's voice reflected his empathy. Then he grinned, his eyebrow arched, eyes twinkling.

"Found a soft spot did we?"

Ace rolled his eyes. "Will you sell me the stupid puppy or not?"

"No." Stan picked up the puppy with another grin. "But I'll give her to you. Pretty little thing isn't she?" he queried.

Ace knew his brother-in-law wasn't talking about the puppy and refrained from comment. Hurrying home, he hoped Lexie would still be asleep. She was. He tiptoed into the den and put the puppy beside her.

* * * * *

Lexie awoke to the sound of whimpering and a cold nose against her cheek. She opened her eyes and looked into the face of the cutest little puppy she'd ever seen. A delighted squeal escaped her smiling lips when she picked it up and nuzzled it.

"For me?" she queried and raised wide, hopeful eyes to Ace.

He grinned. "If you want her."

"Oh! Thank you!" she squealed and jumped up from the couch to give him a hug.

Ace felt the ache in his heart lighten as she cuddled the puppy to her breast, her cheeks flushed, and her eyes sparkling with joy.

Chapter Six

Scott passed the den in time to hear Lexie's excited squeal. He stood in the doorway and watched with surprise when she flung herself in Ace's arms. His eyes narrowed when he noted her appearance. Though dark green in color the short silk pajamas left very little to the imagination.

"What's going on in here?"

"Oh! Scott! Look!" She held the puppy for him to see. "Isn't she the cutest little thing?"

His gaze swept over her in a pointed look. "Don't you think you need a robe?"

She gasped and a flush colored her cheeks. She quickly donned the matching robe then rushed back to him.

Scott noted the silky scrap of material barely reached mid thigh and showed an incredible amount of creamy leg. He grunted. "Not much of a robe Lex," he insisted. "Lord, help me," he muttered, his eyes narrowed into dangerous slits. "Where do you get your clothes?"

"Victoria's Secret," she answered, her tone sweet, loving it -and him- more every time he assumed the role of concerned father. "Don't worry, Dad, you're the only man who's seen me in this."

He arched an eyebrow. "Really?" His gaze cut to Ace who averted his eyes and bit back a grin. Again she flushed, her cheeks a delicate shade of crimson, eyes sparkling with mischief.

"Well," she countered, "you're the only man who's seen me in less."

Scott shook his head in dismay. "I assume you're talking about that scrap of material you call a bathing suit," he hissed, hoping she had enough modesty not to wear the darn thing in public.

She smiled. "Covers what it needs to," she remarked and patted his cheek.

Scott grunted and turned to Ace, his eyebrow arched; the meaning in his dark eyes loud and clear. Ace bit back a grin but his eyes glittered with humor.

"This sounds like a father/daughter conversation," he muttered and made his exit from the room. But the memory of how she looked would remain with him far into the day.

* * * * *

Craig reached for the jug of water and froze. His gaze took in the contents of the refrigerator. Something was missing. He stood in petrified horror when he recognized what it was. The realization hit him with shocking force. He whirled around and glared at the women sitting at the table.

"Where is it?" he demanded of Amber.

"What?"

"Where is your mother's water pitcher?"

Fierce eyes stunned them into immobility. A collective gasp sounded as the moments ticked by, the silence ominous. "Well?" he demanded. The muscle in his jaw twitched as he dug deep for control of the emotions which rioted within his heart and mind.

Feeling like she faced a firing squad, Lexie stood a guilty flush on her cheeks. "I emptied it and washed it. It's in the cabinet."

"I didn't ask you to come here and clean my house," he barked.

Trina and Amber rushed to her rescue.

"Daddy!"

"Craig!"

"I'm sorry," Lexie whispered. Her eyes searched Trina's then Amber's, before returning to his blistering gaze. "I cleaned out the refrigerator like Trina asked. There was mold and mildew inside and out. The water was practically rancid. It was disgusting."

Craig bit back the remainder of his wrath when two tears slid down her cheeks.

Pain darkened his eyes like dark clouds in a stormy sky. Lexie took a step closer to him, then another. "I didn't know it was hers. I'm sorry Mr. Craig. About everything, I wish I could have known her."

Craig realized he'd overreacted and swore softly. "I'm sorry, Lexie," he whispered his voice hoarse and reached for her. He pulled her against his chest, stroked a hand down her hair. "I'm sorry. I wish you could have known her too. You would have loved her. And she would have loved you."

He glanced at Katrina, his eyes begging for understanding and forgiveness.

All three of them sighed with relief when he kissed Lexie's cheek and left the room. Lexie returned to the table and collapsed into a chair. Her shoulders shook, her eyes filled with tears. Never in her life had she seen a man so angry. "I almost threw it away," she admitted, her voice breaking with emotion. "Thank God I didn't."

Katrina reached for her daughter and enfolded Lexie in her embrace as silent sobs shook her slender shoulders. Amber reached over and stroked Lexie's hair.

"I'm so sorry Lexie," she whispered. "I never thought..." her voice trailed off when she realized how deeply her father still grieved.

"He still won't let go will he?" Trina asked her voice soft with concern.

Amber shook her head, tears rolled down her cheeks. "I thought they were getting better. Both he and Ace are having such a hard time. I..." Her voice broke. "I miss her too, especially now. Oh, Trina, I'm so glad you could come," she sobbed.

Stanley walked into the kitchen. "What's going on? Your father looks like he's seen a ghost and why are you crying?"

He pulled Amber close while she relayed the incident. He muttered something under his breath. "You know he didn't mean it," he soothed, his eyes searching Lexie's.

She nodded. "I wish I had known. I would have refilled the pitcher," she remarked, and rose to do so. Her hands shook when she opened the cabinet and reached for it.

Scott walked in. "Craig told me what happened. Are you okay?" he asked and lifted Lexie's chin, his concerned gaze seeking hers.

She nodded.

Torn between his daughter and his best friend, Scott hesitated. Assured everything and everyone was under control, he went back out to comfort Craig only to find he had Ace to contend with too. Two pair of haunted eyes searched his for conformation that Lexie was okay.

"I'm sorry Scott," Craig muttered. "You know I would never hurt her. At all, especially being your child."

"I know that. She knows it too. It's all right Craig. Don't worry about it."

"Maybe I should apologize again," he rose.

"Let it go Daddy," Ace said. "Just let it go. All of it," he insisted, suddenly angry at the load of grief his father still carried around on his shoulders. "You've got to let it go."

Craig glared down at his son, squared off with him, his fists clenched in suppressed fury. "Don't tell me what to do Ace, don't even start that today."

Scott got between the two men before they came to blows, "All right. Enough all ready! Look at you Craig, your own son! And Ace. I'm ashamed you would challenge your father so. Both of you need to get a grip. She's dead and nothing you can do will change that! Grieving is one thing. Fighting is another. You both know damn good and well Tamera wouldn't tolerate this out of either of you!"

His voice softened. "She wouldn't want it either."

They glared at each other for a long, tense moment.

"You're right," Craig admitted, his voice soft. Tears rushed to his eyes. He reached for his son and held him close against his chest. "You're right."

Scott put his arms around both of them, sharing the grief as only a friend could. "Now, what do you say we get this barbeque underway? I'm starving and, unless I miss my guess, everyone else is too."

"Yeah," they agreed. "Let's do that."

Back in the kitchen, Stanley comforted his wife. "Don't cry, My Sweet," he whispered. His lips covered hers in a tender caress. "No more tears. Okay?" he urged and brushed them away with his thumbs while his eyes sought assurance from Trina and Lexie as well. He went back outside relieved to find the tension expelled. They gathered around the barbeque pit in a joint, masculine, effort to provide food for the women and children.

Amber gathered up plates, glasses and silverware while Katrina and Lexie carried out huge bowls of potato salad, green salad and baked beans. She placed everything on a huge tray and accepted Ritchie's offer of help. He carried the tray out while she took the bread. She placed the loaves of buttered French bread on the grill and then everyone gathered around the picnic table to give thanks. She realized the pitcher of iced tea was missing and walked toward the steps.

"Where are you going?" Stan wanted to know.

"Get the tea."

"I'll get it." Four male voices offered simultaneously.

Amber laughed. "It only takes one person to get it," she teased.

"I'll get it," Ace insisted and handed his sister over to her husband. "You sit and rest. Stanley...."

"Right," Stan took her hand and led Amber back to the table. He kicked a crate under her feet and fussed over her until she shook with laughter.

"See what I have to put up with?" she declared. Her eyes encompassed them all and settled on her father.

"You love it and you know it," Craig teased his daughter.

She snorted. "I do not love being treated like an invalid, or an imbecile."

Her husband kissed her cheek and drew her attention back to him. "Well then, how about a cherished wife about to give birth to my son?"

Lexie' giggle cut off her reply. "Can't argue with that, huh, Amber?"

"I guess not," Amber sighed and touched Stan's cheek in a gentle caress.

Time stood still when they gazed into each other's eyes. With a soft chuckle, Stanley kissed her hand then gave it an affectionate squeeze.

"Oh, please," Craig grunted. "You'd think they'd been married ten minutes instead of ten years."

"Ten years? Ten minutes? What's the difference?" Amber queried, her sparkling gaze sought her father's teasing one.

Scott pulled Trina to his side. The movement drew everyone's attention. "There's not a bit of difference when love spans the time," he said and lowered his lips to hers in a tender caress.

Stepping into the intimate scene, Ace put the tea on the table, and grinned at Lexie. "They at it again?" he asked then shook his head in dismay. "Love," he grunted, "Turns a guy from muscle to mush, man to mouse."

Craig chuckled. "Don't worry. Your day is coming," he replied, a meaningful arch to his brow.

"Never!" Ace denied with an emphatic shake of his head. He'd only loved one woman and no one could come close to filling her boots.

"Never, say never," his father warned, remembering the way Ace's eyes had swept over Lexie yesterday and the way he'd looked and acted this morning.

"I think love like this is beautiful," Lexie interjected.

Her eyes sparkled vivid green. She walked over to Craig and reached for his hand.

"Especially when that love spans more than time, into eternity," she whispered, her eyes searching his.

Craig's gaze softened and he pulled the girl to his chest. Here was understanding, deep, unfeigned, complete—

unfettered by personal needs or emotions. He wondered how someone so young could know, could understand something so complex. But she did. He could tell by the look in her eyes, Lexie understood much more than belied her tender age, more than enough to forgive his unwarranted rudeness of earlier.

"Thank you," he whispered then kissed her silky head.

The air filled with love and laughter while plates were prepared and passed around until everyone had a feast before them. Amber closed her eyes and savored the moment. It had been so long since she'd shared this much laughter and joy with her father and brother. The moment filled her with even more poignant emotions when Stanley whispered in her ear, his voice rich with love.

Though she wasn't there in body, Tamera's presence could be felt all around as she watched with the angels while her family began to get their lives back on track. And the God with whom she now dwelled accepted her gracious thanks that such a wonderful young woman had been sent to help her husband and son, one strong enough to help them face up to their grief and heal. Heal with a love that, once recognized, would know no bounds.

The sun began its decent and trailed the sky with splashes of vivid orange, yellow and pink. Everyone gathered on the porch when Stanley tuned his guitar. His heart swelled with joy. Other than the incident over the water pitcher, the day had been wonderful. An easy man to please, he found contentment whether working alone with horses or with his family all around. His eyes shone with love and laughter when he asked for requests.

"Cartoons, Daddy!" Kaitlyn insisted.

"Yeah," her sister cheered. "Cartoons."

He laughed softly when Scott's boys also urged him to sing the song.

'Cartoons' was an adorable little song about how various animated characters would sing praises to God and had swept the nation with its charm. Soft voice on the notes and gentle hands on the strings, Stanley's rendition had the adults laughingly joining in on the chorus and the twins dancing around his chair. Appeasing the children first, he proceeded to entertain the adults after they ran off to play. Craig's eyes sparkled with amusement when he whispered a request in Stan's ear and winked. Stanley paused just long enough for effect then began a short version of George Strait's "She Lays it all on the Line" off the Pure Country sound track.

Lexie squealed and her eyes sparkled with indignation when the evocative words and the emphasis he put on them had all eyes trained on her, which in turn incited a round of teasing. Stanley could tell by the flash of emotion in her brilliant gaze that, had he not had his boots planted firmly on the porch, the chair would fly right out from under him when she kicked it.

Ace watched Lexie, a curious light in his eyes when he wondered—as the song put it—just how far out on a limb she'd be when she loved her man. He clamped a lid on his whirling thoughts and glared at his father. "About as subtle as a freight train," he hissed for Craig's ears only.

Craig just laughed as Stanley started to sing another song. After about a half hour of songs aimed intentionally at piercing Amber's already captured heart, he shook his head. "Geeze, Stanley. Why don't you just drag her upstairs and get it over with?" he grunted.

"Daddy!" Amber squealed. A flush filled her cheeks.

Stan chuckled, took her hand in one of his and raised it to his lips. Something about the soft glimmer of pain which appeared periodically in her eyes told him it'd probably be quite some time before he'd have that pleasure again. "What in the world ever gave you the idea I had such a thing in mind?" he queried, all innocence.

Craig eyed his son-in-law and grunted. "A hundred love songs had nothing to do with it," he remarked.

Amber rolled her eyes with a snort and jerked her hand from Stan's. "You see?" she exclaimed, her eyes beseeching Katrina, her cheeks scorching hot. "You see what I put up with all the time?"

Trina tut-tutted her sympathy.

Stanley grinned and winked at his father-in-law. "She blushes," he remarked, his voice thick with adoration, "Married ten years, about to give birth to our third child, and she blushes. I love it," he added, with a husky laugh and caressed Amber's cheek with his knuckles.

"Jerk," she muttered. Her breath caught on a soft hiss and Stan could tell she tried to remain inconspicuous when she closed her eyes and breathed her way through a mild contraction. He inched his chair nearer in order to watch her closer, and sang another song.

"Get your harmonica, Lex," Scott urged when Stanley paused. She shook her head and flushed.

"You play the harmonica?" Stan asked with interest.

"And the flute, and the clarinet, and the sax," Scott added, his voice thick with pride. "She's real good with her mouth," he remarked, teasing his daughter.

Amidst the talk of seduction and babies, the words took on a different meaning. A thick, uncomfortable silence filled the air. Scott groaned when another blush rushed to Lexie's cheeks. "She gets that from me. Except I'm usually busy putting a boot in mine," he admitted, trying desperately to ease her embarrassment.

Lexie buried her head in Trina's shoulder. "Please take him back to Louisiana," she implored. "Maybe once he crosses the state line he'll get his brain back." Her remark caused a round of laughter and eased the tension somewhat. She turned to Stanley. "Do you know any Alan Jackson?" she asked her eyes pleading with him to sing something, anything.

Stan nodded and took the hint. "Alan Jackson? Yeah," he answered and immediately crooned the words to Alan's hit "All Over Again" which was perfect, since he and Amber had recently celebrated their tenth wedding anniversary.

Lexie placed her hand over her heart with a heavy sigh. "I love Alan Jackson. He's got the longest legs in the world. They reach from the ground all the way to heaven."

"Lexie!" Scott admonished, shocked at the boldness of her statement. She giggled. "Actually, Kristy got me started on that. I prefer George Strait."

Scott bit back a catty remark at the name. Kristy McGee was a beautiful, high-spirited, wild child that he and Lexie had butted heads over more than once. She was also a spoiled little rich kid with a host of problems no one seemed to understand but Lexie. They were the best of friends. Kristy's suicide their junior year of high school, too soon after her father's death, left its mark on Lexie. Going away her senior year, then the trip abroad, had aided in healing her of the pain inflected by their deaths. He watched her intensely when Lexie continued her tale...

"We were all watching the CMA awards. Kristi was always drooling over him. Out of the blue, she made that remark. It was hilarious, had us rolling."

Stan chuckled hoping to ease the sudden tension he sensed emanating from Scott. "Well, that's a pretty loaded remark, Sweetheart, especially when you consider the fact that you're in the company of four very tall cowboys." He glanced up at Ace and grinned. "Two that top six feet, and two, just under."

"Yeah," Ace interjected, tempted to kiss her pretty mouth shut and show her the true measure of a cowboy. "And it takes a lot more than long legs in blue jeans, boots and a hat to make a cowboy."

"Can't prove it by me," she taunted.

Ace grinned. "Hang around, Sweetheart, and you'll see all the cowboy you can stand," he assured, his voice thick with arrogance.

The challenge was on, the rules set: If she hung around long enough, he'd show her a true cowboy. He tossed another challenge at her feet: "You gonna get your harmonica or not, Miss Mouth?"

Her eyes flashed fire but Lexie bit back her retort. They glared at each other a long moment. Then he grinned, his eyebrow arched in a taunting gesture.

Lexie knew the only way to shut him up was to prove herself. She rose and walked into the house as gracefully as possible on legs that wobbled.

"God," she whispered and reached in the bag that contained her harmonica. "I know we haven't always been on the best of terms. But, if You're really out there, and You really care, please don't let me embarrass Scott and Trina. Or myself," she pleaded.

Chapter Seven

Lexie stomped back out on the porch her eyes narrow, cheeks flushed. She glared first at Scott then at Ace, took a deep breath, and turned to Stanley.

"No One Needs to Know by Shania Twain," she said and started to sing while playing her harmonica in the appropriate spots. "How about Clint Black?" she queried afterward, jumping right into "Put Yourself in My Shoes."

For the next hour or so they played and sang. Laughing and breathless, she flopped down between Katrina and Amber while everyone chorused her praises and begged for more.

"Oh, no, no more," she huffed. "Thank You, God," her heart whispered.

Stan grinned up at his brother-in-law. "Looks like she showed you up on that one, Ace," he teased. Ace tipped his hat but refrained from comment.

A shadow of pain crossed Amber's face. Stanley leaned closer, whispered something, and brushed his lips over hers in a tender caress. "One more song," he stroked the strings as he would a lover. "This one's for you, My Sweet."

Craig was not surprised to see Stanley reduce his daughter to a mere puddle of emotions when he started to sing a hit song by one of Country Music's hottest duos. What shocked him was the look on his son's face when Lexie sat at Stanley's feet, turned her back so as not to overpower him, and lifted her voice to harmonize with his in a rendition of "It's Your Love" that would make the original artists proud. Or jealous.

Silence, sweet and poignant filled the air when they finished the song and Stanley kissed his wife once more. Amber sank her fingers in his thick, chestnut locks and wept softly into his shoulder. "I love you," they murmured at the same time.

Craig's heart ached with tenderness at their embrace and he swallowed the thick lump of emotion clogging his airways. His attention diverted to his son when Ace cleared his throat and remarked, "I think I'll go bed down the bulls," before he stepped off the porch.

"What's the matter Adam?" Craig teased. "Can't take the heat?" He could tell by the way Ace glared at him, his son would not be goaded into a response.

"His name's Adam?" Lexie queried. "No wonder he's so arrogant, his name originates back to the first man."

Craig turned to her with a laugh. "My name's Adam too," he stated and could see he'd totally confused Lexie.

"But, I thought..."

Craig chuckled. "Actually his name is Adam Craig Harris the Fourth," he informed her.

"That explains it all," she remarked with a roll of her eyes for emphasis. "Not only does it originate to the first man, but he's fourth generation," she said and flashed a challenging smile at Ace's frown.

"That's right," Ace grunted. "The original man," he muttered, his mind scrambling for a response. "Just don't forget that," he ordered, unable to come up with anything cattier, tempted again to kiss her pretty mouth shut. He turned on his heel and headed toward the barn while Trina jumped to his defense.

"Does he really bed them down?" Lexie asked, undaunted by Trina's fussing, then flushed when she realized how ridiculous she sounded. "That was a stupid question," she muttered.

Craig shook his head. "No question is stupid. But, no, the only bulls he beds down are the babies like the one he brought in yesterday. It's simply a statement Ace makes when he wants a few minutes alone." His attention averted to Amber when a soft moan escaped her.

"Easy, Love." He heard Stanley coax. "Breathe, deep now."

Amber rubbed her stomach and eyed Scott. "Will you deliver my baby?" He looked stunned for a moment, then surprised. A flush of pleasure darkened his skin.

"Yeah." He nodded, grinned. "I'd be honored."

"Would you mind?" she asked Stanley. "I'd really like to have him at home."

Questioning blue eyes searched Scott's a full moment and Craig watched his son-in-law swallow his fear and concern before he turned back to Amber. "I guess not. If that's what you really want, as long as everything goes okay."

"I'd never let anything go wrong, Stanley," Scott promised.

Stan shook his head. "I know. Okay then."

Amber gazed up at Craig. "Do you mind Daddy?"

Craig frowned, a bit puzzled until it dawned on him what his daughter asked. "Here? You want to have him here?"

She nodded then clenched her teeth when another contraction squeezed her middle. "Here," she answered, "Where I can feel Mama's presence all around me." Her voice broke and she struggled with her emotions.

Craig eyed his son-in-law for a moment to gauge his reaction. Stan shrugged. Craig smiled and squatted beside his daughter. "How about in the bed where she slept?" he offered.

Amber's eyes widened in surprise. "Really?" she whispered, as yet another contraction started. Craig nodded and brushed the hair back off her face.

"I'd like that, Daddy," she whispered, clutching his hand when the contraction eased up then quickly rolled into another. "Trina, would you tend to my daughters?" she gritted, when it was over.

"Of course," Trina answered her smile generous.

Craig whistled. "Ace!"

Ace rushed back to the porch at the urgency in his father's voice.

"Get a sheet of plastic and come help me."

"What?" he asked plainly puzzled.

"Amber's going to have the baby. Here. We need to get the bed ready."

Ace froze. His worried gaze encompassed his sister and brother-in-law. "Here? Now?" He knelt at her feet, took her hands in his. "Are you sure?" he questioned, eyeing Stanley.

Amber smiled and stroked a lock of blond hair off his forehead. "We're sure. And soon Brat," she informed him when her middle tightened again. "So hurry," she panted.

He paled, nodded, and jumped off the porch to do as his father bid.

"Round up the girls, Stanley," Amber beseeched. "I want to spend a little time with them," she bit out then choked back a groan.

Stanley whistled. The girls came running. Talking in a quiet, gentle tone, he explained what was happening. He picked up the girls, careful to keep their weight off of Amber, and held them so that she could hug and kiss each one.

"Is there anything I can do?" Lexie asked, touched by the tenderness unfolding all around her.

Amber smiled and reached for her hand. "Thanks, Lex. Help Trina will you? Those two can be a handful."

Lexie smiled. "Sure. C'mon girls. How about a bubble bath?" she urged, and laughed at their enthusiastic responses. Taking them by the hand, she led them upstairs.

Stan, Scott and Trina kept Amber company, and coached her breathing during and between contractions.

Stanley brushed the hair off her face, his expression stayed calm even when his heart raced with each contraction. Soon, very soon, his son would be born! He closed his eyes and breathed a silent prayer.

Craig walked out. "Everything's ready. I think," he told Scott.

Scott gave Katrina last minute instructions and turned to Amber. "Whenever you're ready, Sweetheart. The contractions are less than two minutes apart now."

Amber nodded and prepared to rise. A gasp escaped her when a rush of wetness flowed from her body. Stanley swung her up in his arms and carried her to her mother's bed.

Craig and Ace, each holding a twin, paced the hall outside the bedroom door where Amber, Scott and Stanley worked to bring the baby into the world. Ritchie and Robert played Nintendo in the den while Trina and Lexie waited on the porch. They sat on the swing and talked while waiting for news.

"So, what do you think so far?" Trina asked her daughter.

"Beautiful, everything and everyone. Well, *almost* everyone," she remarked, her tone dry when she remembered the blatant challenge in Ace's eyes earlier.

Trina laughed and hugged her daughter. "Ace is a tender-hearted soul. You'll see," she promised.

Lexie giggled. "He sure got a little green when Amber said she was having that baby soon. What did she call him, Brat? It suits," she decided.

"Lex," Katrina chided. "Be nice. He's very sweet. A bit arrogant I know, but sweet. He loves Amber beyond reason. Always has, the same way he loved, still loves, his mother. Tamera's death has been very hard on him."

"We'll be fine," Lexie promised then laid her head on Trina's shoulder. "As long as he keeps his mouth shut," she added then grinned at Trina's sigh.

Had Lexie seen him in that moment, she wouldn't have thought Ace so arrogant or so tough. And she would have understood what Trina meant. He paled and eyed his father when yet another muffled scream from his sister penetrated the door to his parents' room. His eyes, wide and anguished, reflected his thoughts.

"I didn't realize it was so hard for her." Craig's smile was tender and wise, though his eyes mirrored Ace's concern.

"That's cause in the hospital they wheel them away where you can't hear them cry. Don't worry though; she won't remember one moment of pain once that baby is placed in her arms."

Ace raked his fingers through his hair and snorted in disbelief. "I don't see how Stanley can stand it."

Craig remembered the day his children were born and chuckled. "Because he has to. It's his child too. You'll understand when the time comes for your own."

Meanwhile, Scott urged Amber to push her way through another contraction.

"You better pray this baby is a boy," she grunted between clenched teeth, and glared at her husband.

Stan chuckled and raised their clutched hands to his mouth. "If it's not, we'll just have to try again."

"That's what you think," she hissed then groaned, fighting with each breath not to scream.

Scott's eyes glittered when they sought hers. "Put some of that energy into pushing Amber. I can see the head. C'mon now," he urged.

Craig and Ace looked at each other with relief when they heard one last, muffled, scream and the lusty cry of the child.

"Baby," the twins chorused.

They waited expectantly for Stan to appear at the door. He did, his face wreathed in smiles. "It's a boy!"

Lexie and Trina smiled at the excited shouts from the house. "Oh, Lord. It must be a boy. We're not going to be able to stand them," Lexie teased.

Katrina laughed. She rose and extended a hand to her daughter. "Probably not, especially Stanley, he'll be strutting around here like he's the only one who's done it. They all do, until the newness wears off and they have to get up in the middle of the night. Then it's our entire fault," she teased.

Lexie laughed, shook her head and rolled her eyes. "Men." They entered the house and she checked on the boys while Trina went to help Scott get Amber and the baby cleaned up and settled.

Stanley held his son until Amber was settled back in the bed. Leaning down, he placed him in his mother's arms. His lips covered hers in a tender caress.

"Thank you, My Sweet," he whispered, his voice tender, eyes bright with tears. "He's beautiful."

Amber accepted her husband's embrace then turned her attention to her baby. She un-wrapped him and fingered the tiny hands and feet. "Oh, Mama," she whispered while tears streamed down her cheeks. "I wish you were here," she sobbed and buried her face in the folds of blanket that surrounded her son.

She raised tear-drenched eyes to Scott's. "He is beautiful. Thank you."

He chuckled and kissed her cheek. "My pleasure, Sweetheart." He stroked the baby's face then lifted his eyes to those of his wife. "It's been a long time since I delivered a baby. It's a beautiful thing. Life..." he shook his head, subdued and humbled by the emotions in his soul. That he be granted such a privilege.

Trina wrapped her arms around him for a hug then leaned down for another look at the baby. "He is beautiful, Amber. Congratulations, Stanley."

A knock on the door interrupted their conversation, Craig peeked in. "Hey, how about me? When do I get to see him? I am the grandfather," he grumbled, unable to hide a grin.

Amber beamed at him. "C'mon in Daddy. Ace too. And bring the girls."

Stanley took his daughters while Craig and Ace took turns hugging and kissing Amber and cooing over the baby. Noting his wife's drooping eyes, he signaled for Ace to take the girls. Taking his son in his arms, he let the girls kiss him, each on a cheek, before gently but firmly urging everyone out of the room.

He placed William Stanley Morrison in the bassinet that had been brought up before his delivery then tucked the covers around his wife when she snuggled deeper into the bed. Stanley knelt beside the bed while tears of relief streamed down his cheeks and thanked God for the safe delivery of his son, the quick recovery of his wife, and the other blessings in his life.

Amber woke sometime later to find him stretched out in a chair, snoring softly. One hand rested behind his head, the other was in the bassinet where it lay lightly on the baby's back to feel his breathing. His feet were propped up on the bed beside her. Tears clogged her eyes and throat when she shook him awake. "Stanley?"

Immediately awake and alert, Stan leaned forward to kiss his wife. "What is it?"

"The best thing about having the baby at home is that the bed is big enough for both of us."

He chuckled. "I didn't want to disturb you."

"Sleeping alone disturbs me. I'm awake aren't I?"

He grinned, slipped out of his clothes and under the covers. "Yes, Ma'am," he admitted and pulled her in his arms.

Later that morning Lexie got her first look at the baby. She held him and stroked his soft cheek while humming under her breath then gazed up at Scott. "I want one," she whimpered.

Eyes wide, innocent, and glazed with wonder were perfectly capable of pleading her case. Scott shook his head and grinned. "Don't even go there. I'm not old enough to be a grandfather."

"Hey," Craig interjected. "You're as old as I am."

"And your point might be?" Scott teased him. Turning back to Lexie he continued. "First you go to college, then you get married, then you have a baby. In that order," he declared.

She shook her head and smiled down at the infant cuddled against her breast. "See what you have to look forward to?" she teased. "Rules, rules, rules."

Amber laughed. "Bring him here," she patted the bed beside her.

Lexie obliged. Climbing onto the bed she laid William next to his mother.

"Un-wrap him Lexie. Isn't he beautiful? God's greatest gift, His most precious creation, the most beautiful expression of our love," she added then gazed tenderly up at her husband. "A child. A son," she said her voice reverent, her lips meeting Stan's in a tender caress.

Lexie fingered the tiny hands and feet and agreed. "I've never held one so new or so little before."

"He's big compared to the twins." Amber informed her.

Stan chuckled. "That's because there were two in there instead of one. He had more room to grow."

"Speaking of twins," Amber hinted.

Stanley took the hint. "I'll go fetch them for you, My Sweet. Anything else?" he queried then leaned down for another kiss.

The baby stirred, whimpered. The men left the room when Amber placed him to her breast where he suckled hungrily.

Lexie sat, mesmerized at the special bond linking mother and son and felt a hunger, a need unlike anything she'd ever known tug at her heart.

Amber noticed the emotions in Lexie's eyes and smiled. "You're day's coming Lex. You'll make a beautiful mother some day."

Her smile tremulous, Lexie shrugged. "I hope so Amber. I really do. Trina's the only mother I've known. I hope I've learned enough from her to know how."

Moved by the hope in her eyes and the fear and confusion in her voice, Amber reached a hand to stroke her cheek, the touch of a mother, a friend, a sister. "You will. A mother's instinct is natural, strong, most of the time anyway. All you really need is love, Lex."

Lexie smiled. "I hope to have that kind of love one day Amber. I really do, and a family, a big family."

"Well, you'll get plenty of practice in the next few weeks watching after those two girls of mine. So much practice in fact that you may even change your mind," Amber warned, her voice tinged with laughter.

Lexie grinned not realizing her heart was showing, softening, and opening up more than it ever had. "It's an experience I'm looking forward to," she assured her new friend.

Chapter Eight

Craig walked in the house, surprised at the quietness. Katrina and Scott had taken the boys to San Antonio for a few days. Lexie opted to stay behind and help Amber. To his utmost gratitude, Stanley hadn't rushed his family home right after the baby was born. Nearly two weeks had passed and they were still there. Ace was somewhere out on the range.

He stopped in the kitchen for a glass of water before heading upstairs, and nearly choked when Lexie stepped out of the den. His eyes swept over her, scantily clad in a leotard, tights and tennis shoes. "I hope you don't plan on leaving the house dressed like that," he remarked.

She laughed. "You sound just like Scott, but no, Sir. Mr. Craig, do you mind if I move some of the furniture around in the den so I can work out?"

"Not a bit. Where are the twins?"

"Stanley took them to town for a while. He needed to pick up some feed and stuff. Thought they, and I, could use a break. Amber and the baby are resting."

Craig nodded. "Hey, I've got a better idea. How much room do you need to work out?"

She shook her head. "Not much," she assured him. "But the way the furniture is arranged in the den, there's absolutely no room."

He motioned with his head. "Follow me." He led the way to a room in the back of the house, Ace's work out room which was empty except for a weight bench and stereo.

Her eyes widened. "This is great! I didn't know it was here." Craig's eyes sparkled with mischief.

"This is Ace's hide out. Normally no one is allowed, probably because it stays cluttered. In fact, I'm surprised it's so neat and clean," he observed.

Lexie laughed. "Trina's here, nothing goes unnoticed or unclean wherever she is."

Craig laughed. "Well, make yourself at home."

"You're sure he won't mind? I just need the floor space and the stereo."

Craig shrugged and fought the grin tugging at the corners of his mouth. "It's still my house."

Lexie smiled back. "Okay. Thanks. But, if he tosses me out on my ear, you'll hear about it."

Craig chuckled and left her alone.

Lexie hurried back into the den and retrieved her tapes. She put them in the dual cassette player, did a few stretches to warm up then turned on the music. Her routine was spontaneous, jumps and kicks entwined with dance steps. She'd tried organized routines, but found she worked just as hard when dancing. And dancing was something she loved. She didn't need routine, she needed spontaneity and expression.

Craig hummed to himself and tiptoed upstairs. He peeked in on Amber and was overjoyed to find her awake and alone. He placed a kiss on her cheek, inquired as to how she felt and lifted the baby out of his bassinet. "And how's PaPaw's little man this afternoon?" he cooed and held his grandson close, inhaling the sweet, baby scent of him.

Amber beamed up at him. "He's just beautiful, isn't he, Daddy?"

Craig chuckled and agreed.

She frowned. "What's all the racket downstairs?"

"Lexie's working out. In Ace's weight room," he admitted a sly grin on his face.

"Daddy," she chided. "If I didn't know you better, I'd swear you were throwing those two at each other."

"Not me," he denied, his face a mask of innocence.

She grunted in a very unladylike manner. "When it was me and Stanley you hated it," she teased.

"That's different."

"Why?"

He shrugged. "Cause, it just is."

She grinned, rolled her eyes. "Bull. Can't say as I blame you though, I just adore Lexie. And Ace needs to settle down. Maybe he'll forget about professional bull riding if he falls in love. I never really liked the thought of him doing that anyway. And I know Mama hated it."

Her eyes had darkened with worry. "I hate him riding more now than ever," Craig admitted. The baby squirmed then cried. He handed him to Amber and watched with adoring eyes when she placed him at her breast. He leaned over and kissed her on the forehead then sat quietly while she nursed his grandson. His mind wandered back to the days when her mother did the same with her and Ace.

The pain of missing Tamera was like a raw, open, wound that ate at his heart, mind, and soul. He had to force down the lump of tears in his throat. He doubted he'd ever really get over her death. Or get used to the long, lonely nights. But he couldn't even consider the thought of another woman. No one would ever measure up. Or take her place in his life, or in his heart.

Nearly sixty, he was content to live out the rest of his days watching his children grow and succeed, and spoiling his grandchildren. He, too, hoped Ace would give up the dream of pro bull riding. And that he'd find a sweet, little wife who would fill the void his mother's death had left in his life. And fill the house with children, heirs to the Harris fortune.

* * * * *

Ace guzzled down a drink of water, tossed his shirt on the pile of dirty clothes and headed toward the back of the house. He stopped and a frown marred his forehead when he heard music coming from his weight room. That room was off limits. It was the one place he could go to be totally alone. Lifting weights kept his body toned and strong, and cleared his mind. And his mind definitely needed to be cleared since the last few days it had been crowded, *overcrowded*, with thoughts of a fiery haired wench.

His eyes narrowed when he discovered that same wench in his own private sanctuary. He leaned against the door jam and watched while she danced, oblivious to his presence. The moves she executed reminded him of some he'd seen only in movies. Strong. Sensual. Desire began a slow burn through his system, until he ached from it. The ache infuriated him.

The music stopped.

Lexie froze when she heard clapping. She turned and found Ace watching her. His hands smacked together in short, punctuated, bursts of sound. He looked flushed, angry. Tension coiled the entire length of him. His face was taut, the muscle in his jaw throbbed madly, and his eyes were dark, gunmetal gray.

"Very good, I'll have to take you out sometime," he hissed through clenched teeth. "That is, if you call that dancing. I'm not even sure you can call that music."

Before she could reply, he stepped over to the stereo and slapped a Brooks and Dunn cassette into the player. The hard country sound blared. His eyes raked over her, taunted, and spurred her into action. Her eyes spit fire at him. Without a word, she shook her hair loose from its ponytail and grabbed his hat. She put it on her head then executed a high school dance-line version of a country ho down, complete with fancy footwork, kicks and splits.

Ace shook his head in dismay when he realized that she'd shown him up yet again. He grinned. "You showing me up every chance you get is getting pretty hard to take."

Lexie bowed, tossed his hat, and surprisingly, roped the hat rack. It twirled wildly then settled on a hook.

Ace whistled.

"I'll accept that as a compliment." She remarked, a tad too sweet. "You shouldn't be so arrogant as to challenge me every time you open your mouth. Then I wouldn't have to show you up."

"Let's keep this one to ourselves. Okay?"

His eyes glistened like dewdrops on sheet metal. Lexie's heart skipped a beat. "Why?"

"You're going to ruin my reputation, that's why."

"Which reputation is that?" she queried her voice saccharine, and fluttered her eyelashes. "The one for being stuck up, or the one for being a conceited jerk?"

He straddled the weight bench and grinned. "Take your pick. Now, if you'll excuse me, I have a prior engagement with Bessie here."

"Bessie, isn't that what you name cows?"

He laughed and agreed. "Yeah. And it's because of her that I'm not soft and fat like one," he admitted.

His voice was rich with amusement, his steely eyes danced with mirth. Lexie eyed the broad expanse of chest, the well-defined arms. Not bulging, but well toned and muscular. Excitement, raw and unfamiliar, curled in her stomach.

"You watched me," she argued and locked her gaze with his. Her fingers itched to stroke the dark blond curls which covered his chest. She clenched her fist to stop herself.

Ace shrugged. "Suit yourself." He waited and watched emotions cloud her eyes. Desire poured through him sharp and painful, galvanizing in its wake.

Lexie's heart thundered in her chest. As though in a trance she stepped forward and sank her fingers into the curls. "I wonder if it's as soft as..." she whispered in a thick, husky voice, her eyes alight with curiosity while she ran her fingers through the thick mop of blond hair on his head. "How can someone so tough, so cocky, have hair as soft as a baby's?" she mused aloud.

His eyes narrowed, blood surged, and pulse throbbed in answer. He fought the raging effect of her touch and the urge to kiss her, and grabbed her arm. "Don't play with me, Alexis," he warned in a husky voice, then raked the day's growth of beard over the tender skin of her wrist, proving even his hair wasn't all soft.

Her breath caught in an audible hiss. "Wouldn't dream of it," she said and released her grip. With a small twist, she freed herself from his grasp. Her smile was all the more powerful because of its innocence. "But, I do have permission to knock you off that pedestal you were put on the day you were born," she admitted, her voice bold and haughty.

"Oh yeah, from who?" Ace wanted to know. She regarded him with laughing eyes.

"Your father, he gave me permission the first time we met."

Ace grunted. "Looks like I need to have a talk with my father." Lying down, he gripped the weights out of their rack and lowered them to his chest, allowing her the choice to watch or leave and grinned to himself when she hurried from the room, a bright flush on her cheeks.

The workout did absolutely nothing to clear his mind or ease the tension of unanswered desire. Their next encounter was just as brief and every bit as disturbing.

Ace finished his workout then went to his room, showered, dressed and headed down to the kitchen. He could hear the twins' excited chatter and Stanley's laughter from his father's bedroom. His heart swelled with emotion when he remembered the night the baby was born. He reached his destination and walked straight to the refrigerator, but passed Lexie who sat at the table with William snuggled against her heart.

He reached for the water jug and raised it to his lips while glancing her way. Pulled back in a ponytail, tendrils of thick hair, still damp from her own shower, escaped to curl around her face. Her eyes were soft and tender as she gazed down at the baby in her arms. William's tiny hand curled into a fist around her finger. She stroked it gently.

"Look mighty pretty sitting there holding that baby," Ace remarked, then took a swig of water. And she did, very pretty. He nearly choked when she frowned at him and wrinkled her nose in distaste.

"That's disgusting. Don't you use a glass?"

The admonishment reminded him of his mother. Memories swarmed through him, sweet and painful. He swallowed a guilty grin and placed the water jug back in the fridge when she said something soft and mocking to his nephew then smiled up at him, a tender, teasing light in her eyes.

"I stole him right out from under Stanley's nose," she declared.

He grinned in response, but shook his head at her words. "I can guarantee you Stanley knows exactly where that baby is," he assured her and walked over to where they sat.

"He's so tiny. So beautiful," she breathed her smile ever so sweet. "It's hard to believe someone so tiny, so fragile, will grow up to be as tall and strong and probably as good looking as Stanley."

Ace chuckled. "Looks like my brother-in-law has made quite an impression on you."

She grinned. "Your whole family has made an impression on me. Some better than others," she taunted.

"Touché," Ace replied. He reached down to stroke his nephew's head and fought the urge to take him from Lexie. "And he's not beautiful," he countered, his voice thick with masculine scorn. "He's a might handsome little cowboy," he concluded then leaned to kiss the soft head.

And found his face very near Lexie's breast.

His eyes widened then narrowed, when desire renewed the assault on his senses. He saw the pulse throb in her throat, the faint flush on her cheeks. Her breath caught in a soft gasp as her lips parted invitingly. Her eyes were bright, at once curious and surprised.

Ace struggled with the desire to taste the tender skin which showed through the open collar of her shirt and to feel the rapid pulse beneath his lips. Realizing the direction of his thoughts, he pulled back as if he'd been burned. And he had. The subtle waves of excitement that emanated from her were more powerful than the most practiced flirt he'd ever come in contact with. And he'd come in contact with his share.

The rodeo circuit, college, young and old—women everywhere threw themselves at him with such disgusting regularity, it was a wonder his heart was still intact.

He stood and gazed down at her for a long, tense moment. Her eyes met his, bold and unashamed, sparkling like rare, precious emeralds. A hint of laughter lurked in the depths. They stayed locked in each other's gaze until a movement at the door drew his attention.

Stanley cleared his throat. His eyes danced and mocked when he nodded a hello at Ace. With a grin he walked over to Lexie and reached for his son.

"I'll take him now. Before you drop him," he teased, and chuckled at her blush.

The girls rushed in on his heels, breaking the spell. Kaitlyn threw herself in Ace's arms. Ashlyn climbed on Lexie's lap.

"See you later, Ace." Stanley winked, then turned and left the room. He hurried upstairs and sat in the rocker by the bed. "You'll never guess what I just witnessed," he told Amber. Between chuckles, he relayed the scene he'd observed between them. "I swear, you'd think they were looking at each other for the first time," he concluded.

Amber smiled. "Maybe they were," she remarked, her romantic heart taking flight.

Stan grinned. "Ole Ace looked like he'd been struck by lightning. Or hit by a Mac truck." He leaned forward and his lips covered hers in a sweet caress. "I know exactly how he feels," he assured his wife. "Am, when do you think you'll be ready to head home?"

Amber shrugged. She knew he'd ask sooner or later. She also knew he hadn't asked before now because he was allowing her father the joy of having a full house. The house was too big and empty for just him and Ace.

"I don't know. I haven't really thought about it too much. I," her voice broke. "I guess I've just relished being here, of feeling Mama's presence all around, especially here in their room. I guess Daddy's ready to have his bed back too."

Stanley put the baby in the bassinet and sat beside her on the bed. "You don't have to be here to feel her presence, Sweet," he assured her, his voice soft and tender as he stroked the dark hair off her face. "I see her, feel her, everywhere. I went by there today."

He didn't have to say where 'there' was. Amber knew he meant the cemetery. His eyes clouded as he continued.

"I could feel her touch. See her smile. I know, somehow, I believe she's watching over us. And she's just thrilled about the baby. I know that may sound crazy, but..."

Amber shook her head in quick denial. "That's not crazy. That's faith, eternal life, the core of our hope. I know what you mean too. Sometimes I can hear her voice. In my heart, you know? And I believe the same as you."

He pulled her in his arms. "I don't know what I'd do if I lost you, My Sweet. I know you still worry about your father and Ace. But, they will be okay Amber. I, for one, can understand where your father's coming from."

She nodded and slipped her arms around his waist. "I know. I couldn't bear it if I lost you."

"I'm not about to rush you, Amber. But, whenever you're ready, I'm ready to go home. I want to be in my bed with you by my side and the girls tucked snugly in theirs. I work better when you are all there with me."

"Okay, Stanley. I'm kind of ready too. I'm anxious to get settled into a routine and start writing again. How about when Scott and Trina get back? That way Daddy and Ace won't be alone again."

His smile was as tender as the light in his eyes. "Deal," he whispered in a husky voice before his lips covered hers in a tender caress.

Chapter Nine

Craig walked into the kitchen surprised to find Amber already up and busy. The baby slept in his stroller. "What'cha doin', Sweetheart?"

Amber glanced over her shoulder at her father as though he'd lost his mind and his sense of smell. Bacon sizzled in the skillet, pancakes bubbled on the grill ready to be turned over, fresh coffee brewed in the pot and she was beating eggs to scramble. She grinned and put the eggs aside long enough to tend to the pancakes. "Milking the cow."

Craig chuckled and shook his head. "God, how did I end up with two wise-mouth kids?"

She laughed. "Ask a stupid question...." she began, her remark interrupted when Ace stumbled through the back door whistling.

Craig eyed his son. Unless mistaken, those were the same clothes Ace wore when he left last night. "Where've you been?"

"Out."

"All night?" He shook his head in dismay when Ace shrugged.

"Ain't goin' down till the sun comes up," Ace replied, quoting one of his favorite country artists.

"Ace, I did have a talk with you about the facts of life, didn't I?"

Tongue in cheek, Ace poured himself and his father a cup of coffee. "Yes, Sir."

"Did I leave anything out?"

"Like what?" he asked and handed Craig a cup before reaching for the sugar.

"Love, honor, cherish, respect, abstinence.

Ace bit his lip to keep from grinning. He winked at his sister then regarded his father with wide, innocent eyes. "Abstinence...isn't that what makes the heart grow fonder?"

Craig wasn't so effective in holding back a grin when Amber giggled. "Something like that."

"I thought so. Don't worry, Daddy, I remember every word of your talk. And Mama's and Amber's and Stanley's," he added with a snort. "I'm probably the only guy in the whole country whose entire family lectured him on the facts of life."

Craig nodded with a laugh. "You remember, but do you heed?"

Ace laughed. "Fear not, I know what the Lord meant when he said not to give what's holy to dogs."

Amber turned, her eyes wide with surprise. "Do you mean to tell me, Ace Harris, champion bull rider....?"

He stopped her surprised exclamation with a finger on her lips and a kiss on her cheek. "Shh, let's not let anyone in on the fact that I'm a candidate for Sainthood," he said in a loud whisper.

"Sainthood? Right," she remarked, when he took his coffee and headed up to his room. She and her father looked at each other for a long moment then burst into surprised laughter.

Ace chuckled to himself when the sound of their laughter echoed from the kitchen. He barely had time to take off his boots, finish his coffee and stretch out on the bed with his hat over his eyes before Kaitlyn climbed up beside him.

"Uncle Ace," she whispered, "are you sleeping?"

"Umm, mm."

"Then why are you dressed?"

He bit back a grin and refrained from comment.

"Uncle Ace?" She lifted his hat to peek at him.

Her surprised squeal bounced off the rafters when he grabbed her. "What?" he demanded and tossed her into the air.

Laughter rang out in the room as Ashlyn joined in and an impromptu wrestling/tickle match ensued.

Lexie had just stepped out of the bathroom when she heard the first yelp and was three-fourths of the way up the stairs when she realized it was one of un-abandoned delight. She smiled at him when Stanley exited the bedroom he and Amber shared for the time being.

He smiled back. "Morning."

"Hey."

He peeked in the room and grinned. "You girls aren't jumping in the bed are you?"

"No, sir!" They replied in unison, laughing and giggling while they jumped on Ace.

"Better not be," he warned, though not too fiercely. Shaking his head he arched an eyebrow at Lexie. "Amazing isn't it? How two little girls can make so much noise. Of course their nearly twenty-year-old uncle, a grown man mind you, is as bad as they are."

"I heard that!" Ace insisted. "Like you have room to talk." He'd witnessed first hand the natural disaster that occurred when Stanley wrestled with his daughters.

Stanley laughed and stuck his head back in the door. "A wonder you can hear a single word with all the racket going on in here."

"I was trying to sleep," Ace defended, doing his best to look innocent. "They started it."

"No, we didn't," Kaitlyn denied. Black silk curls danced off her shoulders at the vehement shake of her head. "He started with the tickle monsters!"

Lexie moved up beside Stanley to peek in the door. "Tickle monsters?"

"C'mon, Yexie! Hep us!" Ashlyn urged.

Ace chortled. "Yeah, c'mon Yexie!" he teased.

Lexie took a step back and shook her head. "No thanks. Y'all get him good girls," she encouraged.

"Chicken!" Ace challenged.

Stanley grinned. "I bet she's not chicken. Are you Lex? Ticklish maybe," he teased, with a poke in her ribs. He guessed right. She flinched. He laughed. "Uh, oh. Look here Ace, look who's ticklish."

Lexie guessed his intent and made a dash for the stairs. Stanley was quicker. He grabbed her around the waist and pulled her against him. His fingers dug playfully into her side.

"Stop it! Don't! Stanley!" She giggled and fought off the barrage of fingers while trying to escape his firm grasp.

Ace grinned then gaped at the girls wide-eyed and open-mouthed. "Ticklish." He held up his hands, wriggled his fingers.

"Let's get her, girls!" he urged, and they scrambled off the bed. He rolled off mere seconds before Stanley picked Lexie up and dumped her unceremoniously in the middle.

"I'm going to kill you, Stanley!" she shrieked, when the twins and Ace attacked her full force.

Stanley left her without mercy or remorse and made his way downstairs and into the kitchen. "Morning, My Sweet," he greeted his wife, and slipped his arms around Amber's waist. "Hmmm, smells good in here."

Amber smiled up at him. "Hungry?"

"Starved," he admitted then nibbled on her neck for emphasis. "Why didn't you wake me earlier?"

"I thought you could use the rest."

He grinned, gave her an intimate squeeze, and stole a slice of bacon from the full platter while she poured him a cup of coffee. "Morning, PaPaw," he drawled and greeted his father-in-law with a grin.

Craig's eyes narrowed. "Watch it, Boy."

Stanley chuckled then walked over to the stroller and addressed his son. "Hey, Boy, wake up. Think you're going to keep me awake all night then sleep all day? You've got another thought coming," he teased and tickled William's feet. "That's it," he cooed. "Wake up now."

He lifted him out of the stroller and held the baby up as William opened first one eye, then the other to peer at him. He grunted and stretched and his little mouth curved into a smile.

"Don't think you're going to buy me off with a single smile either, Bucko," Stanley chided. "Come on, give me another one," he urged, and brushed his lips across the baby's mouth and cheek.

Amber laughed, placed the cup of coffee in front of her husband and set the table. "Where are the girls?"

"Upstairs with Ace, I just dumped Lexie in the middle of a tickle monster war."

Craig grinned. "Uh-oh, poor Lexie."

Lexie would have agreed. The twins she could handle with ease. Ace was a different case altogether. He wrestled with, and against, the twins until he held her trapped beneath his long frame.

"Say Uncle," he insisted and laughed when she fought to keep his fingers away from her tender ribcage.

"No," she gasped, and fought desperately to keep him from tickling her. His eyes took on a dangerous glow.

"No?" he queried. "Did you say no?" Keeping both of her hands secured in one of his, he took his fingers on a slow, torturous journey up her side. He poked and prodded while she struggled against him and fought to keep from laughing. The struggle revealed the soft skin covering her midriff, which he promptly attacked with his mouth, gnawing and growling wolfishly while the girls egged him on.

"Where else are you ticklish?" he wondered and trailed his fingers along the tender flesh of her neck and collarbone.

"Here?" He grinned at her shriek.

"Stop," she insisted, bucking in an attempt to dislodge him from his perch.

He laughed. "No way you're gonna lose me, Sweetheart. I'm a champion bull rider. Remember?"

She snorted. "Champion male chauvinist pig."

"Oh, no, that's gonna cost you," he threatened and renewed his assault until she gasped for breath. "Take it back."

"No! Ace! I'm going to skin you alive," she threatened between fits of laughter.

"If I ever let you up."

"Oh, you'll have to let me up sooner or later," she warned. A shrill whistle from the kitchen got their attention.

"Breakfast!" Amber's call followed Stanley's whistle.

The twins jumped off the bed and scrambled for the door. "Walk," Ace insisted his attention temporarily averted.

Lexie sighed with relief at the reprieve. With a twist and shove, she tossed him off her. He rolled to the floor with a thud.

Being quick to your feet made the difference between life and death in the bullring. Ace hastened to his when Lexie lunged from the bed, claws bared. He watched and waited in wary silence for her move. With a quick, boyish grin he held his hand out to her. "Truce?"

"I will get you back," she insisted.

He bowed in acknowledgement of her threat. "I'm sure you will," he agreed, his tone amiable. "How about breakfast now, though?"

She turned with a haughty shake of her head and walked to the dresser, but kept her eyes on him in the mirror. She groaned at her rumpled clothing, and the wild riot of hair that tumbled about her shoulders, and picked up the brush. Her eyes narrowed when he took a step closer. "Ace," she warned and wielded the brush like a lethal weapon.

Raising his hands where she could see them, he watched her try to brush some semblance of order to the thick mass of unruly auburn hair. The simple chore made him want to sink both fists in the silken locks and gave him a whole new insight to the word erotic.

Her cheeks were flushed, her eyes sparkled vivid green and spewed wrath. She glared at him as though the tangled tresses were his fault alone. Her chest quivered with each breath she took. He took another step closer and could feel her tremble. Locking his gaze with hers in the mirror, he reached around her and picked up a bandanna off the dresser. He ran it through his fingers in what could have been a caress then slid the cloth beneath her hair and left it trailing over her shoulders.

With hands that shook, Lexie pulled the ends together and tied her hair back into a ponytail. Those bright eyes had gone soft and warm, like liquid metal. Mouth dry as dust, she swallowed hard.

Ace slid his arms around her waist, surprised at how tiny she was. Surprised he hadn't noticed before. He pulled her back against his chest, his embrace gentle.

"I hope I didn't hurt you," he said his voice no more than a husky whisper. He closed his eyes and committed the picture to memory then turned her in his arms. A soft groan escaped as his hands traveled up her arms to cup her cheeks. He felt her stiffen and opened his eyes to look into the endless depths of her gaze.

Lexie couldn't breathe. All she could do was gaze at him, helpless with longing, for what she wasn't sure, and shake her head. Need curled in her like silken flames followed by a wave of fear. Fear that she was losing some part of herself. A part she'd yet to identify with, or understand. She felt as though her whole body had suddenly transformed into a horde of pretty moths drawn to a flame. Exciting. Deadly.

She could tell by the gleam in his eyes, Ace wanted to kiss her and shook her head. "No." She could hardly force the word through her parched throat.

"Yes," he insisted and brushed his lips across her forehead then pulled her soft form against his chest, his arms like steel manacles around her waist.

"Ace!"

His father's voice from the bottom of the stairs jerked him out of the sensual spell. He stepped away from her and held out a hand. Lexie hesitated a moment then slid her hand in his. Ace lifted it to his lips, waited until she lifted wary eyes to his, then with a tender wink and grin, walked with her to the door. Being a gentleman, he stepped back and allowed her to exit before him, then followed her down the stairs.

Lexie welcomed the noisy, crowded, kitchen and slid bonelessly into a chair when Amber placed a plate laden with eggs, bacon and pancakes on the table in front of her. When everyone was served and seated, Craig said the blessing. After they ate, Lexie helped Amber clean the kitchen while

Craig brought the girls in to watch TV and Stanley left for home.

Amber realized Lexie had been unusually quiet during breakfast and asked if something was wrong. Lexie shook her head. Tears of confusion brightened her eyes. The baby whimpered before Amber could press. She settled him at her breast and watched in silence for a moment while Lexie continued to clear the table and load the dishwasher. A flush rode high on her pale cheeks. Her hands trembled.

"Lexie, if you ever want to talk, about anything, I'm here," Amber offered.

Lexie acknowledged Amber's remark with a slight shake of her head and weak smile. With supreme effort she forced the lump of tears down her throat. She had no idea why she wanted to cry, just that she did. The tenderness in Ace surprised her and reached someplace deep inside, someplace dark and cold. That place responded, opening like a flower to sunlight and answered with a longing she couldn't identify and didn't understand. The sound of an approaching vehicle and blaring horn brought a smile to her lips.

"They're back!" Not bothering to dry her hands she raced out the back door and into Scott's arms. He twirled her around then released her with a hug and a kiss so she could embrace Trina and the boys. Laughing and talking all at once, they walked into the house.

Ace had slipped upstairs for a shower. There was no way he'd sleep now. The wrestling match had done more to energize him than a nap would have. Far above being naive or stupid, he realized it was more than rolling around on the bed with his nieces that had his juices pumping. Regardless, he felt as though he could take on the world, and with that exhilarating feeling pushing him, he went out and saddled his horse. He'd barely left the barn when Scott and Trina arrived in a wave of dust and gravel, the horn blaring. Scott hardly had time to turn off the truck's engine and open the door before Lexie flung herself into his arms.

Watching the family's boisterous greeting, Ace felt a tug at his heart. Tears stung his eyes and he thought about his mother. God he missed her! Changing his mind and his destination, he led the horse back into the barn, unsaddled him and left in his truck. He knelt on the dew-dampened earth, stared at the beloved name carved in granite, and visited with his mother.

"She reminds me of you, Mama," he whispered, and then smiled as the realization sank deep into his heart. A soft breeze whispered through his hair and reminded him of his mother's caress. She'd loved to run her fingers through his hair whenever they were talking. A gesture Amber had picked up and imitated to this day. A gesture of love.

A flicker of hope sputtered to life in his spirit. A splash of joy moistened the parched, cracked soil of his soul. His heart opened a little to make room for feelings he never thought he'd experience.

Chapter Ten

Ritchie and Robert went into detail about their visit to San Antonio which turned dinner into a lively affair, full of love and laughter and familial bonding. A break in the conversation allowed Stanley to address his wife. "How soon will you be ready to leave?"

She smiled. "I've packed all day. I'm ready."

"Y'all aren't leaving yet?" Craig knew the day would come when his daughter and son-in-law would want to take their family home. He knew it was only natural, it was only right. But he didn't have to like it. It was his privilege, his duty, not to like it.

Amber smiled at her father, and gave his hand a gentle squeeze. "Yes Daddy. It's time for us to go home."

Acting on impulse Scott spoke as he stood up. "I was hoping y'all would stay one more night. I've a desire to dance with my daughter," he remarked then pulled Lexie out of her chair and into a waltz around the table. Flushed with excitement from the day, she laughed.

Scott eyed Amber. "I thought, maybe, you would baby-sit."

"That's not fair! I haven't been dancing in months."

"It's too soon for you to go dancing," Scott insisted.

Amber snorted. Her eyes sparkled like rare, precious gems. "Huh! This child is nearly four weeks old! You just want a baby-sitter."

"Now Amber, as the physician who delivered your baby, very nearly delivered you too, do you think I would use that knowledge and experience to trick you?"

"You're a man aren't you?"

Everyone laughed. Stanley gazed up at Scott. "How come I didn't know you delivered Amber?"

"I didn't," Scott corrected. "But I was there. I'll never forget it either."

"Oh, please, do tell," Stanley urged.

He and Craig laughed. "Tamera was calm and cool, Craig was a basket case." Scott chuckled at the memory and continued. "Pacing and growling, glaring at the doctor, demanding to know how much longer. We tried to explain that babies come in their own time, Tamera and the baby were fine, and everything was progressing normally. He ignored us and kept up the tirade until the doctor threatened to throw him out. I swear, I thought there'd be a barroom brawl right there in the delivery room. You are a whole lot calmer than he was during the birth of his children," he assured Stanley.

Stanley laughed. "I don't believe it. Not big, tough, Craig Harris," he teased.

Craig grunted. "I should have thrown you off this ranch years ago," he muttered, when Stanley taunted him without mercy.

Ace cocked back in his chair and drew everyone's attention. "What about me? What about the day I was born?"

Amber laughed. "You've been a brat since the day you were born."

Ace grinned. "Am not." The smile they shared bespoke of memories and recollections of how she would tease him about being a brat all those years while they grew up.

Scott brushed his lips across Amber's cheek and drew her attention back to him and the question he'd asked. "Well?"

She glanced at Stanley. He shrugged and she knew he figured one more night wouldn't hurt. She glanced up at Scott and nodded. "Okay."

Craig winked at his daughter then turned to his son. "Since you went out last night, you can stay home and help her." For the second time in a single day, one of his children looked at him as though he had lost his mind.

"Stanley can help her," Ace countered.

Amber smiled. "Stanley's worked all day."

Ace knew they were teasing and fell right in. He hunkered down beside his sister and gazed at her with adoring, pleading eyes. A look he spent nearly twenty years perfecting. "You don't really need my help, do you Sissy?"

"Of course, Brat, I can't handle all of these kids all by myself. Like I said, Stanley's worked hard all day."

He grinned at his brother-in-law, expecting him to bail him out. "C'mon, Stan, help me out here," he urged.

Stan chuckled. "On one condition."

Ace waited expectantly.

"That some night, in the very near future, you'll baby-sit so I can take my wife dancing."

Ace laughed. "You got it." He glanced triumphantly at his father then headed upstairs to shower and change.

Craig grunted. "And everyone wonders why he's so arrogant," he remarked.

"He gets it honestly," Scott teased his friend, while everyone else rushed to get the kitchen cleaned and then get ready to go.

Hours later, Stanley crept up the stairs to peek in on his wife and son. She smiled up at him while the baby nursed.

"How's it going?"

He laughed. "Okay. We're playing hide and seek."

"So that's what the racket is. Are you hiding or seeking?"

His eyes swept over her in a hungry gesture. "Seeking," he admitted his voice husky. "And look what I've found. Hey boy, you cuttin' in on my territory?" he queried and slipped his finger under his son's hand which rested on Amber's breast. The little fingers curled into a fist around it.

Amber sighed and lifted her mouth for a kiss. Stan obliged. The tender caress of his lips on hers ended on a soft groan of frustration. She smiled again. "There's something Scott failed to consider when he said it was too soon for me to go dancing."

Her eyes glowed. Stanley's breath caught in his throat. "What's that, My Sweet?"

"Another advantage of having a baby at home is a quicker recovery."

Not mistaking the invitation in her gaze, he hummed in anticipation. His lips covered hers in a hungry gesture and he gave her an intimate caress. "Hold that thought while I go round up these heathens and put them to bed," he suggested, his tone husky. Kissing her again, he hurried off.

Less than an hour later he returned to his wife's side. Taking her in his arms, he reveled in her soft sighs of pleasure as, for the first time in weeks, they celebrated their love in a dance as old as time.

* * * * *

The time neared midnight before things started to wind down at the nightclub. Scott watched with a mixture of pride and alarm while his wife and daughter 'pushed their tush' and 'scooted their boots' through the latest line dances. They were quite a pair out there and it was obvious the male patrons of the nightclub were enjoying the show as they entertained the crowd with their moves, especially Lexie. She'd been on the high school dance line for four years along with summer classes in aerobics, tap, jazz, ballet, and gymnastics, all of which toned her body into quite a lovely sight—long legs, slim hips, breasts straining with every move, cheeks flushed, eyes glittering with excitement, a vision that would make any man's mouth water.

Scott swallowed hard the cold lump of dread in his throat. The boys were bound to come around sooner or later and he knew that it was a miracle and a blessing they hadn't as of yet. How he hoped it would be later!

They'd adopted her at age sixteen and he wanted to enjoy her daughterly affection as long as possible before she found love of her own and made him a grandfather. He watched in surprised dismay when Ace's eyes followed her every move.

The dancers whirled into formation for "Cotton Eyed Joe" when the D. J. announced the tune. Scott glared at Ace and whispered to Craig, "Cut him off."

"What?"

He nodded in Ace's direction. "Cut him off," he stated and headed toward the women. He grabbed Lexie by the hand, slipped his arm around her waist and waited for the song to begin. Craig laughed and took Trina's hand. Ace shrugged with a grin and selected another partner.

Lexie laughed and danced with her father, thrilled when the D. J. honored her request for a fast Cajun song. She twirled in his arms as Scott led her into a jitterbug, and then escorted her from the floor slightly winded.

"Girl you're enough to give an old man a heart attack," he teased.

She tossed her head, her eyes laughed into his. "Or help him stay young," she countered. Executing fancy foot moves, she held her hand to Craig. He accepted and led her out on the floor for a fast two-step. They returned to the table breathless and laughing.

"Enough!" Craig insisted. His breath heaved in and out in ragged pants. "It's been way too long since I've done this."

Lexie and Ace protested when their parents suggested it was time to go home.

"It's early!"

"Early? It's well past midnight," Trina replied.

"So? I don't see any pumpkins. Or mice," Lexie teased. She glanced down and gasped a look of pure surprise and delight on her face. "And look! These boots haven't disintegrated into dust yet. Come on, it's been ages since we've gone dancing," she pleaded.

"Yeah," Ace agreed. "Y'all go on if you want to. We'll stay a while."

"You were out all last night, Ace," his father argued.

"Oh bull, I'm fine, besides, I had a nap earlier. Don't worry, I'll be a gentleman, and keep an eye on her."

Lexie snorted. "As if I need some chauvinistic jerk cowboy to watch after me."

Scott eyed her. "The only way you're going to stay any longer is if you two stick together. Lex, you don't know anyone around here. Ace does. I trust he can steer you clear of any trouble." He eyed Ace, a meaningful lift to his brow.

Ace nodded and lifted his bottle of root beer in salute. "Yes sir. I'll keep the little lady out of trouble," he promised in his best John Wayne imitation.

"Lex?"

She glared at Ace, then Scott. With a roll of her eyes she relented. "Oh okay. Take these worry warts home," she implored Trina.

Trina laughed and patted her cheek then turned a firm gaze on Ace. "I'm counting on you to keep my daughter safe."

To her, Ace gave his most charming smile, bowed, and lifted her hand to his lips. "Yes Ma'am," he drawled. "You have my word as a gentleman and a cowboy."

Everyone chuckled at the exchange then Craig, Scott and Trina left. Glad he'd come in his own truck, Ace sighed with relief when they were safely out the door.

Finally! Now he'd finally get to dance with her.

If he didn't know better, he'd have sworn Scott deliberately kept Lexie out of arm's reach. His arms anyway. He gave her a chance to catch her breath while they finished their drinks and then led her out on the dance floor. Several songs later, they took another break. Lexie was on her way back from the ladies' room when he heard her fend off a potential admirer.

"No thanks," she denied his request for a dance with a smile and shake of her head. "Think I'll sit this one out."

When the cowboy became insistent, Ace stood up. "The lady said no."

"And what do you plan to do about it Mr. Bull Ridin' Ace Harris?" he queried in a tone thick with sarcasm. Ace took a step closer, his eyes narrowed into shimmering slits of silver.

"Only what I have to," he warned in a voice all the more dangerous for its calm, steely, edge. "Now back off. The lady said no."

With a snort and a leer, he patted Lexie on the behind. "Next time then, Darlin'."

Lexie turned in an angry whirl and her palm connected with his cheek. "Not on your life, Darlin'," she mimicked in a disgusted tone.

Ace stepped between them when the guy made a grab for her. "Back off, Johnson, or you're in deep trouble."

It irritated Brad Johnson flat-to-no-end to have to look up, even slightly, to Ace Harris. Always had. Though he was broader, Ace was taller, leaner, and more muscular. Being a bull rider, he was evidently stronger and faster. Though he'd never admit it, Brad knew he couldn't hold his weight against Ace. With a snarl, he turned on his heel and stomped off.

Ace turned to Lexie. "Dance with me," he insisted and pulled her against his side.

"I don't want to dance this one," she insisted.

"You want him to bug you all night?"

She shuddered. "No."

"Then dance with me." He led her out on the dance floor and took her in his arms as the D. J. announced the song and encouraged the guys to hold their girls tight.

Ace had looked forward to this all night. He held her close, his embrace firm but tender, and reveled in the feel of her soft form against his. His hand caressed her spine and he urged her to relax. "I won't bite," he assured in a husky whisper.

"Said the spider to the fly," Lexie muttered and heard him chuckle. All night she had avoided being this close to him. After their intimacy of the morning, she had no idea what Ace wanted from her, or expected. Or she, him. Despite his tenderness, she remained stiff and tense in his arms.

After that first slow dance he never let her out of his arms, and seldom out of his sight. He accompanied her and waited nearby whenever she went to the ladies' room or to get another cold drink. By the time the night came to a close, both were aware that something was happening between them. Something neither expected nor was sure they wanted, but were both willing to let unfold and explore.

Ace pulled her in his arms for the last dance of the night. They moved together to the soothing, sensual, sound of a country love song. He held her close, wanted desperately to kiss her. But in a time when kisses were given too lightly and often taken as such, he opted to wait and share that intimacy with her some time and place where he could be more private about it.

He didn't feel strange in that desire. He'd had his share of kisses. He had the feeling though, that a kiss between them would mean so much more than the others he'd experienced. Unable to resist completely, he brushed his lips across the thick, silken mass of hair beneath his cheek and pressed her face into his chest in a hug.

Lexie looked up at him, her eyes alive with questions. He hushed them with a gentle shake of his head and a finger on her lips. His smile was tender as he pulled her close once more to finish the dance. His head jerked up when his name was called.

"Ace! Tailgate, usual spot."

He grinned and eyed Lexie. "Want to go?"

"Where, for what?"

He laughed. "A bunch of us usually get together when we're not quite ready to call it a night—laugh, joke, dance to the radio, bonfire, the works."

"Sure. Sounds like fun."

All you could see were taillights for miles as truckloads of kids made their way to a special spot by the river. They parked in a huge circle then gathered twigs and started a fire. Radio's tuned in to the same country station, they pared up in couples around the fire. Some laughed and told jokes while others danced.

After initial introductions, Lexie found herself the butt of endless "coonass" jokes. She retaliated with her share of Aggie jokes. "Besides," she countered the latest assault to her heritage. "I'm a Cajun."

Someone snorted. "Huh! A Cajun is just a snobby coonass," he remarked and brought on another round of laughter.

One hand flew to her cheek, the other to her heart. Lexie gasped, wide-eyed and presented them with the perfect picture of insulted innocence. "Y'all know what separates a coonass from a jackass, don't 'cha?" she queried, laying the accent on thick.

She played the southern belle to the hilt and pretended to fan herself as everyone waited breathlessly to see what she'd say next. She batted her eyelashes at Ace.

"Why, the Sabine river, of course."

Ace laughed with the rest of them. No one was disappointed with her lively wit and charming personality. As darkness subsided, couples left or slipped off into the remaining shadows for a few moments alone. Ace rolled to his feet and reached down to give Lexie a hand up. The fact that they were leaving was cause for more teasing by his bolder comrades.

Lexie tossed her head and grinned over her shoulder. "Ha! You'll never know if he even gets to first base," she taunted her new friends.

Whistling and jeering, they egged Ace on. He pulled her against him, his earlier thoughts of privacy forgotten. "Ah, little Lexie," he taunted, his voice thick with male pride and arrogance. "You've been challenging me to shut that pretty mouth since the first time we met."

Before she could pull away, he turned her in his arms. His mouth covered hers and hushed her protests. She resisted but a moment before something wonderful began to happen.

His lips were soft, persuasive, his arms firm, but gentle. His tongue traced her mouth, urging not forcing entrance. Once allowed, instead of the rough thrusting she was used to, and expected, he dipped gently inside as though savoring all the sweetness she had to offer.

The woman in her responded with a little cry of delight which sounded more like a purr, the little girl within responded with a whimper of fear as the thought occurred to her once again that she was losing some part of herself.

Blood warmed by degrees.

Ace held her until the moment of tension passed and their senses hummed like high voltage wires. His hands ran over her in a gentle, subtle caress until he cupped her cheeks in his work-roughened palms. Slowly, gently, he released her lips, thrilling in the soft moan of protest that escaped her.

A low wolf whistle reached their ears. "Looks more like second base to me," came the taunt.

Ace released her. His mind and body reeled from the potency of that one kiss. "Don't give them the satisfaction of being embarrassed," he whispered his voice husky. He ran his finger up her throat, lifted her chin, and waited until she lifted wary eyes to his. "Breakfast?"

She smiled and nodded.

He stepped away from her enticing embrace and held a hand to her. Once more shy, she placed hers in it while he opened the truck door. She scooted across the seat while he got in and buckled up. With a gentle tug on her hand, he pulled her by his side.

Breakfast was sweetly romantic and not at all awkward as they laughed and talked and got to know each other on a deeper level, surprised to find they had a great deal in common.

* * * * *

Scott and Craig talked over their first cup of coffee when the kids stumbled up on the porch. Neither of them had realized their children were still out. Scott's eyes narrowed into dangerous slits when Ace chuckled at Lexie's giggle and admonished her to be quiet then opened the door.

One look at their fathers' taut faces and heated glares had laughter bubbling hysterically. "Uh, oh, we didn't beat them up," Ace remarked.

"Where in the hell have you two been all night?" Craig demanded.

Ace shrugged, surprised at the anger he sensed. "Down by the river with some other kids. You know, where we go all the time."

Scott lunged from his chair, fists clenched. "I'm sure your mother will want to have a word with you," he snarled and took Lexie by the arm. The look he gave Craig insisted that he take proper care of his son.

Ace watched in total confusion. "What's the matter with him? We didn't do anything wrong."

"You kept his daughter out all night Ace."

"Oh, please, she's eighteen, not eight."

"All the more reason to worry," Craig insisted and followed his son up the stairs as Ace reported the events of the evening since they left them at the nightclub. He watched with curious intent while Ace laughed and recalled the teasing Lexie had taken in stride.

"You should have seen her, Daddy. She gave as good as she got. No one could get one up on her. You know Brad Johnson?" He continued at Craig's nod.

"Well, I thought I'd have to tear her off of him when he patted her on the behind." He chuckled at the memory. "Man, she is something else."

Craig grinned. "Sounds like y'all had quite a night."

Ace yawned and hooked one heel in the bootjack to remove his boot. "Yeah." He sighed, yawned lustily. "I think I'm in love."

His father chuckled.

"No really. How do you know for sure?" he asked.

"You don't have to ask," Craig informed his son, an elaborate lift to his dark brow.

Ace shrugged. "Well, maybe not then." He stretched out on the bed and lowered his hat over his eyes. Lifting it, he eyed his father. "Think it'll mess things up with Scott if I marry her?"

"Don't know. You'll have to ask Scott."

He grunted. "Better ask Lexie first. She'd think it major chauvinistic if I asked Scott before I consulted her, even if it is the right thing to do."

Craig laughed and sat beside him as Ace began to snore. He shook his head and wished his wife were here to see her little angel now. "Oh, Temper," his heart whispered, "if only you could see him now."

Somehow, he knew she could.

Down the stairs, in another room, Scott had no more luck in chastising his daughter. She sat huddled with Katrina. They whispered, lapsing into snatches of French–which he still didn't understand–and giggled over the events of last night.

"And then," she finished her story, "when everyone started to slip off into the shadows to neck, Ace..." she hesitated for the sheer pleasure of watching Scott struggle for calm. "Bought me breakfast," she concluded.

"I think necking should be done in private, don't you?" She queried and lifted innocent, beguiling eyes to her father.

Scott rolled his eyes in a dramatic gesture and a low growl sounded in his throat when he turned on his heel and stomped out of the room.

Lexie burst into giggles as Trina tried to chide her. "You shouldn't tease him like that, Lexie. You know how protective he is and he's not ready to share you."

Scott met Craig on his way down the stairs. "You'd better keep an eye on that boy of yours," he growled. Amusement glittered in Craig's gaze.

"Are you saying my son isn't good enough for your daughter?"

Scott stuttered. Though he hadn't said a word that was exactly what his actions were saying. Which was stupid. If he had to handpick a man for Lexie, none could equal his best friend's son. He knew Ace well enough to know that he would be a gentle, one-woman-man, like his father and brother-in-law. His grin sheepish, he answered Craig. "I'm saying that not even *your* son is good enough for her."

Craig laughed and slapped him on the back. "Can't stop them from growing up. Take it from me, I know. Been there myself."

Scott smiled. "Yeah, but there's a big difference, you had Amber eighteen years before you had to share her with Stanley. I've had Lexie less than half that much."

Craig clucked his tongue in sympathy and offered his friend a fresh cup of coffee and a sympathetic ear as Scott reminisced over the years he'd watched Lexie grow up.

Chapter Eleven

Lexie walked into the kitchen surprised to find the house unusually quiet. It took her a while to unwind that morning when she went to bed, but once she did, she slept like a log. Dreams fueled by memories of the last hours of the night and the day before had her waking with a smile on her face and excitement in her soul. A quick shower had washed the last dregs of sleep from her eyes and lingering lethargy from her body.

She glanced over her shoulder when Scott walked into the room. "Hi. Where's everyone?"

"Craig and Ace have gone to help Stanley. Seems one of his Arabian stallions decided he wanted to add a Quarter horse mare to his harem. He busted up a stall trying to get to her. Trina rode along with them to help Amber get settled in again."

"Why didn't anyone wake me? I would love to have helped."

He shrugged. "Guess they figured you needed your sleep after dragging the roads until dawn," he muttered.

She could tell by the frown on his face and his tone of voice he was still irritated with her for staying out all night with Ace. She smiled over at him. "So we're all alone?"

"No. The boys are around here somewhere, took the puppy outside to play a little while ago." His eyes narrowed when her shirt moved to show the smooth area of her abdomen as she reached to get a glass. "What in the hell is that?"

She turned wide-eyed. "What?"

He walked over to her and lifted her blouse to reveal the bruises on her creamy flesh.

Lexie smiled at the memory. "Oh. Tickle monsters."

"Excuse me?" Her eyes danced into his and she raised her hands claw like then wriggled her fingers.

"Tickle monsters. Ace and the twins were in the middle of a full-blown tickle war when Stanley, the heathen, discovered I'm ticklish. He dumped me right in the middle."

"Ace needs to watch his hands," Scott growled and fully intended to tell Ace that himself.

"He didn't hurt me, looks worse than it actually is." She laughed at his snort of disbelief and slipped her arms around his waist. "I really love you, you know. You've been more of a father to me these last few years than mine was the first fifteen of my life."

Scott's heart overflowed, his arms wound around her. "You still miss him though. Don't you, Lex?"

She nodded into his chest. "Yes," she replied, her voice soft, thick with emotion. "And feel guilty for it."

"Why do you feel guilty? You don't have to love one less, to love another. Katrina and I both realize that. Neither of us would want you to forget your father."

"I know."

She sighed and looked up at him, her eyes alive with emotions. "The problem is that he was never a real father. Not in the true sense of the word. Not like you've been. When I realize that, I feel guilty, like I'm betraying him. I know it's crazy. How can you betray someone who's dead, someone who was never really alive, or there for you? I mean, I know he loved me, in his own crazy way, but, he was never there for me."

"What brought this on Lex?"

She shrugged, moved from his embrace, and poured herself a glass of milk then reached for the bread and popped two slices into the toaster while Scott waited for her to continue. She knew he'd stand there, oozing patience while she searched her heart for questions and answers and smiled up at him. She spread a thin layer of peanut butter on the toast, carried it to the table, and waited for him to sit next to her.

Scott watched and waited until she finished eating before he spoke. "So, you want to talk to me?"

She emitted a soft laugh. "You're always so patient. I'll never forget the first time I stayed with y'all. You and Trina went out of your way to make me feel at home. Then, while I roamed the house, you smiled up from your paper, so peaceful, so patient."

He laughed. "You challenged me from the start and twisted every word I said to suit your own mood."

Her eyes danced into his. "But you just looked at me with so much understanding, so much love. I think I fell in love with you at that moment."

He reached for her and pulled her against his chest then asked, "What's eating at you now, Lex?"

"I guess I've recently realized how much I missed as a child, and how lucky I've been to get hooked up with y'all and this whole family business." She shrugged unable to express the depth of her feelings.

"I've always wanted to be part of a family. Brothers and sisters, the whole works. I've barely known these people a month, and yet, I feel like I've known them all of my life. Like there's some kind of connection between us, like we were meant to meet, destined to be. I don't know. And, every one seems so content, so peaceful, even with the hole in their heart.

"Amber and Stanley are so beautiful together, so much in love, so right. Like you and Trina, it gives me hope, makes me jealous, and makes me want what they have. What you and Trina have. What Mr. Craig had with Mrs. Harris.

"And Mr. Craig, he's so solid, so strong and loving. You can tell how much he misses his wife, and yet, he tries, really tries to keep going for the rest of them."

She sighed. "There's just so much I don't understand."

"Like?" Scott stroked the hair off her face and waited for her to pour her heart out.

"Like, why? Why do bad things happen to such good people? Why did she have to die when it's so blatantly obvious she was well loved and needed? Why did my father have to be addicted to alcohol? Why did he have to die? Why was my childhood so unstable? What did I do to deserve that, or better yet, to deserve all the love y'all give me now. Why did Kristy have to be so mixed up? Why did she have to die so young? Why couldn't I help her?"

"Lex, you've been raised in the church, attended the best Christian schools, been taught the Bible inside and out."

"Look what good it's done," she interrupted; obviously confused at what she felt and what she was taught she should feel.

He smiled and continued to stroke her hair. "Have you asked, Lex? If you need understanding, all you have to do is ask God for it."

"I'll never understand the reasons why those things happened."

"Maybe not, but, with His grace and love, you can accept the things you don't understand, and have peace about them. True, you didn't have the best childhood, but there are those who are far less fortunate. And, believe me; although we wouldn't wish it on you again, Katrina and I are eternally grateful you were brought into our lives.

"God doesn't make tragedy, Lexie, but He does use it. God doesn't make mistakes, but He does pick up the pieces and bring about good when we make mistakes. Your father had a problem. You needed a home and love. Your father couldn't, or wouldn't provide that for you. We prayed for years for a daughter and God gave you to us.

"Though we can't take away the sadness of your early years, we can, and hopefully have, given you happiness and stability, love and understanding. We can never make up for the loss of your father or the lack of a relationship with him, but we can offer you all the love we have. Which is a whole lot I might add and it's free and unconditional."

"But what about the rest?" Lexie questioned. "Kristy and Mrs. Harris? Sometimes I can feel the pain in Mr. Craig. And Ace too, even Amber and Stan. How long will it take for them to pick up the pieces and for God to make something good out of this situation?"

"He has, Sweetheart," Scott assured. "He's given them so much life all around. Amber and Stanley have three beautiful, healthy children, one of which looks exactly like her grandmother. Craig's not alone. He has his daughter and son-in-law, grandchildren, and son, and I'll always be here for Craig. We've been friends our whole lives. And Trina loves him like she would a brother. Ace will move on. Sooner or later, he'll fall in love, get married, and have children of his own. Tamera will never really be gone. As long as she lives on in her children and their children, and in our hearts, she'll never really be gone."

Lexie smiled and hugged him. "I guess. You know, even though I've never met her, I sometimes feel her, almost like I could talk to her. I know that probably sounds crazy and some would call it scary, but there is such peace in this house."

"I believe that comes from the love that still lingers even through death," Scott said. "Real love, God's love and love ordained and blessed by God lives on Lex, in us, and in those around us. In those who love us and in whom we love." He lifted her chin. "Don't ever settle for less for yourself either. Promise me you won't ever settle for less."

She felt better, still not completely satisfied but better and less confused. And, though she never really felt close to God, she wanted to be. Lexie knew it would be up to her to make the move to get to know Him, to learn to love and trust Him. She smiled up at Scott and silently thanked God for him. "I promise. You are so brilliant, Dr. Hensley. You know that?"

He chuckled. "Not brilliant, Baby. Just been around and seen a lot in my time. As a physician, you have to know you are not God, merely His instrument. Realizing that, you have to let go and let Him work through you. We all do. The Bible teaches us to *lean not unto our own understanding...* that's because we'll never understand the how's or why's of life and human nature. We're not supposed to understand we're just supposed to trust.

"There is so much to life, Lex. So much God wants you to experience and enjoy. So many blessings He has for you. But you have to want them. Want Him. He'll never forsake you. But He will never force you to love Him. Remember First Corinthians?

"Read it again," he urged when she nodded. "Read it with an open heart. Not a questioning one but an open one, willing and eager to hear His voice. I promise you, He won't let you down. And though you may still wonder why, you'll begin to find peace, real peace. Peace that surpasses understanding. And your eyes will be opened to the blessings you have in your life, and all that He has to offer. What He wants for you, His plan for your life."

Lexie hugged him once more then rose to take her dishes to the sink. She turned back to him and smiled. "So, am I forgiven for 'dragging the roads until dawn,' as you so colorfully put it?"

Sweeter than a sunrise after a week of rain Scott couldn't help but respond to her smile, his grin quick and rich. "For a smile like that I'll forgive you just about anything, Sweetheart, still not happy about it though."

She wrapped her arms around his neck and brushed her lips over his head. "How about if I cook your favorite supper?"

He couldn't help but chuckle. "Not above bribery are you?"

"Not if it means you'll not be upset with me. We really didn't do anything wrong, Scott. Ace was the perfect gentleman though if you tell him I said so, I'll deny it to the very end. From what I understand, these kids get together like this real often."

Scott heard the excitement in her voice and understood her need. Lexie never had many close friends. Kristy had been the only person she got close to. After her death, Lex didn't want, or was afraid, to get close to anyone again. This experience might just be what God intended to start her on the road to deep, spiritual healing. He looked up at her, a sly smile played along his lips. "My favorite dinner, huh?"

She nodded. "I think I saw some crawfish in the freezer."

"That might work," he admitted, thrilled at her giggle.

* * * * *

Ace walked over to the stove and sniffed with enthusiasm the aroma that wafted through the kitchen. They'd been home a couple of hours and the smell had haunted him even as far away from the kitchen as his weight room. "What's cooking'?"

"Crawfish Etoufee'," Lexie answered. "Don't go digging in my food," she warned and held a serving spoon in a threatening gesture.

He ignored her, lifted the lid and took a whiff. His stomach grumbled in appreciation. He loved crawfish Etoufee', but for the simple pleasure of teasing her, he choked back a hum of pleasure and frowned. "Crawfish? You mean those little critters that live in mounds of mud?"

"A Cajun delicacy."

He snorted. "You people are weird. What else you got?"

"Homemade rolls, green salad, a lemon and a chocolate meringue pie."

He lifted an eyebrow. "A singer, dancer and gourmet chef? We just might have to keep you around, even if you are a ticklish wimp."

She growled and threw the spoon at him.

Ace flinched to avoid being hit and caught the spoon then clucked his tongue. "Temper, temper," he chided, and laughed at the color in her cheeks and the way her eyes flashed. He took a step closer to her, then another, advancing step for step while she retreated. "Look here, must eat mud bugs so much, you're beginning to walk like one," he taunted.

Though backed against the counter, she lifted her chin in obvious defiance to his teasing. "I'll get you, Ace Harris. When you least expect it, I'm gonna pay you back for all the misery you've caused me."

Ace glanced over his shoulder to make sure they were alone then slid his arms around her waist and pulled her against him. Awareness sizzled between them and he realized that he hadn't imagined how good she felt in his arms. "Is that a threat or a promise?" he asked, his voice a husky whisper.

Footsteps heading their way forced him to let her go and take a step back. He grinned and winked, wishing he'd had time to kiss her. "We'll see if the food tastes as good as it smells."

He turned on his heel and greeted Trina with a smile and kiss on the cheek before he exited the room.

Lexie turned around and plunged her hands into a sink full of dishwater to cover up the fact that they shook.

Trina walked up beside her and noted Lexie's flushed cheeks. "Everything okay?"

Lexie nodded. "Sometimes I just want to strangle him."

Trina laughed. "And the other times?"

Lexie blushed harder. "And the other times I wish I had."

Trina slipped her arm around her daughter's waist and hugged her to her side. "Now Lex, you know it's not polite to lie to your mother."

Lexie rolled her eyes in an exaggerated gesture and snorted. "Well, *you* wanted me to like him," she defended, with a haughty shake of her head.

"I think it's wonderful." Trina's voice lowered to a conspiring whisper. "Let's not tell Scott yet, though. He's not used to being your father well enough to be happy."

"What's to tell? That I'm starting to like the arrogant, conceited, chauvinistic jerk? You're right, let's not tell Scott. He's liable to refer me to one of his friends to have my head examined."

Katrina laughed. "I'll never forget the first time I met Ace. He was about eight or nine and so adorable. He looked up at me with those dancing eyes and asked if my hair was real."

Lexie grunted. "Charming little brat even then."

Trina chuckled and continued. "You should have seen him. Even then he looked so much like his father, so much like Scott that I fell in love with him on the spot. Seeing him I could imagine what my son would eventually look like."

Lexie smiled at the thought of Richard and Robert, both little replicas of their father. "You weren't disappointed, got two that look like their father."

Trina exhaled on a dreamy sigh. "Yeah, they'll be breaking hearts before you know it."

"I can't believe they all look so much alike and aren't related."

Trina shrugged. "From the talks I've had with Scott, they probably are. But, Proverbs teaches us, *a true friend sticks closer than a brother*. They've been true friends all of their lives so I guess they've never felt the need to know more than that."

"To heck with need, I'd *want* to know if I had a brother or sister out there somewhere. It would be nice just to have a friend like that," Lexie admitted her voice wistful.

"You've got one in Amber," Trina assured her. "And you two have the rest of your lives for that friendship to grow. And someday you'll find a love of your own and have the family you long for." She grinned and nudged Lexie with her shoulder. "Maybe even with Ace."

Lexie grimaced then grinned, noting the unmistakable glow Trina always seemed to radiate. "Are you and Scott really always this happy?"

"Why wouldn't we be?"

She shrugged. "I don't know. There's so much going on today it's hard to believe love is, and can be, that real, that deep, and true."

"Well believe it, Sweetheart. Love, true love, is a gift from God, Lexie. It can burn bright and hot as fire, or be soft, warm and intimate, like candlelight. "Look at Amber and Stanley. They've been married ten years too, yet their love is still as sweet as it was when brand new. She still gets that sparkle in her eye when he walks in the room. So does he. Like he's the only thing on her mind and she, his. But love, like anything, has to be nurtured to be healthy and strong. Don't ever let yourself believe it can't be that way for you. Don't ever settle for second best when you can have the real thing. Listen to your heart, Lex. Let God lead you, and you won't be disappointed."

Lexie hugged her mother. "Scott told me the same thing earlier. Now, *Mom*, how about helping me set the table?"

* * * * *

Craig eyed the empty chairs, the ones which, just that morning, were occupied by his daughter and her family, and forced down the lump in his throat. He grasped the hands on either side of him, led them in the Lord's Prayer, and asked for blessings on the food and for loved ones gone as well as those around him, then signaled for serving to begin. While dishes were passed and plates filled, he found that the ache in his heart had lessened and smiled. He watched Lexie eye Ace when he dished up his second plate of Etoufee'.

"For someone who frowned at the idea of eating mud bugs, you sure are making a pig of yourself," she commented.

Ace grinned. "I love crawfish Etoufee' almost as much as I like picking on you," he admitted.

His eyes shone like dew drops on sheet metal. Lexie made a face at him. "Jerk."

Craig chuckled at the exchange. "This is wonderful Lexie. You cook like this very often?"

She smiled then winked at Scott. "I love to cook. This is Scott's favorite dinner. I sort of bribed him so he wouldn't stay upset with me over last night."

Ace's eyes sought Scott's at her admission. "Did she bribe you enough for both of us?"

"We'll have to talk about that young man." Scott tried to sound firm, disgruntled, and fatherly. He really did. The grin gave him away.

Ace heaved an exaggerated sigh of relief. "Good, cause I'm not good at bribery." He grinned when his father snickered. "We just might have to keep Lexie around for a while, huh Daddy? She cooks almost as well as Amber."

Craig chuckled and turned back to Lexie. "Sweetheart, you're welcome to stay around here as long as you want even if you never cook another meal like this one."

Ace kicked him under the table. "Shh. Bite your tongue, Daddy. Don't you remember anything you taught me? There's no such thing as a free ride. She can stay as long as she continues to cook meals like this," he insisted.

Lexie leaned forward her blistering gaze boring into Ace's teasing one. "If you're not nice, I'll make sure you get no desert," she threatened.

"And do dishes," Craig added.

Ace rolled his eyes and grinned. Being a wise man, he knew when to keep his mouth shut. Now was one of those times.

Later that evening, Craig settled into his bed with a book. The house was quiet, too quiet. He answered the phone before it could ring a second time. "Hello?"

"G'night PaPaw," Ashyln's little voice wobbled.

He heard Amber in the background, "Don't cry. You promised you wouldn't cry if we let you call and say goodnight."

His heart clutched at the sound of tears in the beloved little voice. "Good night, Sweetheart. Is mommy right there?"

"Uh, huh," she sniffled.

"Can I talk to her? What's the matter?" he asked his daughter when Amber took the phone.

"We're having a little problem settling into our own bed."

"You want me to come over for a while?"

Amber laughed. "No, Daddy. She'll be fine."

"Okay. Put her back on."

"Sleep tight, Sweetheart and PaPaw will come see you in the morning. We'll go to town for breakfast okay?"

Ashlyn fought valiantly to stifle a sob. "Okay. Katyen too?"

"Yes. Kaitlyn too," Craig assured his granddaughter.

"Okay, 'night PaPaw."

"Night, Sweetheart."

Amber grabbed the phone before Ashlyn could hang up while she relayed the message of breakfast to her father and sister. "Everything okay over there, Daddy?"

"It's quiet," he admitted.

Her heart clenched at the admission but she forced her voice to be cheerful. "Good night, Daddy, I love you."

"I love you too, Sweetheart."

Chapter Twelve

Ace greeted Scott with a nod and a smile then opened the refrigerator. "You know where Daddy is?" he asked then reached for the orange juice.

Scott nodded. "Your father had a date for breakfast."

"Really?" he queried. His voice clearly reflected disbelief.

Scott smiled over his paper. "Yes, with two pretty ladies."

That got Ace's attention, he glared at Scott. "Excuse me?" Scott's eyes danced merrily. Ace shook his head and laughed. "The twins," he concluded. "He spoils them something fierce."

"And you don't?"

"Not me," Ace denied with an emphatic shake of his head. "Between Daddy and Stanley, I don't have a chance."

"It's a grandfather's privilege to spoil his grandchildren." Scott sighed. "I can't blame him, two beautiful little girls like that need to be spoiled."

Ace chuckled. "It'll be a while before you get to spoil grandchildren," he teased. "You're still busy raising children."

Scott laughed. "That's right. And I'll continue raising them as long as God continues to bless us with them. I may even raise children the same age as grandchildren."

Ace eyed him, a curious light in his eyes. "What took you so long, Scott, to settle down?"

Scott shrugged. "Sometimes it takes a while to find the right woman."

"And sometimes it's instant. Like with Stan and Amber."

Scott nodded. "And sometimes you have to see past the outer package to the person within." He chuckled. "Like with your mother and father. Ole Craig didn't know which way to turn. No one had ever stood up to him, challenged him. Along comes this little girl who challenges his every word and action, and tosses water in his face. It took him a while to see past that, and the outer beauty, to discover the beauty within."

Ace thought of Lexie. To say their first meeting was disastrous was an understatement. But he was beginning to see the person she was inside. He kept those thoughts to himself, for now. "Well, you sure got a prize with Trina."

"I sure did. Don't worry, Ace, you're day is coming."

"Day of reckoning you mean?"

"Is that really how you think of love?" Scott asked his eyebrow arched in question.

Ace knew Scott asked more out of concern than curiosity. He sat across from him and regarded him with serious eyes. "Not really."

He shrugged. "It scares me though, Scott. I'm not sure if I could live through what my father has. I'm not sure I ever want to love anyone as much as he loved Mama. Or as much as I loved her."

Scott nodded thoughtfully and chose his words with care. "You can't go through life being afraid to love, Ace. Kind of like the song The Dance. You may miss the pain but in order to do so, you'll have to miss the pleasure. Love is a gift. God doesn't want you to miss out on it just because He called your mother home."

Ace glared at him, his eyes ablaze with pain and anger. "Why did He do that, Scott?"

Scott sighed and placed a hand on his arm. "I don't know, Ace. Have you asked Him what He wants you to learn from this experience and from these last few years?"

"What on earth can I possibly learn from the death of my mother?"

"To depend on Him, and His love, not hers."

Ace snorted. "Right, like that makes sense."

Scott shook his head. "I'm sorry, Ace. I don't have any better answers. You asked. I'm just trying to help."

Ace sighed and propped his feet up on an empty chair. "I know, Scott. It's just so damn unfair."

"You not giving God a chance is what's so unfair. Your mother believed deeply in the power of God, and in His love. Her whole life was proof of that. *You* are living proof of her faith. After the loss of three children she very well could have given up on God and having a son. But she didn't. She continued to believe, kept praying, kept standing on the Word, almost caused a divorce between her and your father. Craig was so afraid he'd loose her that he wouldn't even consider having another child, much less try for one. They argued, terribly, but Tamera's faith and determination wore him down. And, here you are. Would you throw away everything she fought for to have you, everything she believed in, and everything she taught you about that same kind of faith, because of your hurt and anger? True faith lives on, Ace, it learns to trust and to accept even when we don't understand."

Ace squirmed at the truth. He'd heard the story more than once of how he came to be in the world, had even wondered if it were true, especially in light of how very much in love his parents were. His eyes sought Scott's, his gaze plead for advice, encouragement, something, *anything* to hang on to, and found all in the dark gaze of his lifelong friend.

"I know," he admitted, then heaved a deep sigh. "I watch Amber and Stanley, and Daddy, especially with the kids, and I know I have to move on. I have to let go. Heck, I ride Daddy about it all the time. So does Amber. It's just easier said than done."

"You know how you'll recognize when you're ready to let go?" Scott asked and continued at the shake of Ace's head. "When you can remember the joy without pain. Have you begun to do that yet, Ace?"

Ace smiled. "Some. Sometimes a little memory will surface and I'll find myself smiling and not hurting as bad."

"Good. Then you're on the road to moving on. And, believe me I've had some pretty deep conversations with Amber. She has her days too, days when she can't seem to do anything but miss your mother, and cry. You know what she does?" Again he continued when Ace shook his head.

"She prays, Ace. She gets down on her knees and begins to thank God for her blessings and to talk to Him about the way she feels. About how much she misses her Mama and how she wishes Tamera could be here to hold her, and hold the children. Then she prays for you and your father, because no matter how difficult her experience, she knows it's a mere shadow of the pain you two feel."

Ace swallowed hard when he realized he hadn't really considered his sister's emotions and the way she worried over him and their father. "Amber's always been like that. She's always put the feelings and needs of others before her own."

Scott nodded in agreement. "Stanley's a heck of a man to understand her the way he does. To empathize, to know there's nothing he can really say or do but be there. That's love."

"I guess I could learn a lot from my sister and brother-in-law."

Scott chuckled. "You have. You just haven't acknowledged it, or faced up to it. Faith like Amber's, like your mother's and Stanley's, always asks a lot of us. Some people never want to try and live up to it. Your father has that kind of faith too, but like you, he's just too hurt and angry to admit it, and to stand on it. But, believe me, Ace; the day will come when he has to make that choice. God is patient. He's simply waiting for His children to acknowledge Him and to reach out to Him again."

Scott's heart thrilled with relief when Ace leaned forward, his eyes reflecting excitement when he began to see the light of truth in his words.

"You know, I've never really thought of Stanley's strength as being, you know, a spiritual thing," Ace said.

"But now I see it. I mean I've seen him angry and hurt and disappointed. I've seen him cry and rage. But, even then, he always seems to be in control. To accept whatever happens, take it in stride, and move on."

"That's the fruits of the Spirit operating in Stanley's life: Patience, kindness, gentleness, long-suffering, self control. It takes a bigger man to admit he can't do it all by himself and to allow, no, to ask for God's help and direction, than to try and make it on your own. Like you, Stanley was raised in faith. And he realized, very young, that having faith is the only way to make it through this life. That's why he's so prosperous, so blessed. God honors faith, Ace. Not that you'll never have problems, you see that already. But, He'll never forsake you or let you down. You only have to ask." Ace smiled and Scott was reminded again at how very much like his father Ace was.

Once again, Ace's thoughts turned to Lexie. "Lexie has been through a lot too, hasn't she? More than we know."

Scott heard the softness of Ace's voice and saw the flash of tenderness in his eyes. He nodded. "Yes," he admitted. "She has. And underneath that high-spirited, beautiful little spitfire is a very vulnerable, very tenderhearted young woman."

"I kinda figured," Ace confessed.

Scott's ears perked up at the softness in Ace's tone. "Is there something you want to say to me, Ace?"

Ace heard the tension and the concern in Scott's voice. His unwavering gaze met and held Scott's uncertain one. "She's come to mean a great deal to me, in a very short time. That scares me too."

Scott acknowledged the confession with a nod. "Life and love are like being in the bullring. Sometimes you have to roll with the punches. Sometimes you have to pick yourself up and dust yourself off. However, with the right woman, you'll always come out a winner. But, be careful," he added, an edge of steel in his otherwise soft tone. "Hurt her and you'll answer to me."

"I'd never intentionally hurt her, especially with her being your daughter. Know this though, no matter where our relationship goes, or doesn't go, I'll always treat her with the utmost respect. Not only because I do respect her but because I love and respect you and Trina."

Scott nodded with a grin. "I figured, but it means a lot to hear you say it Ace, a whole lot."

Ace sighed and leaned back in his chair. He had a lot to think about, but felt better than he had in a long time. "Thanks, Scott," he said. "I'm glad y'all are here. We've all benefited. Not just Amber with the baby and all, but Daddy in having his house full, and me. I didn't realize how much I miss my father and the talks we used to have until now, with you."

"Have you told him that?" Scott queried. "Have you told him how much you miss him?"

"Not in so many words."

"Maybe you should. Maybe you should just come out and say it."

"It hasn't worked for Amber. He only gets angry."

"Because he thinks you and Amber don't understand the depth of his grief and that you're pushing him back into living when he's not ready."

"That's crazy."

"Is it, Ace? When was the last time you put your arms around your father and cried with him, instead of challenging him to just let it go?"

Ace flinched. "Ouch."

Scott's smile was tender. "I'm not blaming you, Ace, or Amber. But you've got to realize your father has to face this in his own way and in his own time. I know he'll never remarry or search for love in another woman."

"He's too young for that," Ace interrupted.

"How would you feel, really feel, if he decided being alone was just too hard and went looking? Honestly?"

Ace shrugged. "I guess I really haven't thought about it." He paused in consideration. "I don't think I'd like it at all," he admitted a hard edge to his voice.

"Right, you want him to get on with his life, but you don't realize how difficult that is. No one will ever measure up to the feelings he has for your mother. He loved, still loves her too much to defile the memory of what they shared with someone else. I know that's hard for you to understand because you haven't experienced love to that degree yet. Talk with Stanley. He's the same way. If something happened to Amber tomorrow, he'd probably never remarry either, or at least not for a very long time. I'm not saying that's the right choice for everyone, I'm just saying it's for the person involved to decide and that others, especially his children, should strive to support, if not understand, that choice."

"I guess we've, I've, been really selfish and shallow about the whole thing, haven't I?" Ace asked with a guilty flush.

Scott laughed and pulled Ace against him in a brief hug. "You're not selfish or shallow Ace, you just need to stop a minute and consider the circumstances. Put yourself in your father's shoes for a minute. Really try and pray. Then, maybe you'll understand a little better...." His words trailed off when Craig stepped up on the porch whistling.

Ace grinned when his father walked through the door. "Well, speak of the devil...."

Craig smiled. "Morning."

"And where are the twins?" Ace wanted to know.

"Home. Amber wanted them back right after breakfast. I took them to the park for a while so I figured I'd better get them home or she'd have my hide."

Ace grunted. "Huh, you just wanted to hog them all to yourself and then drop them off before I got a chance to play with them."

"Now Ace, would I do that to you, my only son?"

"Does a bear hibernate in winter?"

Craig laughed, so did Scott. Craig turned to him. "Trina and Lexie said they'd call or get a ride home later. Those three are cooking up something. I guarantee it."

Scott groaned. "Probably going to cost us money too," he teased.

Craig shook his head, grinned. "Cost you or Stanley maybe, but not me."

"Well, guess I'll just have to ride over and visit my sister," Ace remarked and rose from his seat. "I'm gonna take Red Bone. Be back in a while."

"Be careful, Ace."

He grinned. "Always," he assured his father. "That's my name, remember, Careful Ace Harris." His heart thrilled when their laughter followed him out the door his father had just entered.

* * * * *

Lexie stepped off the porch and headed toward the small corral where Stanley worked with his horses. "Hey, Stan," she called out, keeping her voice low enough not to disturb those inside, but loud enough for him to hear from where he squatted, a horse's hoof between his knees.

Stan looked up at the sound of her voice and smiled in welcome. "Hey. Where is everybody?"

"The kids are asleep. Amber and Trina are huddled together at the sewing machine, pouring over a pattern."

"I'm surprised they don't have you pinning, tracing or cutting."

She shook her head. "Not me. Sewing is not my bag. I'm lucky to patch a hem or sew a button. I can thread the machine, but that's about the limit to my ability. What'cha doing?"

Eyeing the hoof between his knees, hoof pick in his hand, and tools at his feet, Stanley bit back his humorous retort and grinned. "Cleaning and trimming hooves."

"Does that hurt?"

"Only if she kicks me."

Her giggle ended on a shriek when she came to a dead stop, her eyes riveted to the ground in front of her. Stanley heard the telltale rattle and angry hiss. He dropped the hoof and turned the horse loose then eyed Lexie with studied calm.

"Don't move, Lex," he warned, a thread of steel in his quiet tone. "Don't even blink."

Lexie couldn't move if her life depended on it. And it depended on her standing still. "My knees are shaking, Stanley," she whimpered.

"Just don't move." He reached down, picked up a hoof file and walked stealthily toward Lexie and the hissing, slithering, coil of danger at her feet.

In a flash Sheba appeared from nowhere and got between Lexie and the rattler. The snake struck. Sheba lunged and snapped fierce jaws behind its head. Lexie fainted.

Stanley dropped the file and rushed to catch Lexie as she crumbled to the ground.

Ace rode up about the time Stanley lifted Lexie in his arms and turned toward the porch. He lunged from his horse. "Good God! What happened?"

"Snake, she fainted."

"Oh, God! Is she all right?" He asked and reached for her.

Stanley held her out of Ace's shaking grasp. "Ace. Calm down," he insisted, and caught his brother-in-law's panicked gaze with his. "She fainted. That's all."

"Are you sure?"

Stanley nodded. "Get me some water and a wet rag." He carried Lexie to the porch and cradled her in his lap while Ace jerked his bandanna from around his throat and grabbed the canteen off his saddle to wet the cloth with hands that shook and caused him to spill water everywhere.

Stan stroked the hair off her face and urged Lexie to wake up. She moaned softly, trembled violently. Her breath began to hitch. She opened her eyes with a muffled scream of terror. Stanley strove to calm her, his tone gentle. "Easy, easy now, you're all right. I've got you."

"He bit me," she whined.

"Where?"

"Everywhere," she whimpered. Tears of shock poured from her eyes, sobs wracked her slender frame.

Stanley chuckled and hugged her for reassurance. "No, he didn't. I promise you didn't get bit." He reached for the cloth in Ace's hand and wiped it over her face.

"Is she all right?" Ace queried his voice hoarse, eyes fierce.

Stanley nodded.

"I'm going to be sick," she moaned, then leaned across Stanley's lap to wretch.

"Go get Trina, Ace. Ace!" Stanley insisted when he didn't budge.

Ace jerked his head in compliance.

"Quietly," Stan urged, when Ace staggered through the back door. "Like talking to a bull in a china shop," he muttered when he heard Ace's stumbling footsteps echo in the hall.

Lexie giggled and reached for the canteen. Her stomach heaved in violent protest when she sipped the water, swished it around in her mouth then spit it out. She buried her face in Ace's bandanna, rested her head between her knees and prayed for calm. The strong, masculine scent of his cologne seeped into her senses and caused a quiver of awareness to shimmer through her already overactive system. She wiped the cloth over her face and neck, then held it over her thudding heart and fanned herself with her empty hand, all-the-while praying Stanley couldn't read her mind or sense the emotions which currently wreaked havoc in her body and soul.

Amber and Katrina looked up in unison when Ace appeared in the doorway pale and shaken. "What?" They asked at once.

"Lexie..." was all he managed to say before Trina rushed past him.

Though concerned for Lexie, Amber worried more about her brother. Pale as death and shaking all over, his eyes were dark and haunted. "Sit down, Ace," she insisted, and led him to the bed. "What happened?"

He sank onto the bed and fought the panic bubbling up in his throat. "Oh, God!" he moaned, and buried his face in his hands. "She scared me to death. She was so pale, so lifeless and reminded me of Mama laid out on the couch, not breathing." He began to sob, huge, heaving sobs that shook his whole frame.

Amber wrapped her arms around her brother and rocked him gently, but didn't dare shush his ragged attempt to stem the sobs.

"I didn't want to care this much, Amber," he mumbled. "Never again."

"Sometimes what we want isn't always what's best for us," she replied, and brushed the thick blond mane off his forehead.

"I know," he whispered, his voice raw. He dragged the heels of his hands over his face, pushed himself off the bed, and stalked into the adjoining bathroom.

"I know," he mumbled again at his reflection. The pale face and haunted eyes staring back at him in the mirror made his stomach churn. He turned on the cold water, splashed his face then buried it in a towel, and willed his emotions into some semblance of control.

Amber leaned against the doorframe, watched and waited until he looked at her and nodded to indicate he was okay. Together they went to check on Lexie. She sat between Trina and Stanley still a bit pale, but seemingly fine.

Ace knelt in front of her and asked, "You okay?"

Lexie glanced up into Ace's pale face and raw eyes and nodded. She fought the urge to curl up against that broad chest and seek comfort in those strong arms.

Ace glanced desperately at the others and tried to grin. His lips quivered instead. With a low moan he gave in to the emotions roiling within and pulled Lexie in his arms. He buried his face in her thick auburn hair and inhaled the intoxicating scent, relieved to feel the thud of her heart against his. Assured she was all right, his smile came more easily. "That's two things she's afraid of, tickle monsters and snakes," he observed with a chuckle.

"I'll take tickle monsters over snakes any day," Lexie assured him with a dainty shudder.

He moved her out of his arms and kissed the tip of her nose. "Me too," he agreed, and then gave her hand a gentle squeeze before he turned to Stanley. "I'll help you hunt around and make sure there's no more."

Stanley nodded. "Keep the kids in for a while," he told Amber.

"Trina and I will take them over to Daddy's when they wake up. We're going there for supper anyway," she replied, and helped Lexie to her feet.

The three women went back inside. Stan stepped off the porch. Ace followed in his wake. He picked up the hoof file he'd planned to use to kill the snake and slid it beneath the shredded mess.

Ace gasped. "Good grief, Stanley, you did all this damage with that little ole file?"

"I didn't even get a chance to use this little ole file," Stanley replied. "Sheba barreled in here out of nowhere, lunged at the snake the moment it struck, beheaded it then tore it to shreds. Still think Terrier's are useless?"

Ace paled. "Guess not. Look," he pointed to the remains. "She was full of eggs."

Stanley eyed his brother-in-law. "Shook you up pretty bad, huh?" he asked.

Stanley's eyes were a kaleidoscope of emotions—a hint of worry, a glimmer of understanding, a sparkle of mirth.

Ace nodded.

"Know just how you feel, Sport," Stan assured and nodded into Ace's confused gaze.

Stanley carried the snake to the trash pile and burned its remains while Ace roamed the yard with a hoe in his hand to make sure there were no other unwelcome intruders, paying special attention to the girls' sandbox.

Chapter Thirteen

Lexie followed Scott to the Suburban and helped him load suitcases. "Is that everything?"

"I think so. Trina is checking to be sure."

"You will be careful?"

"Yes, Ma'am," he teased with a laugh.

"Well!" she huffed. "People drive like idiots these days."

He pulled her in his arms and brushed his lips across her forehead. "Don't worry, Honey, I'll watch out for the other idiots on the road. Sure you don't want to come home?"

She shook her head. "I really want to stay, Scott. I can't explain it, but I feel like I'm needed here. It's so big, so peaceful, and so different. And no one really knows what I've been through. I can relax and get to know myself. And others." She shrugged. "I don't know. Like I said, I can't explain it. I just don't want to leave right now, you know?"

He nodded and stroked the silky strands of hair that escaped her French braid. "I know, Honey. I think I understand what you're saying. And what you're not saying. I thought the year away would be enough to get to know yourself and come into your own, but I guess not."

"Oh, Scott, it's not you or Trina or the boys I want to be away from. It's just...Lafayette, and all the memories. I..." She sighed, swallowed hard, and hugged him tight. "Please don't think it's y'all." Her voice quivered.

"I never thought that for a moment," he assured. "I hope you find what your heart is in search of, Lexie. I hope you find the peace we've talked about so often, God's peace. It's there for the asking."

"I know. And I think maybe, here, where there are hours and days of quiet time, maybe I can."

He hugged her again. "Well, you just call when you're ready to come home and I'll be here in a flash to get you."

They stood arm-in-arm and watched and waited while Trina and the boys said good-bye to Craig and Ace. As the two men walked toward him, Scott held out his hand to Ace. "Remember what we talked about," he urged then grasped Ace's hand and gave it a firm shake.

Ace's gaze met his unwavering. "Every word," he promised and nodded in assurance.

After a long, probing look into the gray depths, Scott turned to search those of his best friend. Fifty years of friendship passed in a split-second look that said it all, and he knew Craig would give his daughter all the love, support and protection she would need. She wouldn't be in better hands except for his. Handshakes turned into hugs and they said their farewells.

Lexie stood with Ace and Craig while Scott put the truck in reverse and started to back away. She pressed a fist to her lips and bit back a little cry of distress.

As though he sensed her reaction, Scott stopped the truck and opened the door.

She flew into his outstretched arms one more time. She reached across him to hug Trina and admonished them to call the minute they got home. She then stretched across the back of the seat and hugged each of the boys. Sniffing back tears, she nodded to Trina's query if she were okay.

She moved away from the truck once more, waved, then pressed fingers to lips and blew them a kiss while Scott backed up and turned around to leave. Craig walked up beside her and put his arm around her waist. She leaned against his long frame and gained comfort from the fatherly embrace. "It's so hard to let go," she whispered in a thick voice.

Her words were not without impact. Craig hugged her to his side and swallowed the lump in his throat.

Ace walked up on the other side of them. He reached around Lexie and placed his hand on his father's shoulder. "Well, Daddy, now that we've got her all to ourselves, what do you say we lock her indoors and make her do all sorts of unspeakable things?"

Craig grinned at the husky, teasing tone of his son's voice. "Like what?"

"Oh, all sorts of things like dishes and floors, laundry and windows. And meals, definitely meals." His voice trailed off in a grunt when Lexie's elbow dug into his side.

"I don't do windows," she insisted, not the least bit daunted by his teasing.

He laughed, tickled her once, and slapped his father on the back. "Gotta go to work."

"What exactly does a cowboy do all day?" Lexie queried a bit too sweetly and gazed up at Ace with wide-eyed innocence.

Craig grinned and winked at her. "Actually not much, it's just an excuse to be out on the range."

"I beg your pardon," Ace demanded. "I'll have you know I do plenty."

Craig laughed, then, deciding to ride with Ace for a change, he headed toward the barn to saddle up.

Ace turned to Lexie. "Now to answer your question, my day consists of working cattle. I may have to round some up for shots or to be wormed. While I'm at that, I check fences and mend them when necessary."

"Doesn't sound like much work to me," she taunted. "Besides, you never look like you've done much real work. Stanley, on the other hand, always looks like he's wrestled with the devil."

"It's different when you have half-a-dozen colts to work every day instead of move a few head of cattle. Not to mention the fight to control stud horses who decide they're not satisfied with their mares and want others of a different breed. Especially Arabians," he sneered. "They're useless. Sorry, Mama," he whispered with a hint of a smile. His eyes lifted heavenward a moment then leveled once more on Lexie.

"We used to argue heatedly over that. She loved Arabians and I loved to get a rise out of her. Want to come along? Then we'll see what you consider work and not."

Lexie remained silent, lost for a moment in his dancing gray gaze. She cleared her throat, shook her head. "No, think I'll get started on those unspeakable things you mentioned. Besides..." She gazed off in the direction her family left in. "I want to stay by the phone in case someone needs me."

They headed in opposite directions. He stopped. "Lexie?" he queried then continued when she looked at him. "I don't suspect you'll have any trouble. But Daddy's riding with me so stay close to the house. Okay?" She nodded her smile brilliant. Ace fought not to kiss those inviting lips.

"Okay. And since you're being so nice, I'll leave a note if I do decide to go somewhere."

He nodded in agreement as his father led their horses out of the barn. "Good deal, see you this evening." He mounted up then threw her his best smile. "Cook something good for supper," he ordered.

She tossed her head with a disdainful snort, turned on her heel, and declined Craig's offer to stay with a wave of her hand and shake of her head.

Craig eyed his son with a grin. "So, what's the plan?"

Ace whirled his horse around and outlined his plans for the day as they rode out of the yard.

Lexie locked the screen door behind her but left the exterior door open. She walked through to the kitchen and utility room and did the same with those doors which allowed the beauty of the day to enter the dim recesses of the house. Though a bit warm, a nice breeze eased the heat. She took a deep breath and decided the house could use an airing then went throughout and opened windows and doors. She stood in the middle of the sprawling ranch house and heard nothing but the sounds of birds and insects outdoors, her own breathing and the tick of a clock inside.

There's so much history here, she thought, so much love. Every room had a feel of it's own; vibrant, warm, inviting, peaceful and underneath it all, a wealth of tenderness and love. She closed her eyes and let the sensations envelope her.

"Well, Lord, it's just You and me here," she said. Her voice echoed in the silence. "And you, Mrs. Tamera. I know you're here. I can feel your presence lingering all through this place and I believe, like Scott, it's your love of this home and your family that stays even when you've left the physical realm. If You're really there God, and if You hear me, please let me know."

As she stood, an overwhelming sense of love and knowing filled her heart and soul. She smiled. "I hoped so," she admitted, feeling not the least bit strange talking aloud to an unseen God. "Would you mind terribly if I put aside some of the teachings of my youth and just get to know you?"

The answer came very audibly in her heart. ***I hoped you would.***

Like a child who just discovered a new friend, she communicated with her Lord. She asked questions and listened for His answers, sought Him—His face, His voice.

While they talked, she went about her newly self-appointed duties of cleaning but took a few minutes to linger in each room and explore. By the time evening drew near, she felt like she'd been in this home all of her life. And she felt closer to God than she ever had before.

Excitement stirred her soul when she thought about the long days ahead when she could commune with God on a more personal level, read her Bible, and hoped the Scriptures would come alive for her. She wondered if she were the only woman, only person, who'd ever felt this way about Him. Somehow, she doubted it.

She prepared dinner amazed at how fast the day had passed and how unconcerned she felt. At once she understood the Scripture to "pray without ceasing." She knew the reason she felt so relaxed and yet energized at the same time was because she'd opened up to God and acknowledged Him in all her ways that day.

* * * * *

Craig chuckled inwardly as, for the umpteenth time that day his son gazed off in the distance, his mind evidently occupied elsewhere. He stopped his horse and watched Ace keep riding. After a few minutes Ace stopped and looked back.

"What's wrong?"

Craig laughed. "What's on your mind? Or, should I ask who?" he teased.

"Can you think of a better reason to be preoccupied?" Ace answered, his grin sheepish.

"Not a one," his father admitted and kicked his horse into a gallop. When they arrived at the house, he eyed his son with a grin. "I saddled, you unsaddle."

"Alone?"

"Yes, alone."

"Aw, c'mon, Daddy, be a sport."

Craig declined with a laugh. "I'm going to check things out. You hurry. I'm hungry."

Ace muttered under his breath and led the horses to the barn while his father went into the house.

Craig reached for the screen door, surprised to find it locked. He knocked then waited for Lexie to open it.

Lexie smiled. "I wasn't sure which door y'all would use," she explained.

"We usually come in through the back door, but that's okay. I'm glad you locked them, especially being here alone." He looked around at the sparkling kitchen and exclaimed, "Wow! You've been busy."

"A little," she admitted with a blush. Craig smiled, kissed her forehead, and went to take a shower.

Ace walked into the kitchen door and asked, "What's for supper?"

He eyed her, a curious lift to his brow. There was something different about her, a glow and an inner radiance that drew him like a moth to a flame. His breath caught in an audible hiss, body tightened with need. He took a deliberate step back from her, all too aware of her presence.

"Pizza, green salad and," she opened the refrigerator door for him to look inside.

"Banana pudding," he breathed. "Oh, man, it's been ages since we had that."

She laughed, pleased at his reaction and glad Amber had told her banana pudding was his favorite desert. "All made from scratch," she informed him. "Don't you dare," she warned and slapped his hand away when he attempted to swipe a taste.

Though his mouth watered with want, Ace backed away from the refrigerator. "How long before everything's ready to eat?" he asked.

"Five, ten, minutes," she said with a shrug.

"Good." He nodded. "Time for a quick shower."

While the two men took showers Lexie set the table. Since there was just the three of them, they sat at the small table in the kitchen, instead of the large one in the dining room. They clasped hands while Craig said the blessing and added an extra prayer for Scott and Trina's safe trip home.

Lexie thanked him then asked about their day. They talked while Craig served himself and then passed the food around. She watched in amazement when the two men devoured the feast laid out before them. They decided to have desert later and all pitched in to clean the kitchen before retiring to the den.

Craig looked around the den in surprise. "You moved this furniture by yourself?"

She nodded. "I hope you don't mind. Makes the room seem bigger, gives you more space."

He laughed. "I don't mind. Just don't hurt yourself."

"Oh pooh," she scoffed. "I'm as healthy as a horse."

"Bet you're looking forward to sleeping in a real bed," Craig teased.

She laughed. "Yeah, and I bet you're looking forward to a quiet evening reading the paper in your favorite chair."

He shrugged. "Actually, I rather liked having my house full. Not as lonely."

"I know," she admitted, her voice quiet.

Then she smiled a sweet, innocent smile that belied, but didn't hinder, the mischievous sparkle in her eyes.

"Besides, I had an ulterior motive for moving the furniture," she admitted. A shy flush covered her cheeks.

"What's that?"

She walked over to the piano which had been inaccessible until she rearranged the furniture. "Does anyone play this thing?"

Craig grinned. "No. I don't think it's been played since my grandmother died." He answered her question with a nod before she could even ask it. "Go ahead."

Lexie lifted the lid and checked the keys, amazed that the instrument was still in tune after so many years. She sat on the bench and played something soft and sensual.

Ace watched her in amazement. "The piano too? Is there no limit to your abilities?" She laughed but flushed at the compliment.

"My father loved music. 'Lexie', he'd say, 'God's given you a gift. Be sure to always share it'. He encouraged me to learn as many instruments as possible, but I stuck to mouth horns and the piano."

Ace grinned. "Can you rope a cow? Ride a bull?" he queried. "Useless," he muttered at the shake of her head, his eyes dancing into hers. She made a face at him and played another song. He waited for her to sing, but the melodies she played tugged at the heartstrings, enticed the imagination, and needed no words.

They had just finished eating huge bowls of pudding and sipping coffee, when a knock sounded at the door. Before Craig could get there to answer it, the twins bounded through.

"Hi, PaPaw!" they screeched and flung themselves at him.

He swung them up in his arms. "Hey! How are my girls this evening?"

"We're going to town for ice cream!" Kaitlyn informed him. "Wanna come?"

Stanley chuckled. "Give us a chance to say hello, Kaitlyn."

The girls wriggled out of their grandfather's arms only to rush into Ace's, then Lexie's.

Craig laughed, kissed his daughter and took his grandson out of her arms. "Lexie's been entertaining us on the piano. Y'all come in," he invited and led them into the den.

"You play the piano too?" Stan asked Lexie.

She smiled. "A little."

Ace snorted. "No need to be modest, Alexis," he chided as a flush climbed into her cheeks.

"Play us a song, Lexie," Stanley urged.

"I wanna pay," Ashlyn insisted and climbed up beside Lexie.

Lexie held her little hands and picked out "Mary had a Little Lamb." After three more nursery rhymes, Stanley urged Ashlyn off Lexie's lap.

"Okay Ashlyn, let Lexie play some grown up music now," he ordered and held his arms out to her. She promptly obeyed, climbed up on his lap, and giggled when he nuzzled her neck.

Lexie's cheeks grew warm as they waited. She closed her eyes, took a deep breath, picked the keys and hummed a verse, then sang.

Stan glanced at his wife as Lexie sang a beautiful ballad of love. His heart swelled with emotion at the tears and tenderness in her gaze. He slid his arm around her waist when she leaned over and brushed her lips across his cheek and returned the gesture with a tender wink and grin.

"That's a beautiful song," he assured Lexie when she finished singing. "Were did you hear it?"

"There's a radio station back home that plays a mixture of soft rock and country."

"Can we go to town now?" Kaitlyn asked her father.

"To town?" Ace interrupted. "What for?"

"Ice cream!" the twins informed him.

"Wanna come, Uncle Ace?" Kaitlyn wanted to know.

Craig laughed. "Uncle Ace is too stuffed with banana pudding."

Ace grinned at his niece. "I'm never too full for ice cream though, especially if it comes with kisses," he teased. Kaitlyn obliged by pressing her tiny lips to his, then his cheeks. He glanced up and caught Lexie watching them, a tender light in her eyes. Their gazes met, simmered. Ace's heart thudded thickly in his chest; blood flowed warmly through his veins as it had at the sound of her voice and the words she sang. In that instance, he wanted her with a hunger unlike any he'd known, one he'd only dreamed of feeling. Stanley's chuckle interrupted his thoughts.

"Ice cream and kisses sounds good to me. Come on then, if we're going to go, let's get moving."

Everyone scrambled for the door.

"Want to come, Lexie?" Amber offered.

She shook her head. "No thanks, I want to stay by the phone."

"I'll be here Lex, if you want to go," Craig assured. "You're welcome to call them back when you get home."

She shook her head. "No, thanks, really."

Amber understood Lexie's feelings and nodded. "Okay, how about you, Ace?"

Ace nodded. "Do I need to take my truck?"

"No, we'll bring you home."

"Okay. Be there in a minute." He reached for his boots while his father walked with his sister and her family to the door. He slipped on his boots and then walked over to Lexie. "Sure you don't want to come along?"

She shook her head. Emotions darkened his eyes like billowing thunderclouds in a storm swept sky.

Ace noticed the same thing about her. Her eyes, deep and dark, churned with emotions like an angry, roiling sea. He ran his knuckles over her cheek in a gentle caress then tilted her chin up with his finger, and lowered his lips to hers in a tender gesture. She began to tremble. In one swift movement he hauled her up off the bench and into his arms.

The sound of little girl giggles helped him regain his senses. "Lexie," he breathed. "I've wanted to do that since the first time," he admitted, his voice tender and husky.

"I wouldn't have stopped you," she confessed as warm color rushed to her cheeks.

His chest rumbled with a throaty chuckle. "I'll have to remember that. Want me to bring you something back?"

She shook her head no and slid bonelessly onto the bench once more when he turned and left the room. Watching him walk was like seeing music in motion. His stride contained all the confidence of a man who knew who he was, what he possessed and was confident in that knowledge. Purely male, Lexie thought. Sensual male. Embarrassed at her own thoughts, she drug her eyes away from his departing figure.

"What took you so long?" Craig demanded, when Ace finally joined them.

"I was asking Lexie if she wanted us to bring something back," he replied and lifted innocent eyes into his father's.

"Right," Stanley snorted then flinched when Amber's elbow dug into his side and Ace glared at him, a dark flush on his cheeks.

Chapter Fourteen

Lexie paused on the porch and appreciated the sight as Stanley put a horse through its paces. His muscles flexed under the smooth, bronze skin of his back and shoulders. Sweat glistened, turning his shoulders into a shimmering, exotic, delightful sight. Sunlight bounced off the deep golden highlights in the incredibly rich chestnut hair.

Amber Morrison is a very lucky woman, she thought, then chided herself for ogling another woman's husband. Her friend's husband at that! But, he's so pretty to look at she defended to herself. Ace's image flashed in her mind. Yeah, he's pretty to look at too, she admitted silently. Shaking herself out of the revere, she stepped off the porch.

Stanley turned at the sound of her footsteps, his smile welcoming. "Hey. How's it going?"

Lexie had come early that morning at Amber's cry for help. She was in a creative flow and wanted Lexie to help with the children.

"Fine, the kids are down for their nap. Amber finished, or got to a stopping point. We've been visiting for a few minutes. She decided to take a hot bath." She reached up and petted the neck of the sorrel filly.

"Do you ride, Lexie?" Stanley asked in a desperate attempt to pull his mind from the thought of his wife's enticing body stretched out in the tub, chin deep in bubbles.

She shook her head. "No. I can ski; water and slopes, and surf; waves and the 'Net, skate; blades and rollers, and play all sorts of athletic games, but I can't ride. Don't tell Ace though. The chauvinistic jerk already thinks I'm useless because I can't rope a calf or ride a bull."

Stan laughed at her indignant tone. "Believe me, Honey; Ace thinks you're far from useless. He just hasn't figured out how many uses you're good for. Yet," he teased.

"Besides, if he's such a chauvinistic jerk, what difference does it make if he knows?"

His grin was all knowing. Lexie flushed then shrieked when he lifted her up onto the filly's back.

"Not afraid of horses are you?"

"No. I'd love to learn to ride. Will you teach me?"

He laughed. "Love to. It'll cost you though, an exchange of favors so to speak."

"What?"

"Stay here tonight and take care of the kids so I can take my wife out for dinner and maybe to a movie or dancing."

"What about Mr. Craig and Ace? They need to eat too."

Stanley shook his head. "I've never seen two more helpless creatures. It's a miracle they've survived this long without a female to look after them. If it weren't for Amber they probably wouldn't have. Feed them here," he offered with a sigh.

She knew his complaint was in good nature and out of love and giggled. "Deal."

He helped her down then turned the filly loose. One glance toward the house and his mind was made up. He eyed Lexie, a pointed lift to his brow. "A hot bath you said?" She nodded, smiling as though she'd read his thoughts. Turning on his heel, he walked toward the house in long, purposeful strides.

Lexie felt her cheeks grow hot at the intensity of his gaze. "You shouldn't be so subtle, Stanley," she remarked at his departing figure, a hint of sarcasm in her voice.

His reply was a soft chuckle as he bent down and cut a rose off the bush by the porch.

* * * * *

Amber heard Stanley's footsteps in the hall and smiled to herself. She listened when he paused by the girl's room and checked on them. She heard him enter their bedroom, close the door, stop by the baby bed. Her heartbeat quickened in anticipation.

Stanley stood for a full moment and drank in the sight of her, her skin flushed from the heat of the water. Soft tendrils of black silk curls escaped the clip to frame her face. Desire poured through him with the force of an erupting volcano. She didn't open her eyes, but he could tell by the soft smile on her lips, she knew he was there. He knelt by the tub and caressed her face with the flower.

Amber smelled the sweet floral scent of the rose before it touched her face, before the soft petals caressed her cheek and lips. "I knew you'd come," she confessed in a husky whisper.

"Did you, now?" he muttered, then buried his lips on hers. He reached down, lifted her from the tub and carried her, dripping, to the bed, where he dried her with the warmth of his love and the heat of his desire.

* * * * *

Ace walked his horse around his sister's house and stopped abruptly, mesmerized at the sight that awaited him. Lexie stood on a rail, leaned over the fence and petted a horse. Daisy Duke Cutoffs strained across her firm hips. Desire awoke painfully at the sight.

"Lord," he muttered. "Why is this happening when You know it's not what I want?"

"Sometimes what we want isn't always what's best for us." The memory of his sister's voice admonished and reminded him, it wasn't what he wanted that counted, but God's will. He sat there a moment and struggled with his emotions.

He hated confrontation.

Oh, he could hold his own against any man or woman. Well, you could never win with a woman, especially one who cried, he reasoned mentally, but confrontation with God is a different story altogether. Ace knew from experience it was, though not always easier, definitely wiser, to submit to His will.

"Okay," he muttered. "What now?" He grinned to himself and gave in to the urge to whistle.

Lexie's head spun around and she flushed at the wolfish grin on Ace's face when he rode toward her.

"Sweetheart, if you stretch any further, those cutoffs are liable to leave nothing, and I mean nothing, to the imagination," he remarked while he dismounted.

She perched on the top rail and gazed down at him wide-eyed and innocent. "You think they're too tight?"

"Oh, no," he breathed. "Perfect fit if you ask me."

She placed her foot lightly against his chest and gave a gentle shove. "Jerk."

"Where's everyone? I thought you were here to baby-sit?"

"I am or rather, was. The kids are all asleep. Amber decided to take a hot bath and Stanley...." her voice trailed off, another hot blush stained her cheeks.

Ace chuckled. "Ole Stanley snuck in for a little afternoon delight," he finished for her.

Lexie closed her eyes as desire, raw and unfamiliar, washed over her in angry waves, so hot, so fierce that the sweltering Texas heat seemed like an old blue northern. She shivered.

Ace too, felt the debilitating effects of feelings almost too powerful to resist. He fought them and the urge to touch her. "So, pretty little Lexie, you've grown to like our wide open spaces?"

She tried hard not to notice the huskiness in his voice and smiled down at him. "Yes. The ranch you have is really beautiful. This place isn't so bad either."

"Is that why you decided to stay a while?"

She shrugged.

"I thought maybe you found something about me you were beginning to like, and that's what made you want to stay."

"Fishing for compliments cowboy?" she taunted and laughed into his dancing gaze.

"Always," he teased.

She heaved an exaggerated, lusty sigh. "Well, you are pretty to look at," she admitted, with another, softer sigh.

He grunted. *Pretty?* His eyebrow arched in teasing and he waited to see what else she'd say.

She batted her eyes. "A pretty good kisser too."

"Pretty good?" His voice clearly reflected that she'd challenged his masculinity. Masculine pride anyway. "I could've sworn by your reaction both times, you'd never been kissed like that before."

She lifted her nose a notch and tossed her head with a disdainful snort. "You're right. I'd never been kissed by a chauvinistic jerk cowboy before."

"Is that so?" he queried, fully intending to prove to her his kiss was more than 'pretty good'.

"Kiss me, Lexie," he ordered in a husky whisper and cupped her face in his hands. His lips covered hers in a tender, searching caress. His tongue dipped gently into her mouth and drew a moan from deep within her. "Much better than pretty good," he mumbled and nibbled on the corners of her mouth.

Lexie placed her hands on his shoulders and stiffened against him. "Enough, cowboy," she insisted.

"Never," he muttered, then swallowed her protests.

Unable to resist the tumultuous emotions he aroused in her, Lexie slid off the fence and into his arms. On impulse, her arms curled around his neck which brought her into even more dangerous proximity with his long, muscular build.

Ace pulled her soft frame against him. A primitive grunt escaped when his hands got lost in the luxurious softness of the silken mass of auburn locks which flowed down her back. A tiny whimper escaped her as his hard thighs dug into her soft ones and the fence pressed firmly, and no doubt painfully, against her back. Digging deep for the control he never dreamed he'd need, much less possess, Ace released her lips and ended the kiss by slow degrees.

"Wow," he breathed, while he held her against his chest. His hands ran over her back in a restless caress. "Much better than pretty good," he assured and stroked her hair until the storm calmed. He placed his hands on her tiny waist and lifted her back up on her perch. Biting back a pain-filled groan of frustration, he climbed up beside her, reluctant to let her too far out of his reach much less out of his sight.

* * * * *

Amber stretched luxuriously, sated and utterly content. A purr of pleasure escaped her smiling lips.

Stanley chuckled and caressed her stomach, which was still soft from carrying his son. It took a conscious effort of his will to stop from nibbling on the enticing flesh he caressed. Knowing without a doubt where his thoughts were headed once more, he pulled the sheet up over her and concealed that luscious body from his sight. As though she read his mind, Amber rolled against him and teased his lips with her mouth.

"Oh, no you don't," he groaned. "I've still got work to do today. As it is I've wasted," he glanced at his watch, "an hour."

"Wasted?" she asked, with a caress across his broad chest.

He smiled but grabbed her hand and pressed it to his mouth to put a stop to her sensuous torture. "Willingly and joyfully," he admitted. "Poor Lexie probably doesn't know whether to come inside or walk home."

Amber pouted prettily, her eyes danced with humor. "Let her find her own reasons to waste an hour."

Stan chuckled and brushed his lips over hers. "She has. Though I doubt they've gotten to this point yet."

The baby whimpered.

"Saved by the baby," he whispered and kissed his wife in a long, tender caress. He rolled away from her inviting arms, walked to the baby bed, and picked up his son.

Amber watched her husband walk across the room without shame and marveled at his gorgeous body when he cradled William in his arms and carried him to her. Broad shoulders, narrow waist, firm thighs, long muscular legs, that cute cowboy butt. He certainly was a sight to behold, she thought with a lusty sigh. She reached for her son, placed him at her breast and lifted her face to that of her husband. "Kiss me Stanley, and then go back to work."

Stan obliged with a chuckle. "Yes, Ma'am."

Amber smiled over at him while he dressed. "Check on the girls and put on a pot of coffee too," she suggested, when he sat on the bed and pulled on his boots.

"Demanding aren't you?"

"After the loving you just got, Mister, I deserve to be demanding."

"And it was all one-sided I'm sure," he teased with another kiss then rose to do as she asked. He paused at the door when she called his name, her smile brilliant.

"I love you, Stanley."

He winked. "Love you too, My Sweet."

Stan paused in his task of brewing a pot of coffee and watched Ace and Lexie for a long moment. They sat on the fence, laughed and talked. You could almost see the air around them vibrate with excitement. She sat on the top rail, her hands clasped tightly onto the thin board. He straddled the board with the ease of a man used to sitting in a saddle. Boots hooked between the rails kept his butt firmly in place but freed his hands. One arm rested comfortably on his thigh and he leaned toward her, grinning at whatever she said.

"What'cha looking at?"

Stan turned and smiled at his wife as she put the baby in his swing. "Come and see," he offered, and moved over to make room for her at the sink.

She walked up beside him and looked out the window. "They make a cute couple."

Stan finished his chore and slipped his arms around her waist. "Yeah. Can you imagine all the pretty red-haired, green-eyed babies they'll have?"

She hugged him, pulled his arms tighter, and snuggled in his embrace. "Or blond hair and green eyes, or red hair and gray eyes. You think they're getting that serious?"

He nodded. "Just watch them. It shows every time they look at each other, in their smiles and in those long, lingering looks."

She sighed and leaned back against his strong frame. "It is beautiful to watch," she whispered, feeling very much in love herself. "Do you really have a lot of work to do this afternoon?"

His heart heard what hers requested, he hugged her. "Guess not," he conceded then turned her in his arms and indulged in a luxurious taste of her sweetness. He gave her an intimate squeeze before he walked to open the back door.

"Coffee's on," he called.

"Decided to be sociable?" Ace called back.

"For a while," Stan quipped, and then left them to come inside or stay as they were.

He glanced back over his shoulder and watched with a smile as Ace jumped off the fence then turned and grasped Lexie by the waist to help her down. Hand in hand, they walked toward the house.

Ace went straight to the swing and picked up his nephew. "Hi, Bucko," he cooed, and lifted him high into the air.

"Easy Ace," his sister cautioned. "He's two months old, not two years."

"Nag, nag, nag," he taunted, then lifted the baby gently above his head. "Your mama worries too much, Bucko. Gotta watch that," he teased. "Too much pettin' and coddlin' and she'll turn you into a sissy."

William gurgled and cooed his agreement as Ace continued to talk.

"You didn't turn out so bad Ace and I know for a fact how much pettin' and coddlin' you got," Stanley remarked.

Ace grinned at his brother-in-law. "That's different. It was just Mama and Amber. This poor guy has two sisters *and* a mother to deal with," he said.

Stanley laughed. "You're right."

Amber glared at her husband. "Excuse me?"

"Better watch them, Amber," Lexie warned, though she enjoyed the teasing banter between them. "Or he'll be a chauvinistic jerk cowboy before he's two years old. Don't put him back," she insisted, and reached for the baby when Ace lowered him toward the swing.

"Why not?"

"Cause, that swing's got nails in it." She lifted him from Ace's arms, held little William close to her heart, and kissed his soft head. "Huh, Sweetheart?" she cooed.

Ace chuckled. "Nails?" he queried and arched a brow at Stanley.

Stan shook his head. "Alexis?"

The stern tone of voice couldn't mask the laughter in his expression.

"Sir?" she asked and regarded him with laughing emerald eyes.

"That child will think he doesn't have to sit up, crawl, or walk if everyone holds him all the time."

She grinned. "Don't worry. When he's old enough to sit up, crawl or walk, I won't hold him. Too much," she added.

Her remark brought a round of laughter that was cut off by a terrified shriek from the other room. Ace and Stanley rose in unison to go see what it was all about, when Ashlyn raced in the room, flung herself in her father's arms, clung to his shoulder, and sobbed.

Stanley rubbed her back. "What's the matter, Sweetheart?"

"There's a monster in my room," she cried.

"Let's go see," Stan offered.

She buried her face in his shoulder. "No, Daddy!"

"Okay, okay, shh." He rubbed her back and tightened his embrace. When her sobs subsided into soft, hiccupping sounds, Stanley shifted her so he could look into her eyes. "Where's the monster, Baby?"

"In my room."

"Did Sissy see it?"

She shook her head and rubbed her little eyes. "No," her voice quivered. "She's seeping."

"Okay." He nodded when Ace stood up.

"Show me, Sweetheart, and Uncle Ace will get rid of that old monster for good."

Stanley tightened his grip on Ashlyn for assurance and they walked toward the twins' room. Kaitlyn lay curled up under the sheet, oblivious to what was going on around her.

Stanley held his daughter as Ace looked under the bed. "No monster here," he whispered, and then moved quietly toward the closet. He opened the door and peered in. He shook his head. "No. Wait." He reached in and pulled out an imaginary creature. "This him?"

Ashyln's eyes widened in terror as she envisioned an ugly creature struggle in her uncle's grasp. She nodded then buried her face into her father's shoulder.

Ace headed out the door, punching and shaking the felon in his hands. "Don't you bother my niece anymore, if you ever come around here again, I'm gonna break your scrawny neck," he declared and tossed him out the back door. He brushed his hands together. "Now. He'll never be back. I promise you that," he assured and reached for his niece.

Ashlyn slid into his embrace. "Thank you, Unka Ace," she mumbled. Her little arms trembled as they went around his neck.

"Anytime, Sweetheart," he assured and hugged her tight.

Stanley grinned over at his wife. "He's insane, Amber," he told her in a gentle, teasing tone. "I was going to convince her there was no such thing as monsters. Macho Man here has to beat it up and scare it off. I'm afraid we really need to get him checked out."

Lexie's giggle cut off Amber's reply. "I thought he was convincing enough," she teased. "For a four year old."

Amber looked adoringly at her brother while he cuddled her daughter. "He'll make a wonderful father one day," she predicted.

Stanley rolled his eyes and relented at the triumphant grin from his brother-in-law. As the afternoon wore on, he began to watch the clock with a frown. Nearly an hour had passed since Ashlyn woke up and Kaitlyn still slept.

As though reading his thoughts, Amber got up. "I'm going to check on Kaitlyn. She'll be up all night if we let her sleep too long."

"Let me," Ace urged and rose from his seat. He handed Ashlyn to her mother then walked into the girls' room, knelt by the bed where she slept and whispered, "Wake up, Kaitlyn."

Her little lips curved into a smile and she squeezed her eyes shut.

He took a length of silky, black hair in his hand and tickled her nose with the ends. "Wake up, Sleeping Beauty," he commanded in a gentle tone.

"Prince Charming has to kiss me," she mumbled.

"You're too young for Prince Anybody to kiss you."

"Nuh uh," she insisted and squeezed her eyes tighter.

Ace chuckled and kissed her cheek. With a soft growl he nibbled on her ear.

She giggled and opened her eyes.

"Kiss not bite," she corrected, regarding him with laughing blue eyes.

He grinned. "But you taste so good," he assured, in his best Count Dracula voice, then proceeded to growl and nibble until she shrieked with laughter.

In the kitchen, Amber groaned, "I shouldn't have let him wake her. Now she'll really be wired."

Stan laughed. "That's okay. Lexie will have to deal with her," he remarked, and then explained when his wife's eyebrow arched in question. "She volunteered to baby-sit so we can go out for a while tonight."

Amber smiled over at Lexie. "You don't mind, really?"

"Not a bit," Lexie assured, as Kaitlyn ran into the kitchen with Ace close on her heels.

"Save me!" she shrieked and flung herself in her father's arms. Stanley held her out of Ace's reach when he made a grab for her and a wrestling match ensued.

Chapter Fifteen

The furniture was righted when the wrestling match moved outside. Lexie's mind whirled in amazement at how the four of them could horse around so much without breaking a single piece of furniture. Her eyes sparkled with amusement when Stanley and Ace surrendered and the twins rushed back in the house.

"We won! We won!"

Amber hugged and congratulated the twins, then sent them back out to play. Stanley and Ace joined the women at the table, flushed and breathless.

"I can't believe a chauvinistic, bull-riding cowboy can't wrestle two little girls, with help mind you, without coming away all out of breath."

Ace grinned at her. "I still have the stamina to wrestle with you, Sweetheart."

She arched a brow at him but refrained from comment.

The afternoon wore on and they tossed around ideas on what to do with the evening ahead.

"I know," Ace exclaimed. "Let's get Daddy to baby-sit and we'll all go out. You'd like to go dancing wouldn't you, Amber?" Her eyes lit up and she nodded. He rose from his chair, picked up the phone, and called his father. "Hey Dad, what'cha doin'?"

Craig eyed the bottle of whiskey on the kitchen counter. "Nothing. Why?"

"Have any plans for this evening?"

Again he eyed the bottle he'd yet to open. "Actually, Ace, I'm sitting here, thinking about getting drunk."

Ace's heart leapt in his throat at the anguish in his father's tone. "Why, Daddy?" The pitch of his voice had all eyes trained on him. He turned away from his sister's probing gaze and waited for his father's response.

"Why the hell not?" Craig demanded.

Ace raked his fingers through his hair and searched his mind for a reason to stop his father's self-destructive idea. Drinking would solve nothing. He'd only end up more miserable. His eyes sought Lexie's with an apologetic smile and he forced his voice to be light. "Cause Stanley's called me in on my promise to baby-sit. How about I bring these little heathens over so you can help me?"

Craig picked up the bottle, opened it, and took a swig.

"Daddy?"

His son's worried voice penetrated his anguished, agitated, mind. He took one more drink then smashed the bottle in the sink. "Okay, Ace. Bring them over. Give me time to clean this mess up."

Ace flinched at the sound of breaking glass but sighed with relief. "Stanley will bring them over later. I'm on my way."

"No need to come running, Ace, I'll be all right."

"I know, Daddy," he assured. "But I'm on Red Bone so I need to head back anyway." Without waiting for a reply, or argument, he hung up the phone and turned to Lexie.

"I'm sorry. He needs me there. I'll have to make it another time. Bring the kids whenever you're ready," he told his sister, but warded off her questions with a raised hand and a firm shake of his head.

Lexie rose from the table and met him at the door before he could escape. "Want me to go with you now?" she offered. His smile was strained, eyes haunted, touch gentle when he caressed her cheek.

"No. Thanks."

Lexie watched Ace ride away, a worried frown marred her forehead. Stanley caught Amber around the waist when she headed for the phone. "Let him be, Amber," he insisted and pulled her against his chest when she looked at him, her beautiful sapphire gaze clouded with anguish. He hugged her and stroked her hair in a tender gesture. "I'm going to shut things down around here. You still want to go tonight?"

Amber fought the pain which wrestled with the joy in her soul. Her lips trembled but she smiled. "Yes."

Stan brushed his lips over hers in a gentle caress. "That's my girl. Put on your favorite jeans, Darlin'," he drawled. "And we'll paint the town."

"I doubt if my favorite jeans will fit," she remarked with a frown.

He sighed and rubbed her body in a subtle stroke. "Oh well, love you anyway," he whispered before his lips covered hers. He slipped past Lexie and gave her arm a tender squeeze before heading out the door.

* * * * *

Ace rode home, worried and dreading the mood his father would more than likely be in. He remembered the talk he'd had with Scott and determined to support his father as best he could. His thoughts turned to Lexie and the tenderness in her eyes when she offered to go with him, and he wondered why he'd said no. Why had he passed up the chance to have her arms wrapped around his waist and her body pressed intimately against his as they rode home?

"Stupid," he muttered to himself and kicked his horse into a run. When he arrived at the ranch, he jerked the saddle off his horse and turned him loose then walked in the back door of the house, appalled at the silence. His nose wrinkled in disgust at the strong smell of whiskey which emanated from the sink. He walked toward the den but braced himself for what he might find.

He stood in the doorway and watched for a long moment as his father just sat with his face buried in his hands. The air of despair surrounding him was tangible and tugged at Ace's heart. He walked softly and knelt at his father's feet. "Daddy?" he queried and grasped Craig's wrists with hands that trembled.

"I miss her, Ace." His voice trembled. "I miss her so much. I miss the feel of her body next to mine, her hair on my skin and the sound of her laughter." Craig choked back a sob and swallowed the hard lump of tears in his throat.

"I know, Daddy," Ace replied. "I miss her too. I miss the way we used to tease and the way she'd brush the hair off my face."

Craig looked into eyes which mirrored his own. "She loved you so much."

Ace's smile wobbled. "I know. And I was a terrible son, always picking on her and making her worry."

"You weren't a terrible son. A little hard headed maybe, but not terrible."

"Where do you suppose I got that from?" Ace asked, and regarded his father with innocent eyes, relieved when Craig smiled.

"Your mother."

Ace didn't argue the point but laughed softly when his father grinned. "Kaitlyn reminds me of her so much."

Craig nodded his head in agreement. "Kaitlyn has her spirit, but Ashlyn has her gentleness and sensitivity. It's amazing how they can be so much like your mother but in different ways, how each inherited a special part of her personality."

Ace grinned. "Yeah, and they're all ours, tonight anyway. What do you say we spoil them so rotten that Amber won't want them back?"

Craig eyed him, his expression woeful. "I'm afraid Stanley won't go for it. We can try, but, I doubt we'll get to keep them longer than one night."

Ace shrugged. "So, we'll just run him off with a shot gun."

Craig couldn't help but chuckle. "I should have done that eleven years ago," he admitted and hugged his son. "Thank you, Ace."

"Anytime, Daddy, that's what I'm here for. Now what do you say we put our heads together and figure out just how we're going to occupy those two heathen nieces of mine?" Ace asked then grinned at the steely look he received from his father.

"Better watch how you talk about my granddaughters, Boy," Craig warned.

Ace merely laughed.

*****

Stanley watched out of the corner of his eye as Amber struggled into a pair of jeans. No matter what she tried, and she tried everything, they wouldn't button. He laughed at her hiss of frustration when she peeled them off and tossed them into the closet. "Why don't you just go buy a pair of jeans?"

"I am not about to spend good money on blue jeans just because these are a little tight. I'll get back in them."

"I'm sure you will, My Sweet, but it won't hurt to get a pair that fits now."

She snarled at him. "It's just not fair," she pouted. "Men have their fun and leave all the work up to us, nourishing, giving birth, ruining our figure."

His eyes ran over her in a look as potent as a caress. "Believe me, Honey, that figure is far from ruined."

Her smile was smug. "Really?" she queried and ran her hand down the firm wall of his stomach muscles. He flinched when she tugged at the hair just below his navel. "Well, if it is, it's all your fault," she accused.

"Blame it on me, I've got wide shoulders."

"You have beautiful shoulders," she breathed then nibbled on one for emphasis.

His body tightened, eyes narrowed, breath caught in an audible hiss. "Woman," he growled and grabbed her by the waist then pulled her against him. He picked her up and carried her to the bed where he loved her quickly and completely into oblivion. "If you don't get dressed soon, we may never leave this house," he warned in a husky voice as they trembled in the aftermath of passion.

She laughed and rolled away from him then walked to the closet and picked out a jump suit. She tried it on, relieved to find that it fit. "We're not in a big hurry are we? I want to visit with Daddy for a little while."

Stanley shook his head with a grin. "You mean we can't drop Lexie and the kids off on the porch and leave the truck running while we unload it?" he teased then chortled at the firm, chiding, look she gave him.

Craig met them at the door with a smile and accepted his daughter's hug, relieved when she didn't question him. "Y'all come on in," he offered and took William out of Amber's arms, leaving her to help Lexie and Stan unload the truck.

They walked into the den. Stanley carried his guitar. He eyed Lexie then nodded at the piano. "I want to learn that song you sang the other night."

She sat and ran her fingers along the keys. "Want me to write it down for you?"

He shook his head. "No. Just sing it."

She began to play but allowed him a moment to find the right key on his guitar before she started to sing. By the time she finished, everyone had tears in their eyes.

"Wow," Stanley breathed. "I like that one." He winked at his wife. "It's perfect."

"Perfect for what?" Lexie asked.

"For seducing my wife," he answered in a low voice and laughed when she blushed.

"Again?" she whispered eyes wide, cheeks hot.

"Something wrong with that?"

"I wouldn't know," she admitted, her eyes shining, her cheeks a delicate shade of crimson.

Ace walked into the room on the tail end of their conversation. "Wouldn't know what?"

She flushed harder. "Nothing," she mumbled.

Ace eyed his brother-in-law, an elaborate lift to his brow. "I wish I could sing."

"Oh please, sing solo," Stanley implored with a wink at Lexie. "So low no one can hear him," he said in a stage whisper.

Lexie giggled. "Or tenor," she added, and then lowered her voice. "Ten or twelve miles down the road."

Ace glared at them. "I'm being serious here."

"What would you sing, Ace?" Amber wanted to know.

He walked over to Lexie and Stan and glanced in her direction. "'I Miss You A Little' by John Michael Montgomery."

Amber gasped. Ace eyed her, his eyes pleading for understanding while she shook her head vehemently. He walked over, took her hands in his. "Yes, Amber," he insisted. "It's time we all stop hiding from the truth. We miss her. We all miss her and it hurts."

Stanley agreed. He nodded at Lexie and sang while she played the sensitive tune on the ivory keys. Before the song was finished Amber jerked away from her brother, glared at her husband and marched out of the room.

Craig sat, his face buried in his hands. Tears streamed down his cheeks, soft sobs shook his huge frame. Ace knelt in front of him as he had earlier. "It's okay to cry, Daddy," he said. "I'm here any time you need to," he assured, and wrapped his arms around his father's shoulders.

Lexie watched them with tears on her cheeks.

Amber stalked back in the room. "Let's go, Stanley," she ordered then glared at her brother. "Thank you Ace, for putting a damper on the evening."

With a sad shake of his head, Stan put down his guitar and walked toward his wife.

Ace called his sister's name when they turned toward the door. He went to her. His eyes begged for understanding and forgiveness. He reached for her hand even though she stiffened. "I didn't mean to put a damper on your evening, Sissy," he said, his voice soft and tender. "He needs to let it go, Amber. To work through it."

"Maybe so," she hissed her eyes icy shards of sapphire. "But did it have to be tonight?"

Ace lowered his eyes, sorry and surprised at her anger. He gazed at his brother-in-law, silently begging Stanley for support and felt imminent relief at the slight, imperceptible nod he received.

"We may pick up the baby, but there are enough bottles if we don't," Amber said.

"Don't worry, we'll be fine," Ace assured her. "Have a good time," he insisted.

Amber compelled her voice to be light and called goodnight to everyone then reached down to hug the girls when they ran to meet her. She forced a smile for Stanley when he opened the door and guided her into the truck. They were scarcely out of the drive when he pulled over and stopped.

"As I see it, we have two choices. We can turn around, pick up the kids and do this some other night. Or we can go and try to have a good time."

"You think I'm wrong? I just wanted a carefree night with my husband. Am I wrong for that?" Amber demanded.

"No, Sweetheart. You're not wrong. Neither is Ace."

"What do you mean?"

Stan sighed and searched his mind for the right words. "It's time for your father, and you, to stop burying your grief. It's time to face it, deal with it, and let God heal you of it. Especially your father."

"I haven't asked him to bury it."

"No, not in so many words, but he knows it upsets you to see him hurting. And the more you badger him..."

"I don't badger," she cut in.

"Okay, wrong word. The more you fuss over him, the deeper he buries it. He's having a rough day Amber. It's got to run its course before he can begin to get over it. You forget, My Sweet, I'm here to hold you when you have a bad day. Ace comes to you, or me. But your father has no one and he doesn't want to burden you with his grief because it upsets you so much."

"I just want him to be happy again. The Bible says that *'sorrow will last for a night, but joy will be found in the morning.'* When will the morning come, Stanley, when?"

"It also says, *'there's a time and a season for every purpose under heaven',*" he reminded in gentle admonishment. "But, it's got to be hard. For nearly thirty years he had your mother to share things with. Now he doesn't. Sharing with you or Ace isn't the same. And he's afraid to show how deep he's really hurting because he doesn't want you to worry. Ace has finally seen that and he's right to encourage your father to grieve. Only by doing that, will he be able to start healing. They were together nearly thirty years. She's been gone less than three. Give him a break, Amber. Let him deal with it in his own way and in his own time."

"Are you saying I'm overbearing and domineering to want him to be happy, to finally start living again, and to see him smile and hear him laugh?"

Stanley's smile was tender, as was the light in his eyes.

"No, My Sweet, you're a bit overprotective but not overbearing." He chuckled. "And you get it honestly, believe me. I've seen a big difference in him these last few months, but it's bound to take time. All you can really do is be there and support him no matter how he feels. Rejoice when he has a happy day and support him when he doesn't. But don't force him to hide his emotions from you. I'm afraid if you don't ease up there'll be a breach in your relationship, Amber, and I'd hate to see that. What you and your father share is really beautiful. Don't risk messing it up by being in too big a hurry for him to get over your mother's death."

Though not easy to admit, or face, Amber knew Stanley was right. Scott had tried to tell her the same thing. She'd just been too stubborn to listen, thinking that she knew what was best for her father. What was best for her, and Ace. She sighed, "Why haven't you told me this before?"

"Because you were always so adamant about him getting better and I didn't want to upset you, especially while you were pregnant. I figured you'd see it sooner or later. I didn't bank on Ace seeing it first."

With truth came understanding and with understanding, peace, Amber knew what she had to do. She had to repent and apologize. She'd done all she could, the only thing left was to let go and let God do what she hadn't been able to. "Can we go back? Just for a minute?" she asked her husband.

Stan shrugged. "Sure. I already said we could do this some other night."

She shook her head fervently. "No. I want this night with you."

"Only if you're sure," Stan remarked.

She kissed him. "I'm sure."

"Okay." He pulled her against him. "Kiss me again, My Sweet," he urged before his lips covered hers in a thorough caress. He turned the truck around and drove back to her father's house.

She leaned over, brushed her lips across his cheek. "Keep that thought," she whispered, and gave him an intimate caress.

"I'll be insane before you get back," he assured, his voice somewhere between a groan and a chuckle.

"What's the matter?" Ace asked his sister when she stepped through the door.

She smiled and kissed his cheek. "I forgot something." She walked to her father's side and laid her hand against his face.

"I'm sorry, Daddy," she whispered. Her eyes searched his for a sign that he understood. "I'm sorry I've attempted to rush you through this pain. I promise I'll try harder to be the daughter you need me to be."

Craig pulled her in his arms. "You're a perfect daughter. Thank you, Sweetheart," he whispered, his voice thick with tears he'd yet to shed.

She turned to her brother. "I expect you to keep a good eye on my babies, Ace, and not spoil them any worse than they already are."

He laughed glad she wasn't angry with him any longer. "I wouldn't dare," he assured then grinned at her snort of disbelief while sending up a silent, "thank you."

Amber hugged him then turned to Lexie and grasped her hand. "Thank you for being here to help them, Lex."

Lexie knew she meant more than helping with the children. She squeezed her hand. "We'll be fine Amber," she promised.

Hours later, Ace paused at Lexie's door on his way to bed. He glanced in and saw her rocking William. He leaned against the doorframe and asked, "What are you singing?"

"Rock a-bye Baby, in French."

"It's pretty," he remarked. "Thanks for staying Lex, I appreciate it."

She smiled up at him. "You're welcome. I wanted to go, but got the impression they wanted, needed, a night out alone."

Ace rolled his eyes. "She'll probably be pregnant tomorrow."

"Ace!" she chided, her eyes laughing into his, her cheeks a delicate shade of crimson. Her smile took his breath away.

"Well, good night," he said, but fought the temptation to walk on over to where she sat and kiss her senseless. Just one kiss, he told himself and stepped through the door.

"How 'bout a kiss goodnight?" he queried and braced his hands on the arms of her chair.

Lexie flushed, but lifted her lips to receive his kiss.

His lips brushed over hers in a tender caress. "Good night," he whispered. Her smile was brilliant and tempted him to taste it again.

Lexie saw the glint in his eyes and placed a firm hand on his chest. "Good night," she insisted.

Robbed of the opportunity to taste her lips once more, Ace settled for a brush of his mouth over his nephew's soft head. "Night, Bucko," he whispered, and was rewarded when William opened his eyes and stopped sucking on his pacifier long enough to smile around it.

* * * * *

Craig walked up the stairs. The house was silent. The twins were piled up in his bed, sound asleep. He stopped at his son's door and watched a moment, surprised Ace was already asleep. Making his way to his bedroom, he noticed Lexie was still awake. "Everything okay?" he asked, and adjusted the bedside lamp so she could get better light. He nodded at the Bible in her hands. "Good reading," he remarked, though he hadn't picked up his in ages.

"It is," she agreed, and put the book aside to move over so he could sit beside her on the bed. Craig reached across her and patted his grandson when he began to squirm.

Lexie smiled. "He doesn't seem to like the bottle too much. I think he misses his mama."

Craig smiled back, picked William up and cuddled him. "Probably, I know Ace didn't like to be far away from his mother when he was this age. Amber gives her children bottles of water and juice fairly early. Tamera nursed ours several months before she gave them anything else."

"Shows how much the opinion of doctors has changed," Lexie remarked.

He agreed. "Having twins, Amber probably didn't have much choice in the matter. Lexie, I want to apologize…"

She shook her head and laid her hand on his arm. "Don't, Mr. Craig. There's no need to apologize. Your family has made me feel so much more than welcome, like I'm a part of it. I understand how hard it is when you lose someone you love." Her voice quivered. "I lost my father and my best friend less than a year apart. But it's getting easier," she admitted. "With God's help."

Craig placed the baby beside her once more and kissed her cheek. "You are a part of the family, Lex, a very special part. Don't ever doubt it. Thank you."

"Good night, Mr. Craig," she said when he walked toward the door.

"Good night, Sweetheart."

Lexie watched him walk away and felt a surge of emotions. She closed her eyes and prayed for God to show her how to help this family, to help them heal and to repay them for all the love and kindness they'd shown her.

Chapter Sixteen

Amber awoke to the feel of Stanley's mustache brush gently across her skin. His lips moved over the smooth flesh of her shoulders while his hands stroked her body to life.

"Good morning, My Sweet," he whispered.

Her lusty sigh ended in a moan when he continued to kiss and caress her. "What time is it?"

"Time to get up, and go fetch the kids."

"In numbers please."

He chuckled. "Six thirty."

She groaned and opened one eye to glare at him. "They're still asleep."

"Want to bet? I'll bet William is hungry too."

"I left plenty of bottles," she mumbled and rolled away from him only to be reminded by her full breasts that bottles were not what her son was accustomed to having for breakfast. Though the wonder of breast pumps enabled her to give her baby mother's milk when she wasn't able to nurse him, it didn't stop nature from taking its course. "All I ask is to sleep late one day out of my life," she grumbled.

Stanley laughed and continued to awaken her senses with tender lips and gentle hands. "Want me to go get them and bring them back? Then you can snooze a few more minutes."

"No. The little heathen will be starving by now."

"Hey, watch how you talk about my son."

She grunted. "You nurse him then."

He laughed again, rolled her over and pulled her closer. "I would if I could, My Sweet. But that's the one thing only you can do."

Amber allowed herself to be enticed fully awake by his insistent kisses and caresses. With a soft sigh of pleasure, she surrendered to the sweet ecstasy that always awaited her in his arms.

"Call and tell Lexie not to feed him until we get there," she ordered her husband a half-hour later, then rolled out of bed and headed for the shower.

"Yes, Ma'am," he answered and picked up the phone.

* * * * *

Craig knew instinctively who was on the line when he picked up the receiver. "Good morning, Stanley."

"Morning. Kids up yet?"

"Yes. The girls are eating breakfast. I'm not sure about the baby. Wait, here they come now."

"Tell Lexie not to feed him, we're on our way."

Craig turned to Lexie as he hung up the phone. "Don't feed him."

"Why?"

He smiled. "I would imagine his mother's feeling pretty full by now."

She blushed. "Oh. What am I supposed to do with him?" she queried, when William started to fuss.

Craig laughed and lifted him out of her arms. "Entertain him, and try to keep him calm. There now," he soothed and bounced him gently. "Mama will be here soon."

Soon was not what William wanted to hear and he let it be known. Craig gave him a pacifier but it failed to live up to its name. He promptly spit it out and howled with anger.

Ace walked in the kitchen. "Hey, what's all this fuss about?" he queried and took the baby out of his father's arms.

"He's hungry," Craig replied. "Stanley just called. They're on their way and Amber said not to feed him."

"Oh, really?" he lifted William above his head. "Well, wait till that mean old mama gets here. I'm going to beat her," he promised William, and swayed him gently. "Yes I am," he assured his nephew. "Don't worry, Bucko, Uncle Ace has a cow or two around here."

William stopped crying the moment Ace picked him up and within moments smiled and cooed in response to his voice. Lexie laughed at the tender, teasing conversation between the nineteen-year-old man and his two-month-old nephew.

Amber and Stan walked in. "Hello!" she called, as she made her way into the kitchen. The twins flung themselves at her. "Oh, I missed my babies," she assured them and laughed as they hugged her then flew into Stanley's embrace. She reached for her son and cuddled him tenderly while she unbuttoned her blouse and sat down. "How's mama's little man? Hungry are we? There now," she soothed, when he rooted greedily then began to nurse.

Lexie smiled at Amber. "He was fussing, but all Ace has to do is talk to him and William shuts up."

Stanley's chuckle cut off Amber's reply. "That's because they're on the same wave length."

Ace grunted and gave his brother-in-law a look which clearly said he didn't think the remark was funny.

Conversation flowed easily and lovingly all around while Lexie gathered ingredients for breakfast. She placed heaping platters of ham, eggs, and toast on the table just as Amber finished feeding William. The men began to eat, wolfing the food down as though they were starved.

"Man," Ace breathed and rubbed his stomach. "If a way to a man's heart is through his stomach, you've got mine forever Darling," he assured Lexie.

"What heart?" his sister queried.

Her blue eyes laughed into his. "I gotta heart," Ace insisted with a grin.

"It's a brain or soul bull riders don't have," Lexie interjected, which reminded him of their first meeting.

"Guess I showed you," Ace remarked. Lexie shrugged without comment. He leaned over, tugged on her shirt, and pulled her face very close to his. "Should I show you again?" he queried. Her eyes dared him to kiss her even though she protested. Ace never backed down from a dare. His lips covered hers in a teasing caress. He chuckled when she pulled away and blushed to the roots of her red hair.

"Jerk," she hissed.

Later that afternoon, Amber sighed with relief when Lexie informed her, the twins were finally asleep. Those two had not wanted to take a nap at all. In fact, they'd protested loudly until Lexie agreed to read them a story and promised to play games with them after they woke up.

The men left shortly after lunch to deliver two horses in Amarillo. They would be gone most of the night. Not content with the women and children alone at their house, Stanley had badgered, begged, and downright threatened until Amber agreed to spend the night with Lexie at her father's house. Craig agreed to accompany his son and son-in-law after speaking to the ranch foreman and several of his other hands for assurance the women and children would be well protected.

Amber smiled at Lexie. "I really love my husband, father and brother, but it feels good to be here, just us, where we can talk. Grown-up, female conversation is a rarity for me."

Lexie giggled. "I can imagine it's hard to come by."

Amber laughed and curled up on the couch. "That's an understatement."

They laughed and talked, sharing stories from their pasts and future dreams. Lexie listened while Amber related many of their childhood follies, especially when she told off on Ace.

While they talked, Amber noticed Lexie's interest in anything regarding her brother. "Have you ever been in love Lexie?"

"No."

"Never? As pretty as you are, I'd have thought you'd have been beating the boys off since you were thirteen." Amber noticed the difference in Lexie immediately. She flushed and her eyes darted nervously around the room, avoiding eye contact. Fear, unknown and unfamiliar, took root in her heart.

Lexie stood up and began to pace. "Not exactly."

"Lexie what is it?" Amber asked. Her voice softened to assure the younger woman that whatever they shared would remain confidential. Lexie turned her eyes full of anguish.

"I've never wanted a boyfriend. I've always been too afraid, and ashamed."

"I'm so sorry Lexie. I don't mean to pry."

She shrugged. "You're not prying. That's what friends are for. I haven't had a real friend since Kristy died," she admitted, her tone soft, sad.

Amber took Lexie in her arms and rocked her gently when she began to cry and speak. Her heart broke at the story of Lexie's childhood and the death of her best friend. But it was when Lexie shared her deepest, darkest, secret that she felt such emotion she couldn't put a name to it.

"When I was twelve a friend of my father's came to stay with us a few days. Well, my father was always drunk so it was easy for him to take advantage of the need I had for attention. It didn't take long either."

Amber knew in her heart what was coming. She put a hand on Lexie's arm. "Don't, Lexie, don't re-live it."

"You know, when I first met you, I was so envious. Not really in a bad way, but a sad, painful kind of jealousy. It seemed you'd had it all, perfect childhood, a wonderful husband, and beautiful children." She blushed, ashamed now of her petty emotions. "But lately I've begun to realize how blessed I am too. I need to tell you this Amber, to be honest with you. Your friendship means so much. Do you mind?"

"Of course not," Amber replied in quiet assurance.

"Anyway, like I said, it didn't take long. He came into my room one night and, well, you can guess what happened. He warned me not to tell my father, but he underestimated what little relationship we did have."

"My God!" Amber interrupted. "You were a child!"

"I've never been a child," Lexie denied, then continued before Amber could respond. "When my father wasn't drunk, which wasn't very often, we had an okay relationship. We laughed and talked a lot. It was more like having a brother instead of a father. He was never serious about anything. He liked to play. He was always dreaming, wanting more, but didn't know exactly how to get that pot at the end of the rainbow. He worked hard and played hard. But he tried to take care of me, Amber. He really did. He just didn't know how."

She shrugged knowing she could never fully explain the paradox her father was. "Anyway, like I said, it wasn't too often that he wasn't drunk. After this 'friend' left, I kept the truth from him as long as I could. Then, I started to be sick in the mornings," she looked away unable to stand the anguish and knowing which shone in Amber's eyes.

She nodded sadly. "You're right, I was pregnant. My father was furious and promised to take care of the situation and his friend. His way of taking care of me was to bring me to an abortion clinic in another state. He paid dearly too and made sure it was done quickly, as painlessly as possible, and that there were no complications, which guaranteed I would be able to have children in the future. The only thing he didn't do was defend me when they insinuated about how very young I was. He let them believe it was some young boy and that he'd taken care of the situation."

The tears continued slowly as she finished the story. "As far as the 'friend', I'm not sure what happened between them. I only know that I never saw him again. Not until my father's funeral. He came to me then, and begged my forgiveness. Said he'd given his life to Jesus and that he was so terribly sorry, and would I please forgive him.

"We talked for a long time. I couldn't trust myself or him enough to tell him about the abortion I had to have as a result of his actions. Even though I attended a private, Christian school, I couldn't understand how he could even ask for forgiveness or how a relationship with Jesus could make everything all right. He said that the only thing he lacked for complete absolution from the guilt he carried was my forgiveness. Of course I said the words, but I don't think I ever really forgave him. Even with all of the religious education, I don't think I've truly forgiven him. I want to, hope to, and know that I must in order to continue my relationship with Christ and maybe one day I will be able to. But, that's another story in itself. Anyway, when I was old enough to date, my life was such a mess, as was my father's. So you see I've been too afraid and ashamed to have a boyfriend or to fall in love."

Amber hugged Lexie to her breast when she began to sob and rocked her as though she were a child. "I'm so sorry, Lex, you went through all of that. I can see why you would be afraid, but you have nothing to be ashamed of. What happened was not your fault. You were innocent. Not much more than a baby yourself. Does Scott know about this?"

Lexie nodded. "I told Trina and she told him. I suppose that's why he's so protective of me. He offered to get me a counselor or someone to talk to. Trina wanted me to talk to a Priest. I didn't want to. No one else knew except Kristy. We shared everything. That's why it was so hard when she died. We were so close and I'm so thankful now to have you," she assured Amber with a hug then emitted a bitter little laugh.

"Poor Kristy, she should have been my father's child. They were so much alike, always wanting more. She had it all. Parents who adored her, all the money she could ever want or need. But it was never enough."

"More of what?"

Lexie shrugged. "I don't know, just more."

Amber smiled. "You know, often times when someone continues to search for "more" what they really need is Christ."

"I know," Lexie admitted. "I believe not knowing, truly knowing if they're in heaven is what bothers me the most. Both of them suffered so much on earth, it seems almost sacrilegious for them not to go to heaven. Especially if God is the all loving, all forgiving God the Bible says He is."

Amber brushed the hair off Lexie's face. "How do you feel about your father and Kristy now?" she asked her tone gentle.

Lexie shrugged. "I kinda feel sorry for them. They just didn't realize how truly blessed they were. It's odd, Amber. My father made sure I was raised in Christian schools, but he never went to church himself. He always felt guilty and condemned because my mother died while having me. Her parents hated him and they died with that hatred in their hearts. That, and the fact he drank so much, only served to make him feel even guiltier. He tried to quit, several times, always vowed he would and that everything would be all right. He just didn't have the strength to do so." She shrugged.

"I guess I should hate him for being so weak, but I can't. I've been angry with him a lot and angry with Kristy too, but I can't bring myself to hate them. I always end up pitying both of them."

Amber hugged her again. "You're right. You should not hate either of them for being weak. We are called to love, not judge. And you're also correct in believing that God is all loving and all forgiving. You said your father made sure you went to Christian schools, so he believed in God. What about Kristy?"

"Oh, she went to the same school as I did. She knew the Bible inside out."

"Was she saved?"

"Yeah, we received Jesus as our Lord and Savior at the same time. Only, the experience didn't seem to affect her in the same way it did me. I mean, I've had my share of problems, moments of doubt and disbelief, but somewhere deep inside I just knew God was the only true answer to life's problems. Kristy never reached that point. Then she died."

Amber prayed silently then chose her words with care. "I'm no Bible scholar, Lex, nor am I perfect. But I do believe both your father and Kristy are in heaven. The Bible says all we have to do in order to be saved is to confess Jesus as Lord and believe that God raised Him from the dead. From what you've told me, both your father and Kristy did that. It's true they did not accept all of the promises of God, and they chose a different path than I or even you would. Their suffering was a result of those choices. However, both of them made the most important choice of all, the choice to accept and profess Jesus as Savior. And for that reason alone I believe they are in heaven."

"I hope so," Lexie sighed. "I'm glad you don't think less of me. I've always blamed myself for the miseries of my childhood and I'm usually so afraid other people would too," she admitted.

"Some people might blame you, but true people of God wouldn't. And, sometimes talking is the best remedy, the quickest road to healing. Have you laid this at the feet of Jesus?"

"I've tried and I'm beginning to realize that I was not to blame. I've asked God to give me the grace to really forgive this man and I continue to pray for him just as I pray for my father and Kristy and my baby. Sometimes I feel so guilty about the baby. I know that may sound crazy with so much rhetoric about whether or not it really is a baby, but the Church teaches it's human from the moment of conception. I'm not sure what I really believe but I know there was nothing I could have done. It was not my fault," she insisted, as though determined to convince herself as well as Amber.

"However I'm not sure if I can really say that I've let it all go." She paused a moment, prayed silently for strength, then asked the question that burned deep in her heart. "Do you think Ace or your father would feel the same way as you do?"

Amber thought a long moment knowing how very important her answer would be in aiding Lexie's healing. "Both my father and Ace would probably want to hunt him up and kill him for you. Or in the very least, castrate him."

"Scott said the same thing," Lexie admitted with a giggle.

Amber laughed. "That's love, Lexie, real love of a father for his daughter. Speaking of love, are you in love with my brother?" Amber recognized the flush on her cheeks and the glow in her eyes even as Lexie shrugged.

"He's come to mean a great deal to me, Amber. I'm not sure if what I feel is love or not. I don't have much experience in the matter. But I'll tell you this, I really care about him and I'd never want to hurt him."

Amber hugged her. "You don't need experience when it's true love. Let me warn you though, if he's anything like my father or my husband, and he is, exactly, you'll constantly struggle with the temptation to strangle him as often as kiss him."

"Do you think I should tell him?"

Again Amber searched her heart before answering. She knew Ace well enough to know he would never blame the child. And she knew he had feelings for Lexie. What she didn't know was how strong those emotions were and whether or not her admission would change them. Instinct told her it wouldn't. If Ace loved Lexie, he would love her even more for her honesty. The truth was always best and she firmly believed in complete openness and honesty in a relationship, especially between a man and a woman.

Taking Lexie's hand in hers she looked into the worried, frightened gaze. "Let me put it like this, Lex, if you love him and think you may want to have a future with him, then tell him. In fact, tell him anyway. If all your relationship is, or ends up being, is friends, you could not ask for a better one than Ace. He's loyal to a fault, and I believe his feelings for you are as yours are toward him."

Lexie breathed a sigh of relief and nodded. She knew Amber was right, Ace deserved to know the truth. But she couldn't help but be afraid of his reaction. She vowed to tell him as soon as the opportunity arose and prayed to God for guidance and strength to know when that time came.

Before long the children began to arise from their naps and the fun started. Concentration, Candy Land, games and stories, they played long into the night, until everyone tumbled into bed in exhausted heaps.

Chapter Seventeen

Ace turned the truck toward home. The trip to Amarillo had taken longer than they expected. They'd had a flat on the horse trailer and trouble finding the ranch where the Arabian yearlings were to be delivered. Now he understood why Stanley usually had the new owners pick up their purchases. It was so much easier and he didn't have to leave his family.

He turned the radio down a notch when Stanley stirred in the seat beside him. His father appeared to be asleep in the rear seat of the king-cab pickup.

"You okay? Want me to take over?" Stan asked.

Ace shook his head. "I'm fine. I'm ready to be home though."

Stanley laughed softly. "Me too, Sport."

Ace grinned over at him. "I didn't think I could miss someone so much," he admitted to his brother-in-law.

Stan knew instinctively who Ace missed so much and smiled. "She is a pretty little thing."

"Yeah," Ace breathed.

Craig coughed to cover a chuckle and nearly choked. "And you didn't want me to invite her to the ranch."

Ace glared into the mirror. "I thought you were asleep."

Again he chuckled. "Impossible. There's absolutely no leg room back here."

Stan laughed, sympathetic with his father-in-law's plight but not willing to trade places with him.

When he could stand it no more, Craig insisted they stop to stretch their legs.

"Aw, Daddy, another two hours and we'll be home," Ace protested wishing he'd stayed behind.

"Well, make it two-and-a half-hours," Craig insisted. "If I don't get out of here and stretch my legs I may never walk again."

They pulled into the next truck stop and opted to break long enough for breakfast aware they'd either get home too early or too late to eat with the rest of the family.

Stanley headed straight for the telephone. "Hello, My Sweet," he greeted when his wife answered.

"Good morning. How close are you to being home?"

He consulted his watch. "A couple of hours, we had a flat and then had trouble finding the Double Bar."

"Oh." She sighed. "Okay. Be careful, Stan," she pleaded.

"We will. We're about to grab a bite of breakfast and will see you in a little while."

"Great. I'll have a fresh pot of coffee brewed."

"Sounds like a winner. Give the kids a hug and kiss for me." He turned at the sound of footsteps and grinned. "Oh, and, give Lexie a hug for Ace," he teased, and then laughed at his brother-in-law's glare.

Amber laughed on the other end of the line. "I'm quite sure he'll be able to do that himself when y'all get back."

Stan chuckled. "You can bet he will. Said he never knew he could miss someone so much," he confided.

"And what did you tell him?"

"That I know exactly how he feels. I hate these trips away from you, My Sweet."

"I hate them too. I love you Stanley. Go on and eat so you can hurry home."

"Will do," Stanley promised and placed the receiver back in its cradle.

Amber hung up the phone with a smile, cuddled the baby at her breast and thanked God for the blessings in her life.

Exactly two hours and fifteen minutes later the men arrived with a whirl of gravel, flying dust and a blare of the horn. The twins flew out of the house and into waiting arms.

"Daddy! Daddy!"

"PaPaw! Uncle Ace!"

All three men took turns with hugs and kisses and listened to excited little girl chatter while they made their way steadily into the house.

Stanley immediately went to his wife and son while Craig poured coffee.

Ace looked around for the one person he wanted most to see. "Where's Lexie?"

Amber smiled. "Well, hello to you too, Brat."

Dutifully he bent to kiss his sister's cheek. "Now, where is she?" he demanded.

His gray eyes danced into her teasing blue ones. "She's exercising," Amber replied, brushing a lock of blonde mane off his forehead.

Minutes later they heard Lexie's surprised shriek from the other room when he joined her.

Surprised wasn't what Lexie felt when his arms wound around her waist. Floored, was what she was, flabbergasted. "What?"

"Man, oh man, I missed you!"

"Are you crazy?"

He laughed and twirled her around. "Probably so! Delirious from sleep deprivation and being cooped up with Stan and Daddy for nearly twenty hours."

She laughed. "Put me down you idiot."

"Say please and kiss me little Lexie," he breathed and covered her lips with his.

What started out as a sweet, friendly greeting, turned all-too-quickly into something more, much more. Ace drug his lips away from hers with a tortured groan. He placed his hands on her tiny waist and gently pushed her away from his body.

His smile was tender, his eyes appraising when they swept over her scantily clad figure. "Get dressed and I'll fetch you a cup of coffee."

"But I'm not finished here."

He tilted her chin up with a gentle finger. "Please."

Her heart fluttered, cheeks grew warm. "Okay."

She turned off the music then slipped on her warm-up pants and a T-shirt. Hand-in-hand they walked to the kitchen.

Lexie headed toward the counter where the coffee pot and cups were. Ace stopped her with a gentle tug on her arm. "I'm fetching, remember?"

She smiled. A soft flush filled her cheeks when she sat next to Amber.

Ace turned pot in hand. "How do you take it?"

"In a cup would be nice."

He grinned, rolled his eyes, and shook his head. "My word, one little kiss and she gets all sassy."

"That's cause you did it wrong," Stanley interjected. "You've got to kiss them with authority." He winked at his wife whose giggle undermined every bit of his so-called authority.

"Right, we'll try this again. Cream, sugar?"

Lexie shook her head, flushing hotly. "No, I stopped drinking coffee-milk when I was four," she taunted and laughed when he grimaced. "Just pour it in a cup."

Craig chortled. "You all can sit here and discuss the finer points of kissing and coffee, I'm going to bed." He rose from his seat and kissed his daughter's cheek.

"Good night, Daddy."

"Night, Sweetheart." With a gentle brush of his knuckles across her face, he caressed Lexie's cheek and headed out of the room.

"Can't run with the big dogs, Daddy, stay on the porch with the puppies," Ace quipped.

Craig shrugged off the teasing with a wave of his hand.

"He looks tired," Amber remarked. A worried frown creased her brow.

"I imagine he is. We all are," Stan admitted, "Except, maybe, Macho Man here. But I haven't seen him laugh so much as he has in the last twenty hours. You'd have thought that he'd ordered every mishap we had just to keep us on the road. And the more upset we got, the funnier he thought it was." He rolled his eyes. "Everything was funny to him. It felt good though, to have him laugh and tease. Huh Ace?"

Ace nodded in agreement. Their attention turned to Ashlyn when she climbed up on her father's lap.

"Miss Yexie taught us a new song yast night."

"Really?"

She nodded. "Want to hear it?"

Stanley smiled into the glittering sapphire gaze of his daughter and nodded.

"Are you seeping, are you seeping..." Ashlyn stuttered, flushed, and then turned to Lexie. "You sing it, Miss Yexie."

"You sing it with me," she urged and took Ashyln's hands in hers. First in English then French she sang, "Are you sleeping, are you sleeping, Brother John, Brother John..."

They listened raptly to the thick, southern accent purring in the husky voice and the velvety roughness of the foreign tongue.

"How come you're not in Nashville?" Stanley asked.

"Shut up Stanley, don't give her any ideas," Ace insisted and poked his elbow into his brother-in-law's side.

Lexie giggled. "I could ask you the same," she remarked.

Stan laughed and shrugged. "I love music. But horses are my life, as is my family. Music is just something I enjoy and enjoy sharing. I never thought about, or wanted, to make a career out of it."

"I feel the same way. I'm not sure what my future holds yet, but I know it's not the entertainment business."

"What do you want to be when you grow up, little Lexie?" Ace teased. "If what I hear is true, the sky is the limit. You could be anything from a doctor to a rocket scientist."

She shrugged. "I don't know yet. I do know that I want a family some day, a big family with lots of children. What about you? Weren't you going to college?"

He nodded. "Still am. Just took the summer off. Gonna be a vet."

"Now days, women can have it all. A career and a family," Lexie remarked.

Ace frowned. "I want a wife who wants to stay home and raise a family. Not someone who's here some of the time and gone the rest. Part-time wife, part-time mother, it don't work for me."

"That's because you're a chauvinistic jerk cowboy," Lexie taunted.

"Maybe so," he agreed. "But I know what my parents had. I see what my sister has. I won't settle for less," he vowed.

"Good for you Ace," his sister interjected. "But, there is nothing wrong with a woman doing her own thing as long as she is a good wife and mother. Look at me, I still substitute teach during the school year and I write also. If a woman is fulfilling her dreams and not just some man's wife, her marriage will be happier. She's just got to keep things in balance. And a good husband will respect that and support her. Like Stanley does me and my dreams. Love, respect, and compromise are key ingredients to a good relationship."

"Yeah," her brother teased. "We know who wears the pants in your family."

"Stanley wears the pants," she defended staunchly, and then promptly ruined the declaration when she added, "I just tell him which ones to put on."

Stanley grunted. "Thank you, My Sweet, for that slur against my manhood." Then with a grin and a wink, "it's getting way too deep in here for me. I'm ready for bed," he admitted, rose from his seat, and stretched.

Without grumble, complaint or argument, Amber rounded up the children and went home with her husband.

Ace checked with the ranch foreman to see if there was anything that required his immediate attention before he decided to rest also. The weather was turning nasty, not much he could do in it. Better for him to rest so he could clean up after the storm. He took a shower, stretched out on the couch, and dozed.

Lightening split the sky, thunder rolled. The storm raged. Its intensity snaked into his dreams. Ace tossed restlessly on the couch, wrestling with some inner turmoil.

Lexie looked up from the book on her lap and watched him quietly when he mumbled in his sleep. She put the book aside and knelt beside him.

"Ace," she whispered, and brushed the hair off his forehead. He moaned and pulled away from her touch. She shook him gently and whispered his name. He called for his mother then bolted upright, nearly unseating her. With a groan he buried his face in his hands.

"God!" he sighed. "Sometimes I miss her so much."

"I know," she soothed and took his hands in hers.

Ace grasped one of her hands and lay back down while his breathing settled back to normal.

"Can I get you anything?" she offered.

He shook his head then opened his eyes and looked into her worried gaze. "Stay with me, Lexie. Let me hold you." He patted the area beside him, positive the couch was plenty big enough for the both of them.

Lexie laid their clasped hands against her cheek. Her lips trailed across the back of his hand as she fought the urge to climb up beside him, to feel the warmth of that strong body curled around hers. Since she and Ace hadn't crossed any boundaries of propriety and she didn't know how serious he would interpret such a move, she figured it was best not to do as he asked and as she wanted. She brushed the hair off his forehead and smiled tenderly into the haunted gaze.

"Tempting though it is, I'm not comfortable with that idea. But I promise I'll stay right here until you go back to sleep."

Ace had watched the conflict of emotions in her eyes while she considered his proposal. He smiled despite his disappointment. "That was supposed to be an offer you couldn't refuse. How can you?" he queried.

"It's not easy," she admitted with a shy smile.

"Good," he muttered, and pulled her head down to nestle in the crook of his shoulder. He loosened the French braid down her back, smoothed his fingers through the thick tresses until her hair cascaded around her in a silken mass. He stroked the silky strands until he fell asleep.

Lexie stayed beside him until he snored softly once again then pressed her lips to his cheek, slipped out of his embrace and returned to her reading.

Sometime later, Ace awoke in a mild state of confusion. He still lay on the couch, but it appeared to be getting darker out. A light blanket had been thrown over him. Though a steady rain continued to fall, the worst of the storm had passed. He glanced at the clock and realized he'd slept the better part of the day. He rolled to his feet and wandered toward the kitchen where the smell of food and the sound of music filled the air.

Lexie sat cross-legged on a chair and played a soft, sensual song, something along the lines of Kenny G, only on the flute. He watched in silent appreciation until she finished the song. "Why the sad music, little one?"

She turned with a smile. "Not so much sad as lonely."

"Not much difference. Missing your family?"

"Yeah, I called them earlier. Everyone's fine. Wondering when I'm coming home."

He tried to ignore the fear gnawing at him at the thought of her leaving. "Are you thinking about that?"

"You ready to get rid of me?"

He shook his head. "Not at all. Is my father up yet?"

She shook her head negative, placed the flute to her lips, closed her eyes, and played another lilting tune.

Ace poured himself a cup of coffee and sat down. He cocked back in his chair, closed his eyes, and just listened. The music tugged at his heartstrings and hinted of dreams unfulfilled. He remembered the flare of desire in her emerald eyes earlier when he asked her to lie beside him. His arms ached to reach out for her now. "Real pretty," he remarked. "I thought you were going to stay with me while I slept."

She laughed. "Someone had to start supper."

He took a deep breath and inhaled the aromas which filled the air.

"Oh. Well, in that case, I forgive you."

"How gallant," she remarked.

"I'm going to go check on my father," he remarked and rolled to his feet. Giving into temptation, he brushed his lips across hers. "Don't stop, Little Lexie, you play well, sounds real pretty."

"Yes, Sir," she complied as meekly as possible.

"Kinda like the sound of that," he teased with a chuckle.

"You would," she taunted then smiled at his arrogant, triumphant, little laugh.

Chapter Eighteen

The summer moved slowly onward, hot and humid. Craig and Ace were gone more than home, as they prepared for the Annual Charity Rodeo to be held less than two weeks away. Lexie spent most of her time at Amber's house and true to his word, Stanley was teaching her to ride. They were out back one sultry afternoon when Ace rode up unexpected.

He watched for a long moment while she walked the horse slowly around the paddock. "What's going on?" he greeted his brother-in-law.

"What does it look like?"

Ace grinned. "What's she doing on Dolly?"

Dolly was Stanley's oldest, gentlest, and most prized mare, the horse both twins learned to ride before they could walk. Stanley didn't believe in starting children out on ponies. If they wanted to ride, they needed to learn on the real thing. Of course, he always made sure the horse he chose for his child, or any child for that matter, was as gentle and obedient as he could train it to be.

Ace knew this. Which was why it didn't take him long to figure out that Lexie was a beginner when it came to horseback riding. He whistled. Dolly stopped dead in her tracks.

Lexie turned, her eyes widened in surprise. A mortified groan escaped her and she blushed furiously.

Ace whistled again and Dolly started to walk toward them. Just when Lexie got her up to a trot, he whistled again. Dolly stopped. No matter how much Lexie coaxed the horse, she wouldn't budge. By the time Ace gave the signal for the horse to move again, Lexie was furious.

She dismounted in an angry whirl. "You promised not to tell him anything!" she hissed at Stanley.

"I didn't. All he had to do was watch to know you're an amateur."

Ace laughed. "If you're going to learn to ride, you shouldn't ride a horse that's been trained to move, or not to move, according to a whistle."

Lexie grabbed the reins and with obvious strain, controlled the urge to slap him with them. She glared at him a long moment then turned on her heel. Her sudden movement surprised Dolly who neighed her disapproval. She suppressed the urge to jerk on the bridle and mentally chided herself not to take it out on the horse. "C'mon girl," she mumbled then glared at Ace again. "Chauvinistic jerk."

Ace knew by the tone of her voice, not to mention the emerald daggers which pierced his heart that she was furious as all get out. He turned to Stanley. "What'd I say?" he asked, utterly confused.

Stan shook his head. "You humiliated her, Ace," he scolded, his tone gentle.

"But I was teasing. She should be used to that by now."

"I know you'd never intentionally humiliate anyone, but you need to pay a little closer attention when it comes to females," he said with a chuckle then continued at Ace's blank look.

"There are times when a woman doesn't want to be teased, Ace. They want to be petted and cuddled. And, sometimes, the last thing they want is to be around a man."

All it took was one meaningful glance for Ace to understand what he hinted at. He flushed darkly then climbed over the fence and followed in her wake.

"Lexie, wait!"

Stanley laughed and headed toward the house. Let him figure it out, he thought. And figure out how to deal with it. It's something every man had to learn for himself.

Ace got to the barn just as Lexie took the saddle off Dolly. He reached for it. She jerked it away.

"I can do it," she hissed. "Learning how to saddle and unsaddle is the first lesson," she muttered her tone scathing. "Just go away you jerk. I wanted to surprise you and you ruined it!" she accused and swiped at the tear that escaped her furious gaze.

"Lexie, I don't care if you know how to ride," he chided.

"Right," she sneered. "You're a cowboy, you rope and ride bulls. You own a ranch for God's sake!"

"So, I'm sure there are lots of things you do that I can't."

"Like what?"

"Well," he searched for something to say that would ease her embarrassment. "I can't cook or play any instruments. And, you're a heck of a lot better dancer than I am."

"But at least you know how," she wailed, unable to stop the tears this time.

He pulled her in his arms and tried to shush her ragged sobs.

"Now I've made a fool of myself in front of Stanley, and I don't even know what's wrong with me," she muttered.

Ace wisely swallowed a laugh and rubbed her back in a gentle caress. "I do. Believe me Honey, living with Amber, Stanley understands. Mama was the same way when her time of the month rolled around. She'd rant and rave and tear into my father for the slightest little thing. He'd just stand there and not say a word. When she finished, he'd smile and ask if she was through fussing at him. When she said yes, he'd ask her for a kiss."

He chuckled at the memory. "Always worked too, stripped the wind right out of her sails." He eyed her, a curious lift to his brow.

"You don't even have to ask," she admitted and rose up on her toes. Her arms curled around his neck, her lips reached for his. In the moment before they met, while she could still think straight, Lexie wondered if she'd ever be able to go a whole day without his kiss.

His lips swooped over hers in a hungry caress. Lexie's mind whirled, dizzy with pleasure. She clung to him when he widened his stance and pulled her more firmly against his hard frame. "Do you know how long it's been since you've kissed me?" she breathed then nibbled on his bottom lip.

He remembered very well their goodnight kiss the night before and muttered, "Less than twenty-four hours I'm sure."

"Too long," she breathed, and pulled his lips down on hers again.

The strength and boldness of her kiss forced him to swallow a triumphant little chuckle. Too soon, he struggled for some semblance of control. "Easy little one or you might end up on your backside in the hay."

Lexie realized how close she was to tumbling into sin with him and stepped back. "Not a chance, Cowboy. And don't flatter yourself," she added when he started to laugh.

"I've always wanted to learn how to ride a horse," she admitted. "I've just never had the time, energy, or opportunity to do so."

He stroked the hair off her face. "Now that you've put me firmly in my place, want to ride with me sometime?"

She made an attempt at nonchalance. "Maybe." She glared at him. "Then again, maybe not, especially if you insist on controlling the horse I'm on."

He slipped his arm around her waist, hugged her to his side and promised not to do that again.

"Why did she stop and go only when you whistled?"

"Because that's how Stanley trained her to obey before he taught the girls to ride. Unless he gives her the okay, she won't move."

"It amazes me how he can teach them so much."

"Horses are smart animals, Lex. And, as much as I hate to admit it, Arabians are some of the smartest. Dolly is one of the best. She loves Stanley. She'd do anything for him. My mother once had an Arabian stallion that saved her life."

"Really?"

"I'm surprised Scott hasn't told you the story."

She shook her head. "I can't wait to hear it."

Over coffee, he and Amber told her the story of how their parents met and fell in love, and how, when she was near death from a rattler's bite, her beloved horse Temper, brought the rescue posse to Tamera's side.

* * * * *

Stanley and Lexie entertained the girls and a couple of ranch hands on the porch while Amber helped her father in the kitchen and William slept in his swing.

"Sing something really deep, Lexie," Stanley urged, anxious to hear her really open up on some heartfelt tune.

"Like what?"

He considered a minute and then chose a tune he thought would offer the opportunity to hear her voice at its max. "Sing 'All I Want For Christmas Is You'."

She laughed. "The sun bears down on us in ninety-six-degree heat and you want me to sing a Christmas song?"

He chuckled. "Use your imagination."

She closed her eyes and took a deep breath. "No way," she admitted with a shake of her head. "But I know what might help." She hurried into the house and retrieved her Saxophone.

"How long have you had that here?"

"I asked Scott to send it the other day when we talked and received it this morning." She tuned the instrument, played a few notes then began to sing.

"Wow!" Stanley breathed. "That's some voice you have there, little girl."

She blushed at the compliment then played a few other songs.

Ace walked out of the barn, amazed at the sight of her playing the Sax and the power in her voice when she sang. He rode in early as expected since his sister and her family was due over for supper. He listened for a few minutes before joining them. He nodded. "Afternoon."

Lexie flushed when he brushed his lips across her cheek. "Think I'll go and help Amber finish up," she excused herself.

Ace eyed his brother-in-law when the ranch hands wandered off. "Gonna get her up on stage with you?" As he had for the past several years, Stanley would provide entertainment at the rodeo.

Stanley grinned. "I'm working on it."

"I asked her if she would sing or dance for us. Know what she said?" He continued at the shake of Stan's head. "She very politely said 'not no, but hell no.'" He chuckled at the memory.

Stanley laughed. "You call that polite?"

He grinned. "I asked her how such a pretty little mouth could say such a thing."

"And?"

"She asked me how such a good looking cowboy could be such a jerk," he admitted with a smile.

His eyes shone like dew drops on sheet metal. Stanley laughed again and strummed his guitar. He looked up, surprised when Ace handed him a tape.

"It's the tape she likes to exercise to. When you take a break, throw it in the stereo. She can't help but get moving."

"What if she decides to exercise between now and then?"

"Do I look stupid?" Ace demanded his tone and expression indignant. "I made a copy," he admitted, with a sly grin.

Stan shook his head. "You are bad to the bone, Ace Harris."

"Clever," Ace countered. "Ingenious, determined."

"Sneaky, underhanded," Stan insisted, then grinned. "Brilliant. I'll try and come up with plan B in case this doesn't work."

* * * * *

The day of the rodeo dawned bright, clear, and hot. Huge, white, puffy clouds floated lazily across a flawless summer sky the same color of Stanley's eyes. Lexie sat with Amber and Craig watching the events. She'd never had so much fun at a rodeo before and was amazed at how children as young as the twins could do so much. She was equally impressed that the proceeds, including a large portion of those made from the sale of animals, were going to charity, several different ones both local and national. The older competitors forfeited prizes which added to the amount of money to be donated. So far, Stanley had shown and sold several horses and the twins had competed and won in barrels and poles. Craig had exhibited the Cutting event and sold several horses as a result. Ace was due to exhibit the bull riding competition, which was the last event of the day. The crowd quieted when Stanley tuned his guitar for the third time that day. In between showing horses and helping Amber with the children, he'd entertained the guests.

Stan racked his brain on what to sing next. He'd already performed every rodeo song he ever heard as well as a variety of entertaining tunes. As luck would have it, he still hadn't come up with plan B to get Lexie up on the stage. He'd put her exercise music tape in the stereo earlier and watched her glare and shake a fist at Ace, who merely grinned. Not even half a song played before the crowd began to murmur. He switched the tape to a Country collection of greatest hits to appease the patrons. With sudden insight he realized that there was no way he'd ever coax Lexie to sing, he'd have to force her, challenge her. He grinned to himself and turned on the mike.

"May I have your attention please?" He continued when he had the crowd's undivided attention. "We have a very special guest in our audience today and I'd like to invite her up to help me out."

He glanced over, saw the vehement shake of her head, and grinned. "Now some of you old timers may remember Dr. Scott Hensley? Well, Lexie is his daughter," he announced to the various murmurs of agreement. "Looks like she needs a little encouragement, come on folks, put your hands together and welcome Miss Lexie Hensley."

Lexie buried her head in her lap. "I'm gonna kill him, Amber." She glared at her friend when Amber laughed. Her gaze was invariably drawn across the arena where Ace watched her. Catching his eye, she flushed when he grinned and lifted a challenging brow at her. She turned to Amber in an angry whirl.

"Him too, Amber, your brother with that smug, cocky grin and arrogant, challenging lift to his brow. I'm going to kill them both," she muttered, as the crowd began to earnestly cheer for her appearance. Hearing a chuckle, she turned to face Craig and knew instantly where Ace got that look.

"Make that all three of them, Amber. After today, William will be the only man left in this family to put up with," she huffed, and bolted from the stands to stomp toward the stage.

"Go girl! Show 'em up Lexie!" Amber called after her.

She stormed up on the stage and glared down at Stanley who was grinning like the proverbial cat that ate the canary. "If your wife wasn't my best friend and you didn't have three little babies to support I'd cut your heart out with a hoof pick!"

Stanley chuckled. "You heard it folks, if it weren't for my family, she'd cut my heart out with a hoof pick. Ouch," he remarked and placed his hand over his heart, his expression solemn. A voice from the crowd drew his attention. "And that lovely voice yelling 'don't let that stop you,' is my beautiful wife. I love you too, My Sweet."

The crowd roared.

Tossing her a challenging grin, he urged Lexie to accompany him on the harmonica.

"I don't have my harmonica," she insisted.

With an insolent look similar to that of his father and brother-in-law, Stanley pulled the item in question out of his pocket. "Any more excuses?"

"You are dead meat buster," she muttered and jerked it out of his grasp. It wasn't long before she got into the spirit of things. Her first solo was "I Want to be a Cowboy's Sweetheart" after which, she switched to her own favorite female artists. Strong songs about tough women with passionate ideas of what relationships should be about. She ended her performance with a rendition of Shania Twains "If You're Not In It For Love." She breathed the last line... "I'm outta here...," and stomped off the stage with a sigh. Without a single glance back, she tossed the microphone over her shoulder. She turned in time to see Stanley catch the object as though they'd practiced the move a thousand times, but there was no way he could have rehearsed the surprised expression on his face. With a laugh, he turned back to the crowd.

"Well folks, I guess she's outta here."

The crowd went wild.

Lexie couldn't ignore, or deny, their fevered cry for more. She returned to the stage and accompanied Stanley in a duet, a love song so sweet, so poignant it softened the hardest of hearts and left not a dry eye in the audience.

Stanley gazed into the emerald eyes which glittered with emotion and winked. He rose from his seat, took her hand in his, brought it to his lips, and faced the crowd while they took their bows. He then announced that Ace would exhibit the bull riding event next while Lexie left the stage. He followed not far behind her. Amber met him at the edge of the stands.

"Mighty powerful emotion up there," she commented.

"Jealous, My Sweet?" he queried with a grin.

The warmth in his gaze could have melted a glacier. "Should I be?" she asked.

He chuckled and brushed his lips across hers. "A little bit of jealousy never hurt anyone as long as it's a fleeting emotion and not a deep-seated fear. I love you," he whispered.

They climbed up beside Lexie and Craig as the chute opened and Ace clung to the back of a thousand pounds of madness. Lexie watched her expression one of horror and fear when the bull lunged and twisted in an attempt to dislodge its unwelcome rider. With a tiny shriek of terror, she buried her face in her lap.

Arm high, spurs digging into the animal, Ace rode like he competed for a championship. The horn sounded. He hung on until a rider on horseback provided his escape. He slid off the back of the horse and waved to his family. An angry snort got his attention. He lunged for the fence and climbed quickly out of the bull's reach. With a confident chuckle, he jumped over the fence and strode to the stands only to be met by the blistering gaze of his father.

"If I ever catch you in the bull ring again, I will beat you within an inch of your miserable life," Craig barked. The muscle in his jaw twitched furiously.

Ace laughed and slapped his father on the back. "All part of the show, Daddy."

He turned, disappointed to find Lexie sitting with her head down. With a wink at his sister, he climbed up beside her. "Great show, Lex."

"You!" she glared at him. "You are insane!"

He chortled. "I'm fine. Look," he offered and held his arms wide in a gesture of supplication. "Take a walk?" he offered her his hand.

She slapped at it. "Don't touch me you maniac!" Her heart still hadn't returned to normal.

She was as pale as death, Ace noted. He jumped off the bleachers and lifted her down by the waist despite her protests. "Lex, I'm fine. Walk with me."

"Physically maybe," she hissed. "Mentally I doubt it."

He looked down into her flashing gaze and saw the anger there, and the fear. Fear for him which meant love. He was reminded of another who had looked at him with that same mixture of emotions in her sapphire gaze, and felt a stab of guilt and remorse. In that instance he knew he loved Lexie, completely. He'd never have to ask again. He held out his hand and waited for her to put hers in it.

Lexie watched the flare of emotions in Ace's glittering gaze and swallowed the lump in her throat. A tender light lit his eyes. He was really okay. He stood there in front of her, waiting for her to agree to a walk. With a sigh, she placed a trembling hand in his and felt the strength of his grip. Her heart leapt into her throat when he clasped it firmly, pulled her close, and pressed his lips to it. He breathed her name then glanced around and she could tell he fought the urge to kiss her. He kept her hand in his, turned away from the crowd, and they walked to the house that had once been Scott's family home. In quiet tones, he spoke in fluent Spanish to the woman in charge of cooking and cleaning at the Bed and Breakfast. She smiled at Lexie, pointed to the coffee and fresh tea and then left them alone. She smiled back then turned to Ace while he poured them a glass of tea.

"It's amazing that this used to be Scott's home. I can picture him here, you know? I don't understand how someone could leave a home so beautiful."

Ace shrugged. "Sometimes life has a way of changing everything. If he hadn't left, he wouldn't have met Trina. Or you."

Tell me about it, Lexie thought. "True, I guess," she admitted in a quiet tone. She took a deep breath and geared herself up for the conversation she knew had to come. She'd read more than she expected to, in Ace's eyes. She'd seen love there and she knew the time had come for her to tell him about her past. She loved him and hoped what she saw in his gaze just moments ago would be strong enough to withstand the truth. Before he could corner her for the kiss he'd refrained from earlier, she moved out of his reach. "I need to tell you something," she admitted.

Unable to sit still and face him, Lexie paced around the room while she bared her soul. With eyes wide and aching with unshed tears and hands that trembled, she turned to face the anger which blazed in his eyes and caused the muscle in his jaw to pulsate. She'd never felt so vulnerable in her life.

Nor had she looked it.

The prickle of fear that danced down his spine at her tone of voice had quickly evolved to horror then rage while she told her story. Ace knew his response would make a world of difference in their lives. He also knew she wouldn't have said a word about this if she didn't love him. "Did your father kill him?"

She shook her head.

"Did Scott?"

"No," she admitted with a hint of a smile.

"Guess it's up to me to do it. Where is he?"

"I didn't tell you so that you could defend my honor, Ace."

"Why then?" He had to know. At that moment he loved her more than ever and he had to know if she felt the same.

"Because I," she flushed and hesitated, still afraid to admit her love. "Because I care about you, a lot, and I couldn't think of continuing a relationship with you unless, until, you knew the truth."

He looked at her for a long, tense, moment before he asked the one question that would haunt him for all eternity if he didn't voice it aloud. "There's never been anyone else?" Though her eyes had strayed often from his while she told her story, they remained steadfast, open and honest, when she answered.

"No, never."

"There'll never be another," he muttered, and then lurched from his chair to cup her face in his hands.

She stopped his kiss with a firm hand against his chest. "I've never wanted to," she admitted. Her eyes searched his. "Until now."

Desire shuddered through him. His lips crushed hers in a hungry caress. "Me neither," he admitted huskily then swallowed her little purr of delight.

"I love you," she whispered.

Her voice was tremulous. Her eyes glittered like firelight off the surface of a smooth, flawless emerald. Ace cocked his head with a grin. A chuckle underlined his words,

"What did you just say, you love me? Maybe that bull did get to me after all because I must surely be hearing things."

A little sound of joy bubbled from her in irrepressible laughter. "I love you, you chauvinistic jerk cowboy," she insisted.

"And I love you," he answered then captured her lips in an endless kiss. Sheer force of will stopped him from sliding with her to the floor then and there. "I want you," he muttered, and caressed her gently when she stiffened in his arms. "Not here, and not like this," he insisted. "But I want to know if the rest of you feels as soft as the skin I can touch or tastes as sweet as your lips."

A hot flush rushed to her cheeks. "I made a vow to myself and to God that I would remain pure until I got married. I know that may sound crazy, but it's the way I feel."

Her admission thrilled him and convinced him there'd been no other man after the one who took advantage of her. Ace indulged in one more kiss then they returned to the rodeo. One look and he could tell the whole family noticed the difference in them. His father was quick to pull him aside and question where they'd been and what they'd been up to. Unable to hide his feelings, nor wanting to, Ace took a walk with him and confided in him of their talk.

"I love her," he admitted and noted the satisfied smirk on his father's face.

"How do you know?" Craig asked with a grin.

"I'm not asking am I?" Ace insisted.

Craig laughed and slapped him on the back. "Just mind yourself young man. That's my best friend's daughter and I'd hate to have to castrate my own son."

Chapter Nineteen

Ace rode the fence line, his mind as usual on something besides work, someone really. In the days since the rodeo, his relationship with Lexie developed steadily. Deeper. Hotter. The memory of that afternoon and evening made his blood boil like never before. He'd never forget the look on her face or the sound of her voice when she said she loved him. He wanted her more with every waking breath. From the moment he left in the morning until he saw her again, she occupied his thoughts. And at night she graced his dreams. He wanted to ask her to marry him, but felt he should talk with her father first. Scott, Trina and the boys were due in over the weekend. He could hardly wait.

Scott, on the other hand, was not looking forward to the weekend at all. He knew from the sound of his daughter's voice, and wife's secretive smile, that she probably would not be coming home with them. The knowledge filled him with a mixture of joy and trepidation. He loved Ace and couldn't think of a better son-in-law, but he wasn't ready to give her up yet. He knew it was selfish of him, but that was a father's prerogative. He remembered the way Craig had fought against Amber's love for Stanley and vowed to try really hard not to be as irrational.

* * * * *

Craig and Stanley watched from the fence while Ace tried to temper the stallion brought in from the herd several weeks ago. He was a magnificent specimen of horseflesh, wild and untamed, rich in color, solid in build, sleek and stately, with incredibly strong bloodlines. Ace had seen the colt born, watched him grow over the past two years, and determined that he would be his next champion stud.

But the horse refused to be tamed. Even Stanley's subtle, gentle approach hadn't worked. The most success he'd had was to get a halter on the animal. Not cruel, but determined, Ace worked hard to get the horse to submit, but it looked as though theirs would be a battle of wills to the end.

He snapped a pair of reins to the halter, pulled them tight and tried to mount the agitated animal. The instant he threw his leg over the horse's back, it jerked and swerved away from him. Just as quickly, he turned then kicked out. Ace ducked, dropped and rolled away from the dangerous hooves but before he could regain his feet, the horse reared and attacked him with angry forefeet.

"Oh, God!" Craig jumped the fence and headed toward the horse with Stanley on his heels. Dodging hooves, he knelt at his son's head while Stanley shooed the horse away from them.

"Ace," Craig fought not to move him. "Jesus, Ace! C'mon," he insisted. "Don't let a horse do to you what a bull couldn't," he urged. "I swear, I'll shoot him," he muttered.

"No," Ace rasped, though he barely remained conscious. "Don't shoot him," he mumbled before the world went black.

"Call an ambulance!" Craig called to Lexie as she ran toward them.

"One's already on the way."

"Stay out, Lex," Stanley warned, careful to keep his voice low so as not to frighten or agitate the already enraged horse. "This horse is crazy mad. I warned Ace not to rush him."

The air filled with thick, tense, wary, silence while they waited for the ambulance to arrive. Stanley stood between the horse and the people and kept up a soothing whisper to the animal in an attempt to keep him still, if not calm, while they loaded Ace onto a stretcher and took him out of the corral. When everyone was gone Stanley opened his arms in a gesture of acquiescence to the animal.

"Easy, Boy," he spoke softly. The animal watched him, wary-eyed. Stanley reached for the reins. "Easy now, I'm just gonna get this off of you." He grasped the leather straps gently and walked forward while the horse pawed the ground in nervous agitation. In one swift movement he unsnapped the reins and stepped out of the horses' way as it thundered past him with an angry whinny. He left the ranch, picked up Amber and the kids, and hurried to the hospital.

Craig and Stan paced the floor while Amber and Lexie tried to keep the kids quiet and occupied. The clock ticked slowly by...one hour, two. Worried and agitated, Craig glared at the doctor when he finally made his appearance.

He shook his head wearily. "I don't know. He's out. There doesn't seem to be much damage, but we won't know for sure until he wakes up."

"When?" Craig demanded.

"I don't know, hours, days."

"What kind of damn fool answer is that?" Craig demanded.

"Daddy," Amber's voice held soft warning.

The doctor shrugged. "We've got him in a room. He's got a concussion for sure and he's unconscious. That's all I can tell you other than the fact that from all the tests we've run, there doesn't seem to be any real damage, yet. We'll have to keep a close eye on him."

"I want him in a private room where I can stay with him," Craig insisted and walked toward the door. He turned to the doctor. "Where is he? I want to see him. Now."

They followed the doctor while he explained what to do, what to expect, and what to watch for in terms of Ace waking up. "Talk to him, bring him some music, and pray," he advised.

Craig's face paled at the sight of his son lying unconscious in the bed. Except for the angry, bruised knot on his forehead, he appeared to be asleep. They heard Lexie gasp and watched her flee from the room.

Lexie collapsed outside the door, thankful there was a wall there to hold her up. She knew people woke up from coma's every day. She also knew that sometimes they didn't. Tears streamed down her cheeks and she began to plead with God for his life.

Amber walked to the bed and looked down into her brother's face, so boyishly angelic, and smiled. She brushed her fingers through his hair and spoke. "We're here, Brat. Someone will be here with you until you find your way back. Hurry now. Wake up," she insisted. She turned to her father. "I'll bring you some things back later."

Craig nodded mutely and took her place by the bed after they all took turns talking to Ace and urging him to wake up. Before she left with Amber and Stan, Lexie walked back into the room, whispered to Ace and kissed him on the cheek.

The ride home was quiet. Even the twins were subdued. Stanley dropped Amber and Lexie off at the ranch and then went home to start supper. They would follow in Craig's truck after Amber gathered some items for her father.

Lexie wandered aimlessly around the house while Amber got a change of clothes for her father and a few things for Ace. Stan had spoken to the ranch foreman before he left with the children. She found herself in the den, sat at the piano, and began to play.

Amber walked down the stairs toward the den where Lexie played and sang. Midway through the song, she collapsed in a crumpled heap. Her shoulders shook and sobs tore from her in painful torrents. Amber hurried over to her. "He's going to be all right, Lexie," she soothed, rocking her.

"God I hope so, Amber. I love him so much," she sobbed.

"Just wait. You'll see. Before you know it, he'll be hanging around all day and harassing you. Or wait till you've been married a while and find out that you're pregnant and he starts bossing you around. Then you'll be ready to strangle him again."

"Oh, Amber," she sighed. "I pray I have that chance."

"You will," Amber promised, and brushed the hair off her face. "And you'll come to the house, too. No sense for you to stay here all alone."

"I don't want to impose."

"If it were an imposition I wouldn't ask. Family doesn't impose on family," Amber chided, settling the matter.

Later that evening, Amber brought her father his clothes. "Here's a tape player and some of Ace's favorite tapes," she said, and set the items up on the bedside table. She sat with them a while and talked with her father and to her brother. "I'll be here in the morning to relieve you, Daddy," she promised and then kissed him good-bye.

Craig didn't bother to inform her that he wasn't about to leave until his son woke up. He just kissed her cheek, admonished her to be careful and to call him the minute she got home, then settled in for the first in what would be a long string of sleepless nights.

* * * * *

Stanley sighed in relief to finally be home. He'd been with the foreman at the Rockin' H handling a host of problems. His relief was short lived when he walked in and found both girls sitting silently in a chair on either side of the kitchen. Ashlyn held ice to her face while Kaitlyn glared stubbornly at the door. He took one look around and turned to Lexie. "What's going on?"

She arched an eyebrow at Kaitlyn when the child slid out of her chair. "Did I say you could get up?"

"My daddy's here now," she spouted, her chin lifted in defiance.

"Kaitlyn..."

The thread of steel in her father's voice halted Kaitlyn's movements.

Stanley nodded at his daughter and waited for Lexie to fill him in on the situation. He watched with a worried frown when she began to tremble.

"I warned Kaitlyn several times to stop jumping off the couch before someone got hurt. She wouldn't listen and it happened. She bumped into Ashlyn who hit her cheek on the table."

"Is that true?" Stanley asked his daughter. Her lip trembled but she nodded. "Go to your room, Kaitlyn, I'll be in to talk to you in a minute."

He walked over to Ashlyn and removed the ice pack from her face. A tiny bruise marred her silky cheek. "You okay, Sweetheart?" She nodded and accepted her father's embrace.

"I'm sorry," Lexie whispered through clenched teeth when Stanley stood to go to his other daughter.

He turned to her. "I don't have a problem with you disciplining them, Lexie," he assured her. Tears filled her eyes. He decided Kaitlyn could wait and took her in his arms instead.

"It's okay to cry, Lex," he urged, and stroked her back in a gentle caress as tears began to slide effortlessly from the weary gaze.

"I've called Scott. He'll drive up and get me this weekend. I can't do this anymore."

"I'm sorry we've put so much on you." At that moment he determined Amber would come home that night.

She shook her head in quick denial. "It's not that. I love to watch the children. I just can't stay here anymore not knowing when or if he'll wake up."

"Will it be any easier away from here?" he asked, his tone gentle.

She shrugged, "Probably not. But at least I'll be with my family. I mean...."

"I know what you mean. It's okay to miss your father, mother and brothers," Stan assured his voice soft, smile tender.

"I really love you, you know," she informed him. "All of you. You're like the big brother I always wanted."

"Same goes here, Kiddo. The minute I laid eyes on you I thought, 'this fiery haired wench could have been born into my family'."

He brushed the hair off her face then kissed her on the cheek. "Now let me go take care of my daughter." He went to the twins' room where he found Kaitlyn curled up on her bed her face buried in the pillow where she sobbed her little heart out.

"Kaitlyn?" He took her in his arms.

"Is Uncle Ace going to go meet MaMaw in heaven?"

Stan's heart twisted in his chest. "I hope not, Sweetheart. Kaitlyn, you know why I sent you to your room, don't you?"

She nodded into his chest. "Cause I hurt Ashlyn and was bad for Miss Lexie."

"Right, and what do you think I should do about it?"

"Punish me," she admitted.

Her lips trembled. Tears clung to her thick lashes and clouded the beloved sapphire gaze. "Maybe so," he agreed. "But I think if you apologize to both your sister and Miss Lexie, and promise to behave, I can overlook it. This time."

"I promise, Daddy," she said and wrapped her little arms around his neck.

Stan hugged her for all he was worth and whispered his love and forgiveness. He watched with a father's pride as she marched into the kitchen, kissed her sister's bruised cheek and apologized, then turned an imploring gaze at Lexie.

"I sorry, Miss Lexie."

Lexie opened her arms to the little girl. "Thank you, Kaitlyn. I know you're not a bad girl," she assured her, when Kaitlyn flung herself in them.

Stan left the house and headed for the hospital for the second time that day, determined it would be the last time for a while, the ride even more stressful after an afternoon of confrontations.

One day had slipped into two, then three, and agonizingly into ten. Ten days, and still no change in Ace. He just laid there. Doctors and specialists had run every test in the book and found no medical reason why he hadn't woke up yet. And everyone was at their wits end.

At first it hadn't been too bad. Amber started off by just going during the day. But as the days slid one into another, she began to stay longer and longer until the only time Stanley saw her or his son was at the hospital in the evenings. Deciding it wasn't good for William to be cooped up in his infant seat all day, he took him home to Lexie and toted bottles of breast milk back and forth from the hospital to the house. Well, enough was enough, he thought with a weary sigh. Whether Amber liked it or not, she was coming home with him tonight.

Lately, it got to where he didn't know what to expect anymore when he got to the hospital. What he didn't expect was to find Amber and her father locked in a clash of wills over the very same issue. He listened for a moment as she admonished Craig about how unhealthy it was to stay by his son's bedside day in and day out. He saw the muscle in Craig's jaw begin to twitch and his eyes narrow into tiny slits of steel.

* * * * *

Some say the comatose walk between two worlds. Ace would attest to that if only he could find his way back to where they were. In the time he'd been away, he'd heard them talk to him and plead with him to wake up. He had heard Scott's voice as he talked with his father, and tried desperately to reach out to them. He wanted to speak with Scott, though for the life of him, he couldn't remember why. He only knew that it was important. But he hadn't made it, nor had he heard any voice other than his father, sister, and Stanley, in quite some time.

He'd also spent a few precious moments with his mother. She sat by his bed, talked to him, and urged him to return to the living. He'd begged to go with her. She shook her head, a serene smile on her face and brushed her fingers through his hair.

"No, Ace. Go back. You have a long life ahead of you. And love now."

"There's no life or love without you, Mama," he insisted and reached for her. But she was gone.

He hadn't seen her again, or heard her voice. He'd only heard the others. If only he could find his way back... Maybe then they would stop fighting over him. He struggled through the thick, gray, fog of unconsciousness when his brother-in-law's voice joined his father and sister's.

* * * * *

Stanley stepped forward and addressed his wife. "Enough Amber, you can't dictate your father's life like this," he said, and had her anger turned on him. He stopped the torrent of angry words with a gentle shake of his head and single, soft command. "Don't."

She brushed by him in an angry huff.

"She needs to go home," Craig growled.

Stan walked to his father-in-law. "She is. Whether she likes it or not, she's going home tonight. But, she's right you know. It wouldn't hurt for you to get out of here for a while, an hour, or two at the most. Have a hot shower, decent meal. I'll stay until you get back. Think about it," he urged. Before Craig could utter the first angry denial, he turned toward the door.

"Now I'm going to face the tongue lashing I'm sure awaits me right outside that door." He heard Craig's weary chuckle and smiled to himself.

Before Stanley could settle himself in the chair beside hers, Amber turned on him. "I'm not trying to dictate my father's life. I'm trying to save it," she hissed.

Her eyes narrowed into icy shards of sapphire. Stanley nodded. "I know that, My Sweet. I want you to come home tonight."

"I can't leave him," she insisted.

"I'm not asking, Amber," he told her, his tone gentle but firm. "Don't make me pull rank on you."

"As if you could," she muttered, surprised when he put a firm hand on her arm. She turned on him in an angry whirl, only to be brought up short by the hurt in his eyes.

"My father needs me," she insisted in a lame effort to save face.

"Your children need you. I need you. And Lexie needs a break. The kids are at each other's throats, William is probably more used to the bottle than the breast, Lexie's called Scott to come and take her home." He watched with concern when tears of fatigue and frustration filled her eyes and she pressed trembling fingers to them.

He pulled her against him and kissed her dark head. "You can't be everything to everyone, Amber. I know your father needs you, but so do we."

He held her tenderly when she began to sob into his chest. After the sobs turned to soft, hiccupping sounds, he pulled her up from the chair and into his arms. "Let's go."

Amber leaned against him and let him lead her back to her brother's room. With an imploring look at her father, she walked toward him. "Drive me home, Daddy," she pleaded softly.

"Would you mind?" she asked her husband glad when he shook his head.

"I said earlier that I wouldn't," Stanley assured with a pointed look at Craig.

Craig emitted a weary sigh and raked his fingers through his hair. He knew the only way he'd get them off his case would be to leave. "Okay," he agreed his tone sour. "But only for a while."

Stan nodded. Amber sighed with relief. She smiled weakly at her husband already regretting the harsh words between them. "We'll probably stop at the Chapel on the way out."

He nodded, kissed her cheek, and heaved a sigh of relief when the door closed behind them. He walked over to the bed and gazed down at his brother-in-law. "All right, Ace," he muttered on a sudden surge of anger. "Enough is enough. It's time for you to quit lollygagging around in La La Land and snap out of it." He snapped his fingers for emphasis.

I'm trying Stanley, keep talking; Ace pleaded silently and struggled through the fog toward the sound of his voice. For the first time in his long journey away, he began to pray for God to guide him back.

"Everyone's at each other's throats," Stanley continued. "The twins are fighting. Your father and Amber are fighting. Lexie's ready to go home."

No! Ace struggled harder and listened to the sound of Stanley's voice, following it, searching for him. God, please! Suddenly his mother appeared and urged him onward, through the fog to awareness.

Stanley walked over to the window and gazed out. "It's a beautiful night, Ace," he kept talking, hoping somehow to reach his brother-in-law and draw him back to the land of the living. "A billion stars on the backdrop of a cloudless, midnight sky. A huge lover's moon. A night to be curled up with your best girl Ace, not laid up in nowhere land."

He turned when the monitors that gauged Ace's heart rate and brainwave activity began to beep erratically. His heart thundered in his chest when his brother-in-law's eye lids began to flutter and his muscles began to twitch. He rang for the nurse. "Something's happening."

"We heard. Doctor's on his way."

"Ace can you hear me? C'mon, Ace, pull out of it," Stan urged then moved aside when the doctor rushed in the room and began to check Ace's pupils.

"Keep talking," the doctor urged. "He's responding."

Stanley did what the doctor said, he urged, coaxed, and pleaded with Ace to wake up.

* * * * *

Amber knelt in front of the tiny alter in the small hospital Chapel. She knew her father occupied the pew nearest to the door. She closed her eyes and although her shoulders shook with silent sobs, she began to pray. "Lord, I know I questioned You when Mama died, but I accepted Your will. Please God, we can't keep going like this. I'm asking You for a sign. Whatever Your will, just give us a sign."

Craig watched his daughter and knew without a doubt, she knelt there and pleaded with God for her brother's life. He felt the sharp stab of anger in the region of his heart. *Why, God? First my wife, now my son! Why? What have I done?*

His heart cried out in frustrated fury. For the second time in his life, he heard the very audible voice of God call his name.

What, God? What do You want from me now? I'll do anything, just don't take my son too!

Craig knew you couldn't argue with God, or bargain with Him, but at that point he was ready to do either, or both, whatever it took, to assure his son's survival.

"I've told you before Craig, the only thing you can give me is your whole heart and your trust. I love you and want to comfort you, yet you've been angry at me for so long."

The truth struck like a shaft of hot iron, branding his heart. He'd been angry at God since the day his wife died. Not once had he thanked Him for the blessings that continued to pour into his life.

"I'm sorry," he whispered his voice hoarse, thick with regret and apology. He felt Amber's arms go around him. For once Craig let himself lean on his daughter. Sobs began to shake his huge frame. "I've been so wrong against God and you. Now look what's happened."

"It's going to be all right, Daddy," she whispered. "I just know he'll pull through. You know God doesn't punish us. Ace chose to rush that horse, that's what happened. God didn't do it. I love you, Daddy."

The peace of God seeped in, filling, healing, and overflowing. They looked at each other in surprise when their names were called over the intercom to return to Ace's room.

* * * * *

Stan prayed Amber and her father hadn't left the hospital. The doctor still worked with Ace, but it was evident he was coming out of the coma.

"C'mon," he heard the doctor say. "It's time you return to the land of the living."

Stan pushed past him, "Ace? C'mon Sport," he urged.

Ace looked back at his mother and hesitated. "Mama?"

"No Ace, go back and give them my love," she said with a smile.

She then blew him a kiss, turned away, and disappeared. Ace took a deep breath and stepped through the fog into the light of consciousness. "Stan," he rasped. "They're not fighting."

"Who, what's he talking about?" The doctor asked.

Stan looked at him. "His father and sister were arguing earlier."

"Do you remember? Did you hear them?" the doctor questioned Ace. Ace nodded, sighed heavily, and closed his eyes. *So good to be back.* At least he thought he was back. But he was exhausted. He stirred when his father rushed into the room.

"What's wrong?" Craig asked.

"I believe he's come back," the doctor answered.

Craig sat on the bed, afraid to hope. "Ace?" he queried.

Ace looked up into the worried gaze. "Hey, Daddy," he rasped.

"Oh, God, Thank You! Thank You, God!" Craig pulled his son in his arms and huge, heaving sobs of relief shook him.

Amber knelt by the bed, bowed her head, and thanked God that her brother was awake.

After the initial wave of relief passed, Craig laid his son back against the pillows. "Ace, can you hear me?" he asked, and brushed a lock of thick, blond, hair off his son's brow.

Ace nodded. "Yeah, I can hear you. I've heard you all along. All of you. I just couldn't find my way back to you. It's like I was lost in this thick, gray, fog. I could hear you but not see you. Where's Lexie?"

"She's with the kids," Amber informed him, then hugged him to her breast. "We're headed that way now."

He nodded. "How long have I been out?"

"Ten days," his sister informed him.

"I'm not about to leave now," Craig insisted, afraid if he left, Ace might slip away from him again.

Ace opened his eyes. His father looked as though he'd aged ten years in the past ten days. "Go on, Daddy; take her home like you promised. Bring Lexie back with you later."

His father reluctantly agreed to leave, and promised to be back in a couple of hours.

"Will you call Lexie for me?" Ace asked his brother-in-law once his father and sister left.

Stan dialed the number. When the phone rang, he placed it by Ace's ear.

"Lexie?" Ace flinched then grinned at her shriek.

"Ace, you're awake! He's awake!" she informed the twins, who came running at her excited cry. "Oh, thank God!" She began to sob.

Ace smiled into the receiver. "Yeah, I'm awake. Let me talk to them," he responded to the twins fevered cries. "I love you girls," he whispered, thrilled to hear their excited, little girl chatter. When Lexie got back on the phone, he urged her to come back with his father.

Stan hung up the phone and sat beside Ace on the bed.

"Daddy didn't shoot my horse, did he?"

Stanley shook his head. "No. I've been working with him, Ace, but it's going to take time."

"Don't break him."

"What?"

"I've decided that I don't want to break him. Just get him tame enough to be around people and run through his paces. I'll stud him out. Anyone who's interested and knows horseflesh will be able to tell he's one-hundred percent quality."

Stan nodded his approval. "That's the second best thing I've heard all day, the first being your voice." Cupping his head in his hand, he rested his forehead against Ace's.

"Welcome back, Sport," he whispered, his voice husky with emotion.

"Good to be back," Ace assured him.

Chapter Twenty

Amber and Craig arrived to find the twins excited, their chatter unabated while they colored pictures for Ace. "Mommy! Mommy!"

"PaPaw! PaPaw! Uncle Ace is awake!"

"We know," Craig answered relief evident in his voice. He hugged them and turned to Lexie. "I have strict orders not to return without you." She flushed. Her eyes sparkled.

"I wouldn't dare let you go back without me."

Amber hugged her daughters and took her son from Lexie's arms. "Thank you, Lexie, for all you've done. I apologize for leaving you so much. I know it's a lot to handle."

Lexie hugged her. "Don't worry about it. I'm glad I was able to help."

"I love you," Amber whispered through her tears, tears of fatigue, tears of joy and relief.

"I love you too, Amber." She looked at Craig. "And you."

He pulled her against his chest, "Same here, Sweetheart. How long will it take for you to get ready to go?"

She shook her head. "I'm ready when you are."

"Daddy, you promised to rest a little. And eat."

Craig hugged his daughter. "And I will. We're going to the ranch so I can check on things there. I'll get a shower and..."

"I'll fix you something to eat while you do all you need to do," Lexie interrupted.

Craig nodded. "See, just as I promised."

"Okay," Amber agreed. She had hoped he would rest a while longer than that. Too tired to argue, she walked with them to the door, and waited until they were on their way before she turned back to her children. She placed William in his baby bouncer then pulled the girls in her arms and hugged them to her breast. By the time Stanley got home things were close to normal. She met him at the door.

"How's everything over here?" he asked.

She attempted a smile, her lips trembled instead, and she swallowed the hard knot of emotion in her throat. "Okay. The girls are still awake. They wanted to wait for you to kiss them goodnight. William has been nursed and bathed. He's playing in his bed."

She took a step closer, her eyes searched his. "I'm sorry, Stanley for leaving you to shoulder all of this alone." His smile was tender as was the light in his eyes.

"That's okay, My Sweet, I've got wide shoulders."

She smiled at the familiar joke. "You have beautiful shoulders. But that's not the point. I should have been here for you and the children."

Stan pulled her in his arms. "You're forgiven, Amber. It's all over now. He's awake and he's going to be fine," he soothed when she began to weep softly into his chest.

Amber dried her eyes and brushed her lips across his. "Thank you. Go and kiss your daughters goodnight. I have a hot bath ready for you."

Stanley sank gratefully into the hot tub of water. With a sigh, he surrendered to her tender administrations as she scrubbed his back and massaged his shoulders in little acts of service and submission that he knew were meant to bolster her apology. Though appreciated, he didn't like it. Her apology was enough.

When she left to turn back the bedcovers, he quickly dried off and wrapped the towel around his waist. He walked into the bedroom and pulled her in his arms. "You've apologized enough, Amber. Now come here," he whispered his voice husky.

His lips covered hers in a tender caress. He knew how tired she was and had no intentions of making love with her, but she clung to him so sweetly. Need swept through them, so powerful it demanded to be assuaged.

Lifting her onto the bed, he assured her of his love and forgiveness in the best way he knew how. He lay in her arms, trembling in the aftermath, and brushed feathery kisses across her face to dry the tears off her cheeks. "Why the tears, My Sweet?"

"Because I love you, and am so blessed to have you as a husband. I never intend to hurt you, Stanley, and when I realize I have, it tears at my heart."

"That's what I love about you the most, My Sweet, your unbiased passion for everyone and everything you love. I know sometimes your loyalty between the family you were born into and the one you have now is strained to the limit. It's only when I see the scale tip in one direction over the other, that I'm forced to speak up. I know it's never intentional. I love you, Amber," he assured his voice soft and husky.

"I love you too," she whispered. She snuggled deeper into his arms and let the warmth and strength of his love lull her into a sound sleep.

* * * * *

Though Lexie had called them when Ace woke up, Scott drove in for the weekend anyway. He wanted to see Ace for himself, to look at his chart. And he wanted to be assured of his daughter's wellbeing. He shouldn't have worried, she was ecstatic, in love, and it showed—in the sparkle in her eyes and the constant flush on her cheeks. He was visiting with Ace when she arrived at the hospital looking lovely as ever.

"Hi!" She kissed him, then Ace, on the cheek.

Scott continued his conversation once she settled on the bed beside Ace. "As I was saying Ace, your test results are remarkable. There are some things you may have to get the hang of again, walking, riding, but other than that, complete recovery is imminent."

"What about kissing? Think I'll have to get the hang of that again?" he queried.

His eyes danced like dew drops on sheet metal. Scott chuckled. "I don't know about kissing."

"Kiss me, Lexie," Ace insisted and pulled her toward him. "Call it therapy."

She flushed sweetly when his lips covered hers in a tender caress. Ace glanced over at Scott after he released her. "I'm not the only one who'll need to get the hang of things, Scott. You'd better start to practice walking your daughter down the aisle."

"You call that a proposal, Cowboy?" Lexie asked before Scott could respond.

"Not really, just assuring your father of my intentions."

Scott frowned over at him. "Tell you what," he remarked and rose from his seat. "When you can get out of bed and down on one knee to propose properly, we'll discuss the possibility of me walking my daughter down the aisle." He held out his hand and waited for Lexie to take it.

Lexie took her father's hand and winked at Ace. "Guess we'll see you later."

"Okay."

The door had barely closed behind them when she hesitated. "I'll be right back," she insisted, and turned back into the room. She walked over to the bed and knelt over Ace then cupped his face in her hands and brushed her lips across his.

"Yes," she whispered. "The answer is yes, Cowboy," she assured, and buried her lips on his, forcing him to swallow a triumphant little chuckle. After the kiss, she didn't wait for a reply, but turned on her heel and marched out.

Scott eyed her, his eyebrow arched in an elaborate gesture. "You told him yes, didn't you?" She flushed, slipped her arm through his, and nodded. "I'm sure your mother will be thrilled," he muttered.

"Aren't you thrilled?"

"A father is not supposed to be thrilled when his little girl grows up and falls in love."

She turned and put her arms around his waist. "But your little girl was half-grown when you got her," she reminded in a gentle, teasing tone.

"All the more reason not to be thrilled," he mumbled, then grinned when she threw back her head and laughed.

"I want to go home with you tomorrow, Scott."

"For awhile I hope."

She shrugged. "Long enough to pack up my room," she teased, then giggled at his grunt of disappointment.

* * * * *

Ace glared at his father and Stanley when they finally made their appearance later that morning. "Get me into some clothes and out of this bed," he insisted.

"Whoa, take it easy. Shouldn't you make sure everything works okay before you're in such a hurry to get up?" His father asked.

He looked down in disgust at the hospital gown which did absolutely nothing to cover his large frame, especially the part of him that responded to Lexie's kiss. He felt an agonizing pull just thinking about that kiss. "Trust me, everything works," he muttered, and then swung his legs over the side of the bed.

"What's the rush, Ace?"

"Scott said when I could get out of this bed and down on one knee to propose properly, then and only then, would we discuss the *possibility* of me marrying Lexie. I swear," he hissed. "Where is it written that a man has to act like a jerk when his daughter falls in love? If you dare pull that on the twins I'll beat you into a pulp," he threatened Stanley.

Stanley chuckled and tossed a duffel bag onto the bed. "Pretty big talk for someone who's been in bed for two weeks."

Ace sighed with relief when he pulled the blue-jean cutoffs out of the bag. Sliding his legs into them, he stood shakily to pull them up over his lean hips. His father was beside him the moment he sank weakly back onto the bed.

"Promise me you'll take it easy, Ace. Think about the long haul here, Son. You hurt yourself now and you'll pay for it in the long run."

Ace glanced imploringly at Stanley in hopes of some help.

Stanley shrugged. "Sorry Sport, but I have to agree with him. You've got to take it easy."

Ace groaned. "Okay, okay. Just get me to the chair. And give me a shirt," he muttered, and flung the gown off his shoulders with a disgusted snort.

Craig chuckled and helped him put on a T-shirt. "I need a ring Daddy, something special."

"How about your mother's?"

"Really? But you still have yours on."

His father smiled. A tender light lit in his gaze. "The rings belonged to my grandmother, Ace. They were designed long before three-piece sets came into style. This is just a single, gold band with diamonds inset on special occasions. You'll have to get your own. Unless, of course, Lexie would prefer something else"

Ace grinned. "Okay, it's a start." He grabbed his father's arm for support and walked to the chair. He hissed a curse as he sank down into it, hating the fact that his legs trembled like those of a newborn colt.

Craig brushed his fingers through his son's thick mane of blond hair. "It'll take time, but it'll get easier, Ace. I promise," he assured him. "So you asked her to marry you?"

Ace smiled. "Sort of. Scott was informing me that I'd need to get the hang of a few things again. You know riding, walking, etcetera. I told him he needed to get the hang of walking her down the aisle. That's when he got all sullen and huffy." He rolled his eyes. "But she said yes," he admitted.

A triumphant gleam danced in the smoky eyes. Craig chuckled. "Good for you, Son."

"Yeah," Stanley agreed. "She is something else. You'll have your hands full the rest of your life. Keep you out of trouble," he teased. "Maybe you ought to hold out for some docile little thing with no opinion for herself," he suggested and regarded Ace with laughing blue eyes.

Ace grinned and shook his head. "No way. She reminds me of mama," he confided.

Craig laughed. "Me too, grab her and hold on for life."

"I intend to."

Later that evening Lexie prepared to go to the hospital while Scott visited with the rest of the family. They were watching a video tape of the rodeo when she approached him. He took her hand in his when she held it out for the keys. "You make me proud up there," he said and kissed her palm.

"Proud? She threatened to cut my son-in-law's heart out with a hoof pick," Craig remarked.

"Keys please?" Lexie said to Scott.

"I don't want you out and on the road late, Lexie."

She shrugged. "Maybe I'll just spend the night then," she suggested but knew without a doubt what his response would be.

"Maybe not," he insisted. "Be careful, Lex," he whispered and kissed her cheek. "Call when you get there and before you leave."

"Yes, Daddy," she teased with exaggerated sweetness.

Craig handed her a bag, "For Ace. A few personal things I forgot to send earlier. You know underwear, socks, and things like that," he insisted, praying she wouldn't look inside.

"Leave it to a man to pack," Amber muttered, and winked at her father. She knew what was in the bag and hoped Lexie wouldn't peek so she added a huge bowl of banana pudding to the gift pack. She imagined Lexie would be too busy making sure it didn't spill to worry about what was in the bag.

Lexie didn't care what was in the bag; she just wanted to get to the hospital. Without much further ado, she kissed her father's cheek and left. She arrived to find Ace thumbing through a magazine with a frown on his face.

"Finally," he breathed. "It's awfully boring here all alone."

His mumbled complaint reminded her of a sullen little boy. She kissed him. "Boring? With all those nurses and nurses' aides hanging around to make sure you're all right?" she argued, unable to mask the jealousy in her voice.

He grinned. "Those are the only advantages to being here," he said and grunted softly when she shoved her elbow into his side and called him a jerk.

"You said it," he insisted, with a laugh. He pulled her toward him and indulged in a long, luxurious taste of her sweetness. "You're the only nurse I want," he assured her, his voice thick, husky.

"Maybe I'll become one."

"And have you bathe some other guy? I don't think so," he declared. He realized but didn't care that she'd turned the tables on him. With a smug smile on her pretty face, she snuggled beside him on the bed, took the remote control, and surfed the channels until she found C. M. T.

"I'm going to go home with Scott tomorrow, Ace," she told him.

His heart sank. "Why?"

"Because, I miss my family, I want to see Trina and spend some time with the boys."

"How long?"

She shrugged. "A week or two, a month at the most."

"A month! Why don't you wait until I can go with you?"

"Because Scott's here now. Besides, you're going to be very busy the next few weeks with physical therapy and all. You won't even miss me," she commented.

"Bull," he huffed. He saw the need in her eyes and relented. "Promise you'll call me every day?"

She nodded with a tender smile. "I promise."

He pulled her in his arms, missing her already. "When do you want to get married?"

"I thought maybe over the Thanksgiving holidays, or Christmas. That way my family can come for a few days, whenever you're up to it."

"I'm up to it now."

She laughed. "You get out of here and on the road to recovery, Cowboy, and we'll set a date later."

"Thanksgiving sounds good," he asserted, determined to be fully recovered by then. When she went to the bathroom, he took advantage of her absence and dug around in the bag until he found what he wanted. When she came out, he took her hand and raised it to his lips. "I love you, Lexie. Will you marry me?" he asked and held the ring for her to see.

She gasped at the simple beauty of the tiny diamond in an antique gold setting. "Where did you get that? And when?"

"It was my mother's, and great-grandmother's before her. We can get something else if you'd prefer."

She shook her head. "Oh no, I'd be honored to wear your mother's ring. Does your father know?"

Ace nodded. "He suggested it. It was in the bag."

"It's beautiful," she gasped, and leaned to kiss him as he slid it on her finger.

She stayed until visiting hours were over. She kissed him good-bye and promised to see him the next morning before she left with her father. She returned to the ranch and hurried in to see Amber before they left. She held her hand out for Amber to see the ring and locked her gaze with those of her best friend. "You sure you don't mind about this?"

Amber was quick to hug her. "Not a bit. I know my mother would love you and be happy about it too," she assured her.

Lexie turned to Craig. "Thank you, I'm honored."

Craig hugged her. "You're a Godsend, Lexie. I'm honored you would consider becoming my daughter-in-law," he assured, and kissed her cheek. He turned to Scott. "And I couldn't ask for better in-law's," he admitted then shook the hand of his best friend of a life time.

* * * * *

Ace left the hospital just days after Lexie left with Scott. "You're home?" she asked, when he called her.

"Yeah," he mumbled, so lonesome he could scream. "I'm here, in this big, empty house, all alone."

She giggled. "I miss you too. I'll come back soon, Cowboy," she assured him.

But Ace wasn't going to wait. He determined to go meet her as soon as he was well enough to drive. She had been gone nearly three weeks when the doctor gave him a clean bill of health, amazed at his recovery. He wasn't riding yet and still wasn't in the same physical shape as when he was injured, but, other than that, the whole ordeal was recounted as a miracle. Wanting to surprise Lexie, he spoke with Scott to set things up on his end and rented a car, but switched vehicles when he crossed the state line.

Lexie and Trina had been shopping all day when they returned home to find a strange car in the drive. "I wonder whose car that is."

Trina did her best to keep a straight face. "Probably a friend of Scott's." She had fallen in with their plan and deliberately kept Lexie out long enough for Ace to arrive.

Lexie grabbed a handful of bags and opened the front door. The first thing she heard was his voice coming from the living room where he sat with Scott.

"Ace!" she screeched and dropped the bags. Racing in, she flung herself in his arms.

Ace picked her up, whirled her around, and pressed tiny kisses all over her face. "God, I missed you!" He put her down and dropped to one knee. "Alexis Jayne Morgan Hensley, will you marry me?"

"Yes!" she assured him with a laugh and a hug, nearly toppling him over with her exuberance.

Rising, he kissed Trina.

"It's good to see you, Ace," she whispered thickly and ran her fingers through his hair.

"Same here, Mom," he teased his future mother-in-law with a hug.

The wedding plans started immediately upon their return to Bandera. When Lexie confided that she hadn't been able to find a dress she liked, Amber approached her father. Tears filled his eyes at her request, but he couldn't deny it. Bringing the dress out, she showed it to Lexie.

Lexie gasped at the beauty of the Victorian-style wedding gown. "Yours?"

Amber nodded. "And my mother's before me. Please don't feel obligated Lexie, but you're welcome to wear it."

She searched Craig's eyes seeing the love there, and the tears. "Are you sure?"

He nodded. "Tamera would love you. She'd have been honored."

She held the dress against her and gazed into the mirror, amazed at how perfect it looked with her small form and vibrant coloring. Something old and borrowed was covered. Though she adored the hat, she chose a waist length veil as something new. A lacy blue garter completed her ensemble. The only snag in the plans happened when she asked Stanley to sing "Butterfly Kisses" at the reception.

Stan's heart clenched at the thought, he shook his head. "I'm not singing that song."

Though he loved it, he doubted his ability to get through an entire song about a father's love for his daughter during the different stages in her life. "I'll buy you the tape. I'd be honored to sing for you, but that one's out."

"Please," she implored, and regarded him with wide, pleading eyes while everyone else waited and watched.

Stan felt his resolve slip. He grunted. "See that look?" he asked Ace. "They'll pull it on you every time," he complained.

Craig laughed. "I warned you years ago to build a wall of defense against it. But no, you don't listen to me," he teased, and then winked at his daughter. "Frankly, I think you ought to sing the song."

Stanley snorted. "Since when does what you think count?"

"Watch it, Boy it's never too late to run you off with a shot gun."

"Suppose I want to dance with my daughters? I can't sing the song and do that too." He tried desperately to get out of it.

Amber killed that chance of escape. "I think they'd rather sit at your feet while you sing it," she declared, and wrapped her arms around his waist.

"Who's side are you on?" he challenged.

She giggled.

Lexie stepped forward with her last weapon. "You gave me no choice when you goaded me up on that stage at the rodeo, Stanley Morrison. You have no choice now."

Ace watched Stanley crumbled under the assault of feminine wiles. Though he also wanted to hear him sing the song, he'd remained loyally silent. He grinned when Stan surrendered with a defeated sigh. "Sucker," he teased.

Stan grinned. "Sometimes Ace, you just have to give them their way."

"Sometimes, or all the time?"

Stan laughed and slapped him on the back. "Yep."

Ace shook his head. "Not me. I'll wear the pants in this family," he determined with a grin.

Lexie turned to him, a mischievous sparkle in her eyes. "I'm sure you've heard the joke about the football player and the cheerleader?"

It was an old joke, one about how a tiny cheerleader wife put her big jock husband in his place on their wedding night over his chauvinistic attitude. Ace knew it well. He nodded, flushed.

"I'd suggest you remember it," Lexie told him in a saccharine voice and patted his cheek. With a giggle, she and Amber escaped to savor the sweet taste of victory.

Epilogue

Thanksgiving Day dawned bright and clear, its cool, crisp air a welcomed relief from the heat of a long, drawn out summer. The wedding was set for the next day. Lexie took a moment to revel in the love that surrounded the Harris' dinner table before Craig said the blessing.

Everyone was there: Craig and Ace, Amber, Stanley and the children, Scott, Trina and the boys. Family. She'd never known the joy or fully expressed the gratitude she felt in her heart for the blessing of family, a family in which tomorrow she would become an even bigger part of. After plates were full and blessings were said, she gave into the desire burning in her heart to voice her feelings aloud. She cleared her throat.

"May I say something?"

Everyone waited.

"In the past, the joy of Thanksgiving has always been tempered by sadness and sorrow." Her eyes searched every pair that watched her and she held each gaze a full moment while she spoke. "There are no words to truly express the gratitude I feel toward God for placing me in the midst of such a wonderful, loving family. Thank you, all, for accepting me so unconditionally."

Ace squeezed her hand. Craig remembered the first time she and Ace met and chuckled.

"Bet you never, in your wildest imagination, thought your dreams would come true on a west Texas ranch in the arms of a chauvinistic jerk cowboy," he teased.

She wrinkled her nose daintily, her eyes laughed into his. "Ugh. I never thought about it that way."

"Never too late to back out," her father insisted.

She looked at Ace. His gaze swept over her with such warmth, such love, such blatant desire and raw masculinity that she nearly melted into her chair. "I think I'll give it a try," she admitted.

He leaned toward her. "To quote our favorite female artist darling, 'if you're not in it for life....'" He shook his head. "I'm outta here."

"Same goes for you, Cowboy," she whispered, after he brushed his lips over hers.

The next morning found her awakened by his soft knock and urgent whisper to open the door. She rolled out of bed and reached for the door knob when she heard Craig's voice.

"Ace, what are you doing? Tradition has it bad luck to see the bride the day of the wedding before the ceremony."

She imagined Ace glare at his father and smiled when he hissed, "Tradition stinks."

She heard the laughter in Craig's voice and could tell by the thick emotion coloring his tone he was remembering his own wedding day when he remarked, "I know, Son, been there myself."

Lexie leaned her head on the door when Ace knocked again, "Lex? You don't believe that superstitious hogwash do you? This is the twenty-first century for crying out loud."

Lexie giggled. "That's debatable. Most say the twenty-first century begins next year. However, no I don't believe in all that superstitious hogwash, but I'm not taking any chances, Cowboy," she insisted, and then laughed at his muttered curse.

As the day wore on, Ace's patience wore thin. He paced the floor at Amber's house, glared at the clocks and swore the darn things were wrong.

Stanley chuckled. "Having second thoughts, Sport?"

He sank into a chair with a sigh and shook his head. "Not at all. Regretful I was so picky though, otherwise I'd have a little more experience," he muttered. His eyes begged his brother-in-law for assurance and advice for the night ahead.

Stanley understood why Ace was so worried and knelt in front of him. "Just be gentle Ace. And take your time. The flesh is yours to control. Let your heart lead you. Your love and natural instinct will take care of the rest," he assured him.

Stanley's eyes shone with love, joy, and pride. Ace whispered his thanks, closed his eyes and prayed for the clock to strike two.

The ceremony was blessedly short and sweet. Stanley outdid himself with the singing and Lexie joined him on the piano for a song or two during the reception after which, Craig and Scott danced with their daughters while Stanley, the twins at his feet, his voice thick and husky with emotion, poured his heart out over "Butterfly Kisses."

Ace danced with his mother-in-law, but wished desperately his mother was there.

Trina brushed her fingers through the thick blond mane of her son-in-law's hair, and whispered her love. The joy in those expressive eyes was tempered by a hint of sadness. She held him tight when he hugged her close and thanked her for Lexie. Her smile was tender. "Thank, Scott, it was he who first set his heart on having her as a daughter."

"I'm not sure he would be willing to accept my thanks right now," Ace teased, his eyes following their every step as his lovely wife danced with her father.

Trina laughed, her eyes shining with the love she had reserved just for him. "You're right. Probably not, especially since you've just taken her away from him. But, believe me, he knows he couldn't ask for, or hope to get, a better son-in-law."

Ace kissed her cheek then changed partners with Scott while Stanley sang one last song. "I love you Alexis Jayne Morgan Hensley Harris," he whispered, his voice husky as his hands caressed her back and shoulders, to pull her closer to his body.

His gaze, warm and soft like liquid metal and touch like tempered fire sent shivers of anticipation down her spine. Lexie smiled up into his eyes. "And I love you, Adam Craig Harris the Fourth," she assured.

When Stanley finished singing, Scott cleared his throat. "A toast and a challenge," he said and lifted a glass of champagne. Glasses raised, everyone waited.

"My beautiful wife has informed me that we are going to have a baby," he announced, then pulled Trina close in his embrace and covered her lips with his.

After the cheers of excitement simmered down, he raised his glass again. "Now for the challenge, the first girl born into the family gets the honor of bearing the name Tamera Joy."

"That's not fair," Ace said. He nodded at Trina. "She's already pregnant." He pointed at his sister. "She could be..."

"Bite your tongue Ace Harris," Amber interrupted.

"I've loved that name from the moment it left my sister's lips months ago." Ace admitted. "Besides, we may not want children right away," he added.

"We do," his new wife cut in.

"We do?" he asked. She nodded and her eyes sparkled like rare, precious gems.

"Yeah, I figured the best way to keep a bull-riding, rodeo cowboy home, is to saddle him with a house full of kids."

Ace grinned. "Who needs bulls?" He chuckled when a hot flush stained Lexie's cheeks. "I mean..."

"Don't worry Sport, we know exactly what you mean," Stanley cut in with a laugh.

"That didn't come out like I meant it to," he whispered to his sweetly blushing wife as everyone gathered around Trina and Scott for hugs and kisses and best wishes.

* * * * *

Ace knelt at the headstone which marked his mother's gravesite. Not a day went by that he didn't miss her, or remember the time when he lay in a coma and she came to visit him and to urge him to return to the living. Not a day went by that he didn't thank God for the opportunity to assure his family of the truth and the reality of everlasting life. And not a day went by when he failed to thank God for the many blessings that continued to pour into his life.

From the first moment he took Lexie in his arms and made her his wife, he truly understood and appreciated the joy, the pleasure, and the honor of being a man. It was a glorious experience and one he'd not soon forget. He was reminded every morning when he awoke in her arms, or she in his. It was an honor to know he was her first, and only, love. Though her body had been violated as a child, her heart had remained pure. Now it was his, only his—a blessing he'd never take lightly. Her love gave his life meaning and purpose, and a whole new reason for being.

He rose to wrap his arms around her when she put her hand on his shoulder. He took the tiny, squirming bundle from her, brushed his lips over hers in a tender caress and held Lexie against his chest with one arm. The other cradled his newborn daughter. When Lexie told him she was pregnant, the news had thrilled more than frightened him. Now, they stood together and introduced little Tamera Joy to her grandmother. Though they'd also been blessed with a girl, Scott had graciously forfeited the name when they discovered Lexie and Ace's child was female. Ace vowed his daughter would know her grandmother as fully as if she were physically with them.

"Wish you were here to hold her, Mama," he whispered his voice husky. "She's beautiful. Just like her mama."

His lips brushed over Lexie's in a tender caress. "Her hair is a gorgeous shade of red-gold and her eyes are baby blue. I think they'll probably be green," he whispered.

"I hope so anyway," he confessed. Nothing would please him more than for his daughter to inherit the brilliant gaze of her mother.

* * * * *

Craig and Scott sat at the kitchen table and enjoyed the peace and quiet as the house settled down around them.

Amber and Stanley had taken their children home, excitedly anticipating the visit of one jolly old elf. Trina nursed little Riki Jayne upstairs in hopes of getting her settled down for the night. At a little over five months old and crawling, the sites, sounds and excitement of Christmas fascinated the child. The boys, Richard and Robert, were asleep in the den. Ace and Lexie had long since retired with the baby tucked in her bassinet.

"What a day," Craig sighed, stretched his legs, and wished aloud that he was in front of a roaring fire.

Scott nodded. "It's been a full one," he admitted, but wondered how to broach the subject uppermost in his mind. "You know, Lexie has asked several times how we could go so many years without knowing if we were blood relations. I told her that we've never felt the need to know and that we were closer than many blood brothers ever were. But when I consider her childhood, I can understand why she would feel the need to know, especially since she's become a mother herself."

Craig eyed him, a curious lift to his brow.

"Are you feeling the need to know?"

Scott shrugged and thought about his mother's letter. They'd always been brothers at heart, blood or the lack thereof had made no difference then, wouldn't change things now. "Not really a need. I've always been happy and satisfied having you as my friend. I truly don't believe anything would ever change that."

"But?" Craig queried at the hesitancy in his voice.

Scott sighed, tears filled his eyes. "But the events of September eleventh stirred up old questions. I can't believe it's been over three months, the pain is still so raw."

"Neither can I," Craig assured him, his voice solemn, then smiled. "But you're right, nothing will change the way we feel about each other, not this late in the game anyway. We're too old and set in our ways to alter how we feel about each other now," he said with a grin then sobered. "You've been more than a friend to me these fifty-plus years and I'll always be grateful you are a part of my life."

Scott hadn't realized until that moment how much those words truly meant. He took a deep breath and smiled. "In that case, how about a drink?" he asked, and then got up to retrieve a bottle of whiskey and two glasses.

Craig accepted the glass with a sigh of appreciation. He raised it in salute. "To little Tamera Joy, may she grow into the name and grace her parents' lives with joyful misery." He chuckled.

"Just as her grandmother graced ours and would expect of her namesake."

Scott laughed and took a sip then raised his glass again. "I was thinking more along the lines of...to you, *my brother*, and to our beautiful granddaughter."

Tears burned the back of Craig's throat, the truth burst to life in his heart. Joy settled in his soul like a warm sunset. The light in Scott's eyes answered any questions he may have asked. The why's and wherefores didn't matter, all that mattered was, Scott was at peace with what he'd discovered when he read his mother's letter. He touched his glass to Scott's with a nod, smiled at his lifelong friend, and swallowed hard the lump of emotion which clogged his airways.

"Alright then, for the blessing of family."

Dear Readers,

I hope you've enjoyed living and loving, and laughing and crying with these characters as much as I have. There's no greater pleasure than that which comes from using the talent God gave me to glorify Him.

I pray you've been blessed by the timeless truths revealed in these stories. Out of all the Scripture references in this series, one thing remains true.....***Only when hearts are tempered, minds are opened and wills are softened can man discern the will of God for his life.***

Therefore, soften your heart, open your mind and surrender your will to the Father that He may bless you richly.

Sincerely,
Pamela S. Thibodeaux
"Inspirational with an Edge!" ™
http://pamelathibodeaux.com

Fate deemed them neighbors, scandal had them brothers. Not caring whether or not they were blood relations, Scott Hensley and Craig Harris spent their entire lives as the best of friends. Until the day tragedy struck America and brought to life unanswered questions from the past. Can Scott handle the truth? Better yet will the truth really set him free?

Prologue

Scott Hensley sat in the den of his Louisiana home, his heart heavy, overwhelmed with the same sense of shock and grief that rocked the nation. His wife, Katrina, was upstairs nursing his infant daughter and his sons were in their rooms doing homework, all seemingly normal activities in a world that was far from normal.

One week ago, on a beautiful fall morning much like this one, terrorists waged an attack on America the likes of which he'd never expected to see in his lifetime. Scott sat in frozen horror as the events were relived on the television. He hated seeing the terror and panic replayed over and over, yet seemed unable to tear himself away from the set. Since that day, his wife had been in tears, his sons subdued and afraid, their innocence stripped away by an unknown evil. The only innocence left was that of his three-month-old daughter.

Lexie, his adopted daughter, (who was due to make him a grandfather before the year was over) called daily just to hear their voice and to reassure herself—and his friends of a lifetime which she had married into—of Scott and his family's wellbeing.

Scott's mind wandered back to another act of terrorism that had affected his life so deeply. The memories surfaced as though it happened yesterday...

The airplane rising boldly against a brilliant summer sky...the sound of an explosion...the sight of that ball of fire and black smoke billowing out of the plane as it spiraled toward the earth to crash into a crumbled heap of burning metal and flesh.

He felt the same sense of loss and helpless anger now as he did back then. Getting up, he poured a liberal amount of whiskey into a glass, slammed it down in one gulp and poured another then strode across the room to turn the television off.

A sound, much like that of a wounded or enraged animal escaped his throat when he knocked back the second shot of whiskey and all but slung the glass on a surge of impotent fury, then buried his head in shaking hands. How he made it back across the room to collapse on the couch once more would always remain a mystery.

It didn't take a genius to figure out he was conceived in wartime, but being an only child, Scott had never been called upon to defend his country during the wars to follow, though he'd seen enough carnage in his years as a physician to suffice for a lifetime of war.

His mind circled through the years of his life until it rested once more on the matter in his heart that had never been completely settled.

Who was he?

Though the question had arisen at different points in his life, Scott never felt the need to have it answered. He knew who he was: *Dr. Richard Scott Hensley, born of Rosa Sanchez Hensley and Jonathan Scott Hensley, Bandera, Texas, 1944* with roots as deep as the rich Texas soil. But now, with the country in turmoil, the existence of his children, and his daughter about to give birth to his first grandchild, the answer seemed imperative.

Scott only hoped he had the courage and strength to withstand whatever that answer turned out to be.

Rising once more he picked the glass up off the floor, carried it into the kitchen and rinsed it out. Returning to the den, he fixed himself another drink, pouring whiskey until it danced at the rim of the crystal shot glass. Scott didn't down this one, only took a sip so it wouldn't spill onto the carpet as he walked over to his desk and retrieved the envelope which had lain unopened for nearly a quarter of a century. Though faded and yellow now, he still felt the deep-seated fear and panic he'd felt the day the letter was given to him.

His palms began to sweat, hands to shake. Scott took another sip of whiskey and walked quickly over to the couch before his knees gave way. Tossing the envelope onto the coffee table, he placed his glass next to it, buried his face in trembling hands and prayed.

God, why? *What difference will opening this thing make now?*

The answer came as in usually did, in a well known, much loved scripture. *And you shall know the truth and the truth shall set you free.*

Still, Scott hesitated knowing somehow, somewhere deep down inside, once he opened the envelope a part of him would never be the same.

Reaching over he picked up the glass with one hand and the letter with the other then leaned back into the soft cushions of the couch, sipping the whiskey while slapping the letter against his thigh. His mother's handwriting beckoned him to open the envelope. He had only to close his eyes to see her face, smell her perfume, feel her touch, and hear her voice...

"I love you, Scott, and I'm so very proud of you."

Quickly, before he could change his mind, Scott put the glass down, slid his finger beneath the flap of the envelope to break the seal then ran it along the edge until it lay open in the palm of his hand. Again he hesitated, his breathing sharp, almost painful. His heart thundered in his chest.

Taking a deep breath he withdrew the pages from the envelope, resisting the urge to crumple it up like so much trash and throw it away. He picked up the glass again, sipped.

With a silent plea to God to get him through this, he put the glass back down and unfolded the letter. A wave of grief washed over him at the sight of his mother's handwriting, so bold and beautiful. Scott blinked back the tears with determination and read...

My darling son, your father has encouraged me for years to write this letter...

Don't Forget Books 1, 2 & 3!

Tempered Hearts

Rancher Craig Harris and veterinarian Tamera Collins clash from the moment they meet. Innocence is pitted against arrogance as tempers rise and passions ignite to form a love as pure as the finest gold, fresh from the crucible and as strong as steel. Thrown together amid tragedy and unsated passion, Tamera and Craig share a strong attraction that neither accepts as the first stages of love. Torn between desire and dislike, they must make peace with their pasts and God in order to open up to the love blossoming between them. It is a love that nothing can destroy when they come to understand *that* **only when hearts are tempered, minds are opened and wills are softened can man discern the will of God for his life.**

Tempered Dreams

Dr. Scott Hensley (introduced in Tempered Hearts) has built a wall around his heart since the death of his wife and parents. Katrina Simmons is recovering from scars inflicted on her as a battered wife. Can dreams be renewed and faith strengthened? Can they find joy and peace in God's love and in love for one another?

Tempered Fire

Amber Harris is a good girl on the brink of womanhood. Stanley Morrison is a young man at the start of his life. For each other, they have always felt the fireworks that two people in love should feel. However, the questions about his past, his pride, and Amber's father might be the end of what could be a strong relationship. As the two try to protect their budding romance, some unlikely but powerful forces conspire to keep them apart. Will they survive the wishes of everyone around them with their relationship intact?

About the Author

Pamela S. Thibodeaux grew up in the town of Iowa, Louisiana. She is a mother, grandmother and deeply committed Christian who firmly believes in God and His promises.

"God is very real to me and I feel that people today need and want to hear more of His truths wherever they can glean them. People are hungry for practical (and real) Christian values, not some 'holier-than-thou' beliefs that are impossible to believe and impossible to live up to," Pamela says.

"I do my best to encourage readers to develop a personal relationship with God. The deepest desire of my heart is to glorify God and to get His message of faith, trust and forgiveness to a hurting world."

Email Pamela at: pthibo7@gmail.com
Visit her website: http://www.pamelathibodeaux.com
Or blog: http://pamswildroseblog.blogspot.com

Other Titles by Pamela S. Thibodeaux

Love is a Rose

Music is the magical entry into the spirit world; the golden gate into the Kingdom of God. But we mustn't be of the mindset that God only uses Christian music to reach out and touch our mind, heart and spirit. God uses any and every means available to speak to His children.

Our job is to be open and receptive.

In this devotional, Pamela S Thibodeaux shares how God opened her spirit to a deeper understanding of the abundance of His grace and mercy through the words of the song, The Rose sung by Country & Western artist Conway Twitty.

Pamela offers Seeds to Ponder and a prayer as she parallels the love of God and the Christian life to each verse of the song.

Lori Strickland (introduced in *Tempered Fire*) has always been known as her father's "wild child" with no desire to change until she meets ex-bull-rider-turned-preacher Rafe Judson. Her attempts to change her wanton ways come to naught until she realizes redemption only comes with true repentance. Can she find redemption and win the heart of the cowboy preacher? Find out in ***Lori's Redemption***

A visionary is someone who sees into the future Taylor Forrestier sees into the past but only as it pertains to her work. Hailed by her peers as *"a visionary with an instinct for beauty and an eye for the unique"* Taylor is undoubtedly a brilliant architect and gifted designer. But she and twin brother Trevor, share more than a successful business. The two share a childhood wrought with lies and deceit and the kind of abuse that's disgustingly prevalent in today's society. Can the love of God and the awesome healing power of His grace and mercy free the twins from their past and open their hearts to the good plan and the future He has for their lives? Find out in ***The Visionary*** ~ Where the awesome power of God's love heals the most wounded of souls.

   The Inheritance *is about the chance we all long for...the chance to start over.* Widowed at age thirty-nine and suffering from empty nest syndrome, Rebecca Sinclair is overshadowed by grief and loneliness. Her husband has been deceased for a year, her oldest child has moved to New York in pursuit of an acting career and her youngest child is attending college in France. Having spent over half of her life as a wife and mother, she has no idea what God has in store for her now. Will an unexpected inheritance in the wine country of New York bring meaning and purpose to her life and give her the courage to love again?

US Postal worker Raymond Jacobey has been in love with the little widow since he first set eyes on her. A wanderer searching for the ever-illusive soul mate, Ray has never stayed in one place too long. Raised by self-centered, high-power executives, he's longed for the idyllic life of residing in a cozy house in a small town with the love of his life. Will he gain the heart of the lovely widow or will he lose her to the wine country of New York?   Find out in ***The Inheritance***

   Single mom Cathy Johnson is tired of running her life alone...what she needs is a well-trained angel to help out. Jared Savoy gave up the dream of having a family when he discovered he is sterile. Can a confirmed bachelor and the mother of four find love amid normal daily chaos? Find out in ***Cathy's Angel***

   Best-selling novelist and songwriter, Camie Rogers has penned numerous accounts of the secret love she holds in her heart. Country-Music Superstar Kip Allen has changed from the shy, humble boy, to the epitome of "star." Can the two rediscover each other after one night of his Home is Where the Heart is Tour? Find out in **Choices**

Anthony Paul Seville is known as the 'most eligible bachelor' in New Orleans, possibly even the entire state of Louisiana, but finds himself alone—completely and explicitly alone. Jessica Aucoin is a writer on her way to fame and fortune, but is haunted by a man from her past. Will the "champion" lawyer and the author of romantic suspense find love written in their future?   Find out in **A Hero for Jessica**

Sienna has survived what most succumb to - the death of a spouse and child and has maintained her faith despite her troubles. William has never met anyone who actually lived out what they say they believe. Is it true love between the faithful optimist and broody pessimist or simply **Winter Madness**?

Grade school teacher Carson Alexander has a gift—a gift that has driven a wedge between him and his family. Worse, it's put him at odds with God. Feeling alone and misunderstood, Carson views God's gift of prophecy as the worst kind of curse...that is until he meets Lorelei Conner, landscape artist extraordinaire, and perhaps the one person who may need Carson and his gift more than anyone ever has. Lorelei Connor is a mother on the run. Her abusive ex-husband has followed her all over the country trying to steal their daughter. Distrusting of men and needing to keep on the move, she's surprised by her desire to remain close to Carson Alexander. Through her fear and hesitation, she must learn to rely on God to guide her—not an easy task when He's prompting her to trust a man. Can their relationship withstand the tragedy lurking on the horizon? Find out in **In His Sight**

Jason Stockwell has been commissioned to interview Kylie Erickson and to review her books. Only problem is, she won't give the time of day much less an interview to someone whose type of writing she deems not worthy of respect. Can they suspend their judgmental attitudes and find true love? Find out in ***Review of Love*** (A FREE read from White Rose Publishing!)

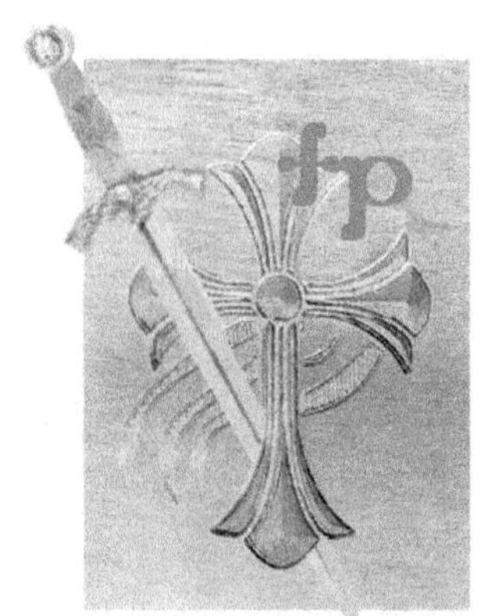

**Temperance
Publishing**